D0512243

SUDDEN

The man's hands were bound. From a branch overhead dangled a lariat, the end in the hands of two burly men. Someone was raising a hand as a signal when Sudden stepped forward, guns drawn.

'Mebbe one of you will tell me what's goin' on?' he suggested.

'We're stringing up a cattle thief,' a broken-nosed man snarled. 'Ain't that plain enough?'

'What's your name?' Sudden asked quietly.

'Lanty,' the man replied. 'What's that to you?'

Sudden grinned, a cold and mirthless grin. 'I might need it for your tombstone.'

Other SUDDEN Westerns
by OLIVER STRANGE

SUDDEN—OUTLAWED
SUDDEN
THE MARSHAL OF LAWLESS
SUDDEN—GOLDSEEKER
SUDDEN MAKES WAR
SUDDEN RIDES AGAIN
SUDDEN TAKES THE TRAIL
THE RANGE ROBBERS
THE LAW O' THE LARIAT

by FREDERICK H. CHRISTIAN

SUDDEN STRIKES BACK
SUDDEN—TROUBLESHOOTER
SUDDEN AT BAY
SUDDEN—APACHE FIGHTER
SUDDEN—DEAD OR ALIVE

and published by CORGI BOOKS

Oliver Strange

Sudden Plays a Hand

CORGI BOOKS

TRANSWORLD PUBLISHERS LTD

A National General Company

SUDDEN PLAYS A HAND
A CORGI BOOK 0 552 08728 9

Originally published in Great Britain
by George Newnes Ltd.

PRINTING HISTORY

George Newnes Edition published 1950
Corgi Edition published 1961
Corgi Edition reprinted 1962
Corgi Edition reprinted 1963
Corgi Edition reprinted 1964
Corgi Edition reissued 1965
Corgi Edition reprinted 1966
Corgi Edition reprinted 1968
Corgi Edition reprinted 1969
Corgi Edition reissued 1971
Corgi Edition reprinted 1972

*This book is copyright. No portion of it may be reproduced
by any process without written permission. All inquiries
should be addressed to the publishers.*

Condition of sale—this book is sold subject to the
condition that it shall not, by way of trade *or otherwise,*
be lent, re-sold, hired out or otherwise *circulated*
without the publisher's prior consent in any form of
binding or cover other than that in which it is published
*and without a similar condition including this condition
being imposed on the subsequent purchaser.*

This book is set in Plantin 9 pt.

Corgi Books are published by Transworld Publishers, Ltd.,
Cavendish House, 57–59 Uxbridge Road, Ealing, London, W.5.

Made and printed in Great Britain by
Richard Clay (The Chaucer Press), Ltd., Bungay, Suffolk.

To
the memory of my nephew
FLYING OFFICER G. J. HARDEN, D.F.C.,
R.A.F.V.R.

SUDDEN PLAYS A HAND

CHAPTER I

'KEEP yore han's mighty still an' explain yoreself.'

The curt command was delivered in a tone which was, in itself, a menace, and the appearance of the speaker did little to lessen it. A big fellow, seemingly in the mid-thirties, with enormous shoulders and a gross body to match. From beneath the brim of his slouched hat black eyes gleamed fiercely, and his thick lips, unhidden by a straggling moustache, were pursed in a savage pout.

The man to whom the order was given seemed in no hurry to reply. He, too, was big, but less heavily built, and perhaps eight years younger than the other. His clean-shaven face was hard and reckless. Sitting their horses, some dozen paces apart, on opposite sides of a tiny break in the woods through which a faint trail led, they eyed one another steadily. At length the younger man spoke:

'What right you got to hold me up thisaway?'

The ghost of a grin passed over the other's lips. 'No right, on'y a left,' he replied, raising that hand enough to reveal a levelled revolver. 'This is my country.'

The threatened man merely shrugged his shoulders. 'I ain't passed any fences,' he pointed out.

'You wouldn't—my name's better'n barb' wire,' came the boast. 'Bardoe—Bull Bardoe. Mebbe that wises you up some?'

'Not—one—damn—bit,' was the drawled reply. 'Never heard tell o' you.'

Bardoe did not detect the lie, but he was very sensible of the sneering tone, and it deepened his scowl of aggression.

'You must shorely be a pilgrim,' he gibed in turn. 'What might yore name be?'

'It might be Judas Iscariot, but it ain't,' the stranger retorted. He appeared to be deliberately trying to incense the other. 'You'll have heard o' Old Nick? Well, I'm Young Nick. I was called after the Devil, an' have been on the way to him ever since.'

'Cease foolin' or I'll shorten yore journey,' Bardoe snarled, and then a surprised look of comprehension widened his eyes. 'Tellin' me yo're Nicholas Drait, o' Shadow Valley? And you never heard o' me?'

'Brother, that was a slip,' Drait returned mildly, but his narrowed eyes watched warily. 'What I meant to say was that I

9

never heard *any good* o' you. Rustler, road-agent, train hold-up, murd——'

He saw the movement he was waiting for, and his own weapon—long held in readiness—came up. The reports merged into one, shattering the silence and causing a frightened fluttering in the greenery overhead. The younger man felt the burn of a bullet on his cheek, and then saw Bardoe lean forward and pitch sideways to the ground.

'Hell!' he cried.

The exclamation was one of amazement; where he had looked for an empty saddle he saw a girl astride the stricken man's horse; Bardoe's bulky body had effectually concealed her from his view. She was young—not much over twenty, he judged, and was dressed in a worn calico gown, clumsy shoes, and an old sun-bonnet which had slipped back to reveal an untidy mop of golden-brown hair. She seemed pitifully small on the back of the big beast she bestrode. Drait got down, dropped the reins over his pony's head, and stepped towards her. As though frozen with horror, she remained bent and motionless, her gaze glued to the sprawling form of the shot man.

'Who the deuce are you?' Drait asked roughly.

Getting no answer, not even a look, he muttered an impatient oath and turned to his victim. With cold, callous eyes the victor surveyed his work, stooped to lift the wide-flung left hand, let it fall limply back to the ground, and began to search the body. In a vest pocket he found a slip of paper, and on it, scrawled in pencil: 'One hundred three-year-olds at 10 a head—1,000 bucks.'

'C'rect,' he commented grimly, and thrusting it into his own pocket, bent to his task again.

Around Bardoe's middle, concealed by the slack of his shirt, he discovered a money-belt—a heavy one. He began to buckle it about his own waist, but on second thoughts, rolled it up and placed it in one of the saddle-pockets of the owner's horse. This brought his attention back to the girl, and he stood considering her with a sombre puzzled expression. At length he appeared to have reached a decision. She was looking at him now, her large eyes full of fear.

'Climb into the saddle,' he said. 'We've a long way to go.'

She scrambled over the cantle, while he shortened the stirrup leathers so that her feet could reach. Then, handing her the reins, he mounted his own beast and rode out of the glade. Sitting slackly, head down-bent, she followed. They moved slowly, for the nature of the country, rough and broken, made speed only an invitation to accident. Several times he spoke to her but received no reply, and with a lift of his shoulders, he relinquished the attempt to make her talk, and gave his attention to the tricky trail they were traversing. But from time to time, when it was possible for them to ride abreast, he found himself studying her. The sun-bonnet had been pulled on, hiding the face, but he noted the youngness of her, and the smallness of the toil-worn hands which gripped the reins.

'Bull Bardoe's woman,' he told himself. 'Well, if that's the best he could give her in the way o' clothes, I guess she won't lose on the exchange.'

When the dropping sun set the western sky ablaze, warning that the day was about to die, Drait halted on the bank of a small creek and turned off the trail, following the water, to stop finally on a little grassy level shut in by undergrowth.

'We'll camp here,' he said. 'Get down an' rest—you look tuckered out.'

She obeyed in silence, seating herself on a slight mound, whence she watched listlessly while he unsaddled and led off the horses to picket them some fifty yards away where the grass was more luxuriant. Returning with an armful of dry wood, he built a fire, and while it was burning up, opened his blanket roll to unearth a battered coffee-pot, a frying-pan, and a tin mug. He surveyed the latter with a half-grin.

'On'y got one,' he remarked. 'We're a mite short o' grub, too. You see, I warn't expectin' comp'ny.' If the girl heard, she gave no sign, and he went on, 'Mebbe Bull can help us out.'

A search of Bardoe's blanket revealed another mug, coffee-pot, part of a loaf, a slab of cooked deer-meat, and a tin which Drait took to be salt, but on tasting, found to be sugar.

The coffee-pot, filled from the creek, was set on the glowing embers. When it boiled, he cut two slices of bread, put a layer of meat between them, and poured steaming liquid into one of the mugs.

'Cawfee should be hot as hell, black as a nigger's soul, an' sweet as sin,' he grinned. 'Come an' get it.'

'I'm not hungry,' the girl said.

It was the first time he had heard her voice, and he was struck by the low, vibrant tone—clear-sounding, like the note of a harp. The effect was curious—it made him angry.

'Allasame, you'll eat, drink, an' like it—I don't want a sick woman on my hands,' he grated, and when she still made no movement, 'Do I have to take my quirt to you?'

This brought her to the fire, where she ate and drank in sullen silence. Drait took no futher notice, devoting himself to the meal, and the fact that it had been mainly provided by the man he had shot did not appear to have affected his appetite. When they had finished, she looked up and said abruptly:

'Why did you kill him?'

Drait laughed harshly. 'To save myself. His gun was out first; he meant to get me—a stranger he'd never set eyes on.'

This silenced her; she had seen Bardoe furtively draw his weapon the moment they had met. Moodily she looked on while he replenished the fire and spread the blankets, one on each side, with the saddles for pillows.

'There's yore bed,' he said. 'Better turn in—we'll be makin' an early start.'

He set the example, rolling himself in the blanket, and in a few moments, regular breathing told that he was asleep. The girl lay down, but only to stare, wide-eyed, at the dark dome above, in which points of light were now beginning to peep. The one thought in her mind was to get away, somehow, somewhere. Presently she raised herself, making a little noise, and gazed at the recumbent form across the fire. It remained motionless, and satisfied that her captor slept, she stood up and stole in the direction of the horses.

No sooner had she melted into the shadow than the sleeper flung aside his blanket, a heavy scowl on his brow. Cat-footed, he followed, reaching her as she stooped to pull the picket-pin of Bardoe's mount.

'Tryin' to run out on me, huh?' he said, as she shrank back in alarm. 'Well, I treated you fair, but now . . .'

He left the sentence unfinished, and gripping her wrist, dragged her back to the camp. Obeying his gesture, she sank on the bed again. Drait fetched his own blanket and saddle, arranged them, stretched himself beside her, and slid an arm about her shoulders.

'I ain't trustin' you no more,' he said gruffly.

Swift-born panic seized her and she struggled to rise. Her resistance infuriated him, and his fingers, vice-like, bit into the soft flesh of her arm as he pulled her nearer. She fought back, to her own undoing, for contact with her lithe young body roused a devil of desire and rendered him ruthless. His hot breath scorched her cheek, and then avid lips found her own, and held them.

* * *

When she awoke, the day was but a few hours old. On the other side of the fire, Drait was preparing breakfast. He pointed to the creek.

'A sluice'll freshen you up, an' you'll be needin' food,' he said. 'We got some hard ridin' ahead.'

The roughness had gone from his voice, but she was too crushed to notice. Wearily she went to the stream, and kneeling, bathed her face and hands in the ice-cold water. Back at the fire, she swallowed mechanically the bread, fried bacon, and coffee he passed to her. She was vaguely conscious that he was regarding her with an air of puzzlement. At length the silence proved too much for him.

'Why'n hell didn't you tell me—'bout yoreself?' he burst out. 'How was I to know? I figured you were——'

'Bardoe's plaything, and therefore, anybody's,' she finished stormily, roused by his attempt to put the blame on her. 'I wasn't—I never saw him until an hour before we met you. He offered me work—at his ranch.'

Drait's lips curled in a sneer. 'An' you believed that?'

'Why not? Are all men liars?' she retorted. 'I'd run away, and was lost in the woods.'

'What were you runnin' from?'

'Another beast like you,' she flashed back.

Bit by bit, he got the story. She had lost her parents early, and was raised in an orphanage. At sixteen, she had been found employment with a small farmer. She had been well-treated, and for nearly four years, was happy. Then misfortune came, the family returned to the East, and she took another situation. Here she was wretched; the wife was cruel, and the husband wanted to be kind—too kind. In the midst of a terrible scene, she fled, not even waiting to collect her few possessions.

'What's yore name?' Drait asked.

'Mary,' she replied shortly.

'We'll be on our way,' he said.

He fetched and saddled the horses, packed the gear, and threw water on the blazing sticks; whatever laws he might break, that of guarding against the forest fires was not one of them. She was struggling to get astride the big horse when two strong arms lifted her into position. In another moment, he was in his own saddle and heading for the trail.

At the end of five miles, they paused on a lofty bench which gave them a view of the surrounding country. Away on their right, several columns of smoke indicated a settlement.

'Burnt Hollow,' he muttered. 'Find what we want there, mebbe.'

'What are you going to do with me?' she asked fearfully.

'Marry you,' he replied bluntly.

The reply deprived her of speech; she could only stare at him round-eyed. The hard jaw and sombre expression told her he was not joking; he would do it, and she was powerless. Dimly, she understood that he was trying to put things right, but her animosity remained. She shrugged her shoulders in contemptuous despair; what did it matter?

The tiny township of Burnt Hollow was just awakening when they rode in. Drait drew rein outside a building labelled 'General Store,' through the open door of which a man in his shirt-sleeves was sweeping yesterday's dirt.

'Got any duds for a woman?' he asked.

'Shore,' was the reply. 'Step right in.'

They hitched their horses and followed him into the store. 'I want a complete outfit for this girl,' Drait said. 'Can you do it?'

'Well, if you ain't lucky,' the tradesman smiled. 'Got one for the darter o' Lem Wilkins, the big cattle-man, you know.' He cast a measuring eye over the girl. 'She's just about yore build, ma'am. My missus 'll fix you up.'

An angular grey-haired woman answered his call, and when he had explained, said to the girl, 'Come with me, my dear,' and to Drait, 'It's goin' to cost you somethin, Mister.'

'Go the limit,' he told her, and turned to the storekeeper. 'I need some cartridges an' smokin'. Got a parson?'

'I don't stock 'em, but there's one in town—'bout twenty yards along the street,' the merchant grinned.

The customer nodded, perched himself on the counter, and rolled a cigarette. He smoked that one and another before the woman reappeared, and then he had to look twice ere he recognised his fellow-traveller. The calico dress had been replaced by a neat riding-skirt, with a shirt-waist, and a light coat; the clumsy shoes by high boots, and the sun-bonnet by a soft, black felt hat beneath which the trimmed, golden-brown curls showed to advantage. In one hand, the girl carried a small grip. The clothes set off the shapeliness of her youthful body, and Drait suddenly realised that a smile on the cold, immobile face would have made it beautiful.

'There's extras in the bag,' the woman said anxiously. 'You said for to make a good job of it.'

'You've done fine, ma'am,' Drait replied, as he paid the bill. 'I'm obliged.'

They went out and walked down the street. The storekeeper laughed. 'That's a weddin'-dress you've sold, mother,' he said. 'Askin' for a parson, he was.'

'Looks more like she's goin' to her funeral,' the woman retorted.

Meanwhile, the pair they were discussing had stopped at a small log cabin on the door of which a notice announced, 'Josiah Jones, Minister.' Drait rapped, and the man himself appeared. A frail figure, prematurely grey, utterly unfit it would seem to 'fight the good fight' in a place where the laws of neither God nor man were of little avail. Yet there was a simple dignity, derived, no doubt, from his calling.

'We want you to marry us,' Drait said.

The minister nodded and took them into the parlour. It was a small room, neatly but poorly furnished with plain wood chairs, a desk, and table on which lay a Bible and prayer-book. They sat down, and he asked their names, ages, and whether either had been married before, entering their replies in a book. He knew quite well that he could not prove or disprove anything they told him, but the formality satisfied his conscience.

'Mary Francis Darrell, twenty-one, and Nicholas Drait, twenty-seven, both single,' he read out. 'We shall need two witnesses; my good neighbours usually oblige.'

He went out and presently returned with two youngish men who favoured the bride with an immediate stare of admiration, which ceased abruptly when the groom turned his own narrowed eyes upon them.

'Cut out the frills, Padre, we're pressed for time,' Drait requested.

A runaway pair, the minister decided.

He began the service, omitting all but the essential portions. The girl listened with a face of stone, but made her responses clearly and firmly.

'With this ring——' The minister paused and looked expectantly at the bridegroom.

Drait bit back an oath, then grinned, and fumbling in the breast of his shirt, produced a narrow gold band hanging round his neck by a string. Snapping this, he slipped the ring on the bride's finger and became aware that her hand was icy.

Having pronounced them man and wife, the minister recorded the event, all present signed their names, and the ceremony was over. The witnesses went out, richer by easily-earned dollars, and the minister handed a copy of his entry to the bride.

'Take good care of that, my dear, and I hope you will be very happy,' he said.

'Thank you,' she murmured, and for an instant there was a gleam of warmth in her sombre eyes.

Drait laid a bill on the table. 'Will that cover yore fee?' he asked.

'More than five times,' the little man smiled.

He watched them walk up the street, mount, and ride away. All was not well there, but he could do nothing. 'A pretty lass,' he mused. 'She reminds me of someone; but it was long ago.'

Clear of the town, the newly-wedded couple came to where the trail forked, and Mary Drait, without a glance at her husband, said acidly:

'Where are we going; to your ranch?'

15

'I don't have any,' he replied. 'An' in case yo're beginnin' to regret Bardoe, you may as well know that he was a cattle-thief, an' worse. His "ranch" was just a place where he kept stolen steers till it was safe to sell 'em.'

'You said you had never heard of him,' she reminded.

'Shore,' he admitted. 'His gun was out an' mine warn't—then.'

'Is it worse to steal cattle than money?'

'Guess not, but Bardoe would 'a' stripped me s'pos'n the luck had gone the other way. Besides, if you'd been what I figured, the coin was due to you, an' that's why yo're sittin' on it right now; I should 'a' pointed you for the nearest town an' that would 'a' been the finish.' He read the unbelief in her eyes and a gust of anger swept over him. 'Ten miles along that trail to the right'll fetch you to Midway; it can still be the finish—if you want.'

With a furious look, she snatched the quirt hanging from the horn of the saddle and for an instant he thought she was about to strike him. But the lash fell on the flank of her horse, and sent it dashing along the trail to which he had pointed. Drait swung into the other. In less than five minutes he heard the pad of pounding hooves, and smiled mirthlessly, but did not slacken his pace.

'Better the devil you know,' he muttered. 'Reckon I guessed correct—for once.'

He was not travelling fast, and she soon overtook him.

'Changed yore mind, huh?' he asked.

'I come with you only on your promise to keep secret this—marriage,' she said.

'Ashamed of it?'

'Yes,' was the furious retort.

'Folks will have notions,' he offered.

'I don't care what they think. You promise?'

'Suits me,' he replied indifferently. 'An' now, Miss Darrell, we've got quite a piece to go afore we get home.'

There was a gibe in the last word.

CHAPTER II

TWO riders were loping lazily along a little-worn track which had begun to dip down into a patch of scrub and larger trees. They made an odd couple, for apart from being obviously cow-punchers, they were entirely unlike. The elder, lean, long-limbed, and wide of shoulder, was not yet thirty, but his tanned, clean-shaven face, with its firm jaw and steady, grey-blue eyes, was that of a man who has seen life and its many problems, and death, which solves them all, and is prepared to face either unflinchingly. To the casual observer, the crossed cartridge-belts slung about his hips, and the shiny butts of two six-shooters protruding from their holsters, would have proclaimed a person perilous to provoke. The casual observer would have been right, for this was 'Sudden'—wanted, unjustly, as an outlaw in far-away Texas, and reputed throughout the South-West for reckless daring and dexterity with any weapon.*

His companion did not appear formidable. Still in his teens, he was of small but wiry build, his features thin and angular, with eyes ever alive. He wore one gun only, but his hand was never far from it, a fact the older man noted with a smile.

'Expectin' trouble, Yorky?' he asked presently.

'Guess not, but there's no harm in bein' ready,' the youth replied. 'She's liable to be just round th' corner. Don't you reckon we'll get some excitement this trip, Jim?'

'You're a bloodthirsty young devil,' came the answer. 'This is just a holiday, an' we're mindin' our own business, yu sabe?'

'Figure you can, Jim?' Yorky asked slyly.

'Meanin'?' with an assumption of fierceness.

'Well, if you'd made that a rule, I'd be fillin' a hole in th' ground right now, an' Dan an' Doc Malachi wouldn't be arguin' over which of 'em has th' finest kid.'

The grin which made a boy of him again softened Sudden's saturnine features. 'Awright, yu win,' he said, and then checked his mount as a rasping voice reached them.

'Anythin' to say, Drait, afore we jerk you into the next world?'

Sudden twisted his reins round the saddle-horn, pulled both guns, and forced his horse through a break in the underbrush. Yorky followed.

The scene upon which they burst was a curious one: a man with hands bound behind, standing beneath a tree. From an overhead branch dangled a lariat, the loop around his neck, and the other end in the hands of two burly ruffians. A couple more stood a few yards away, gazing with malevolent satisfaction at the prisoner, whose expression was one of sneering contempt. On one side of the open space, four horses nibbled contentedly at tufts of grass, and on the other a further two, on one of which sat a girl, wrists tied and head bent. A dark-faced, broken-nosed fellow was raising a hand as a signal to the executioners when Sudden spoke.

* Related in *Sudden Outlawed.*

17

'Put 'em up, *pronto*,' he said, and there was a bite in his voice which told that delay would certainly be dangerous.

The command was promptly obeyed, the pair holding the rope letting go as though it had suddenly turned into a rattle-snake. This stranger on the black horse appeared to know exactly what he wanted and to be capable of raising Cain if he did not get it. True, they were four to two, but each of them was well aware that a bullet could travel faster than the hand of the greatest gunman. The unknown accepted their obedience as a matter of course.

'Now that we're all comfortable, mebbe one o' you will tell me what's goin' on?' he suggested.

'We're stringin' up this fella,' the broken-nosed man snarled. 'Ain't that plain enough?'

'As plain as yore face, an' that's Gawd-awful plain,' Sudden replied, adding sharply, 'What's yore name?'

'Lanty,' was the unthinking reply, and then, 'What's it gotta do with you, anyway?'

'I might need it for yore tombstone.' Lanty looked alarmed; this two-gun stranger was not his idea of a humorist. 'Why are yu hangin' this man?'

'He's a cattle-thief.'

'Appearances shorely are deceivin'; I'd 'a' picked yu for that part, Mister Vigilante,' Sudden said. 'I don't see any cattle. Have yu searched him?'

It was the accused who answered, with a grin. 'Did so, an' all they found was a couple o' calves—on my legs; they took my wad instead.'

'That warn't noways right, Mister Vigilante,' came the re-proof. 'Dollars ain't evidence; they might 'a' been earned honest.'

'My name's Dirk,' Lanty snapped. 'We didn't need no proof. That's Nick Drait, a nester, an' they all steal stock. That hoss the gal's on bears Bardoe's brand.'

'I borrowed it for the lady,' came the prompt explanation.

'Was Bull there at the time?' Lanty wanted to know.

'Shore, an' raised no objection.' This with a grim smile.

Sudden did not understand, but his heart warmed to a man who could find anything amusing in his present situation. 'One of us,' he reflected, and turned his attention to the other horses.

'You ridin' for the S P?' he asked, and got an affirmative nod.

Drait spoke again. 'An' that's a lie. The S P has a new cook; ask 'em to tell you the colour of his hide.'

The challenge met with sullen silence. At a word from his friend, Yorky slid from his saddle, released the girl's wrists, and

18

performed a like office for the accused. Then the two of them collected the weapons of the four, Drait taking his own and his money from Lanty. Standing in front of him, he said:

'You hit me after I was tied up. Well, a blow for a blow is my motto, an' I'm actin' up to it.' Measuring his distance, he drove a fist into the scowling face, with a force that lifted its owner from his feet and dropped him on the back of his neck several yards away. Spitting a tooth and a torrent of oaths from his gashed mouth, the prostrate ruffian gasped:

'I'll git you for that, Drait.'

'Try, an' I'll send you to hell so quick they won't be ready for you,' was the reply. He went to the S P horses, slung the saddles to the ground, and knotted the bridles together. 'I'm takin' 'em back to the S P—mebbe,' he said.

The prospect of being set afoot brought immediate protest from the victims; a cowboy would almost rather ride in a hearse than walk. Their leader appealed to Sudden.

'Them hosses was loaned us,' he explained. 'Our'n was played out an' we left 'em in exchange.'

'Comin' so late, an' on top o' yore other claim, that's a pore tale,' Sudden told him. 'Toddlin' home'll give yu a chance to think up a better one. Yo're lucky; I've seen men swing for less.'

Driving the tied animals ahead, the nester and his party turned back into the trail, Sudden and Drait in the lead, with Yorky and the girl behind.

'I'm shorely obliged,' the rescued man said. 'It was curtains for me if you hadn't shown up.'

'Forget it,' Sudden replied. 'One look at that Lanty fella's face told me yu were gettin' a raw deal. So yo're a nester?'

'Sort of. I'd like fine for you to see my place, Mister.'

'Green is the name; it ain't a long word, but "Jim" is shorter,' the other smiled. 'My side-kick is called "Yorky" an' he's a good kid; we're just takin' a look at the country.'

'She's worth it, but reptiles is mighty prevalent,' was the sardonic answer.

Meanwhile, Yorky was endeavouring to thaw the human iceberg riding beside him, and meeting with little success. Hardeyed, she stared at the trail before them, and replied to his remarks in words of one syllable. At length, he fell back on his favourite topic—his friend. So she learned of the coming of the cowboy to the Circle Dot, the restoration of his own health, and the amazing adventures which followed.* Despite herself, she was interested, and her gaze went from the trail to the broad back of the man she was hearing about.

* Related in *Sudden Makes War*.

'Why are you called Yorky!' she asked.

'Just a name th' boys give me. You see, I was born in li'l old Noo York.'

'I never would have taken you for an Easterner.'

That made a friend of him; for many months he had been striving to eradicate all trace of the East from his speech, and only in moments of high excitement did he now relapse.

'Don't you ever want to go back?'

'No, ma'am. Look!' He swept a hand towards the distant mountains. 'Me for th' West, every time.'

'It's a cruel country, and its men are like it,' she said bitterly.

'Fella has to be tough, but that don't mean bad,' the boy defended. 'Now yore—friend, Drait,'—he did not notice her shiver—'he's tough, but I'd trust him; he has a straight eye. An' wasn't that the gran' daddy of a wallop he give that Lanty jasper?'

'Is brutality the only remedy for evil?'

'I guess so, in a land where there ain't no law.'

'Oh, I might have known,' she said. 'You men always hang together.'

Yorky grinned delightedly. 'If hangin' together keeps us from hangin' separate it gets my vote.'

She did not smile, and if she had intended to reply, the distant report of a rifle, followed by several more, drove it from her mind. Drait straightened up in his saddle, and swore.

'Damnation! That's Shadow Valley way; somethin' wrong. We gotta hurry.'

The big Mexican spurs rasped the ribs of his mount, quickening its pace. Very soon he swung off the main trail to the left, plunging into thick scrub with only a few hoofprints to point the way.

'This'll save some miles, but it's tricky travellin',' he explained. 'Them hosses is goin' to hamper us.'

'Easy settled,' Sudden replied, and beckoned to Yorky. 'Put yore loop over one o' the broncs an' lead 'em behind us.'

He watched approvingly as the boy made the throw and held the captives until the two men had passed.

'Ain't forgot all I taught yu,' he smiled.

'Not any, an' learned a lot more,' Yorky retorted, as he resumed his place by the again silent girl.

They descended a long slope by means of a series of wooded shelves, and as Drait had warned, care was essential and speed out of the question. No more firing was heard, but a column of black smoke staining the sky some miles off brought another curse to the lips of their leader.

'If that's my place some o' the cattlemen round here are goin' to need new ranch-houses afore long,' he gritted.

Presently they reached a level expanse of short grass, on the far side of which was what appeared to be the mouth of a gorge. Barely forty yards apart, rock walls rose abruptly on either side, curving inwards as though to meet at the top to form a gigantic natural arch. Huge boulders lying near supported the theory that once it had existed, but now only the pillars remained.

They passed through this gateway, and Sudden was surprised to find, instead of the stony gully he had expected, an open oval valley, shut in by miniature cliffs. A bend prevented him from seeing the full extent of the valley, but it appeared to be about a quarter of a mile in width, and the floor was carpeted with good grass. An imprecation from the nester stopped further observation.

On the fringe of the brush the charred remains of a log hut were still smoking. Only when they were close did they see, hanging from a tree-branch, the horror awaiting them. A little while earlier it had been a man, but now, the sagging head, with its bloated features, outthrust blackened tongue and goggling eyes presented only a hideous travesty of God's handiwork. The girl screamed, Yorky's face whitened, but the two men stared at the thing in hard-lipped silence; they had seen the like before. Drait rode forward, and standing in his stirrups, slashed through the rope and lowered the body gently to the ground. Then it was he saw the paper pinned to the shirt. Printed in crude capitals, it read: 'Get out, Drait. Yo're next.'

He folded and put it in a pocket. Then came the hammer of hurrying hooves, as four riders raced up and slid to a stop. At the sight of the dead man they removed their hats.

'So they got Eddie,' commented one of them, a small, grizzled bowlegged cowboy, older than the others. 'We didn't know that.'

'What do you know, Quilt?' Drait asked.

'Mighty little. We was up at the other end, blockin' the outlet like you said. We saw smoke an' come a'bilin'. O' course, they spotted us an' ran, the damn cowards. We see it was on'y the ol' cabin an' took after 'em, loosin' lead, but havin' no luck. They'd got too big a start, an' when they split in the brush we lost 'em.'

'How many?'

'Nine, I reckoned. No, couldn't pin a name to any—we on'y saw their tails. There was a biggish chap who might 'a' bin Cullin, but I wouldn't swear to him.'

Drait's eyes went again to the limp, pitiful figure, over the contorted face of which he had put his own hat. 'Think of it,'

21

he said bitterly. 'He was crippled for life—his hoss rolled on him—an' the bastards had to hang him, for no reason 'cept he worked for me. By God! Eddie, they shall pay, in full.'

'Haven't yu got a sheriff?' Sudden asked.

'I ain't, but the cattlemen have,' was the ironic reply. 'They appointed him an' he wants to keep his job; figure it out for yoreself.' He got back into his saddle. 'Quilt, you an' the boys take care o' Eddie—next that *palo verde* he used to sit under. Where's Beau?'

'Took the buckboard to Midway for them supplies you ordered. Be along any time now.'

The nester nodded. 'Want you all to feed at the house this evenin'. We gotta talk things over.'

Some two hundred yards further along the valley brought them to the house. A low building, constructed of squared logs, it covered considerable space. There was a raised veranda along the front, and at the back the ground had been cleared halfway to the overshadowing cliff. On the left was a small horse-corral, and a little to the right was the bunkhouse. Having unsaddled and corralled the horses, they walked to the house. A stout, middle-aged Negress met them at the door.

''Lo, Lindy,' the nester greeted.

'Sho' am pow'ful glad to see yoh, Massa Nick,' she replied.

'What happened?'

'Eddie tells me go hide in de brush 'case dere's trouble. He went to fin' out what dem riders was afteh. I ain't seen Eddie no mo'.' she ended fearfully.

'You won't—they murdered him.' He saw her mouth open and eyes fill with tears, and spoke roughly. 'He died doin' his duty, an' weepin' won't help.' He pointed to an open door. 'Jim, there's the parlour; you an' Yorky make yoreselves to home; grub'll be ready soon.'

When they had gone he turned again to the black woman. 'Lindy, this is my friend, Miss Darrell; she's stayin' here. Do all you can to make her comfortable. Just now she's tired an' would like to wash an' tidy up. See to it, an' then fix a meal here for all of us.'

For the moment the Negress forgot her grief, and beamed. 'Yuh come wi' me, honey,' she said.

The girl hesitated, and Drait said quietly, 'You can trust Lindy, as I would, with anythin' I possessed.'

Plainly fitted as the bedroom was, it should have represented luxury to Mary Drait, but the events of the past twenty-four hours, culminating in the awesome sight of the murdered man, had produced in her a state of stunned hopelessness; it seemed like a terrifying nightmare from which she could not wake up.

22

The Negress helped her remove hat and coat, and poured water into the basin. Her motherly gaze noted the white, drawn face, the haggard eyes. 'Yoh et sence mawnin'?' And when the girl shook her head, 'I jes' knowed it; dat Nick thinks we all strong as bullocks, like hisself. Now yoh lie down an' rest while I git a meal foh yoh an' nine'—her voice faltered—'eight hungry men.'

She hurried away, and the exhausted girl threw herself on the bed and presently slept.

Having entrusted his 'guest' to the care of the black woman, Drait joined his guests in the parlour. It was a large room, and the big centre table suggested hospitality, the solid chairs, comfort. A high, old-fashioned dresser with cupboards, and a writing-desk relieved the bareness of the walls and rugs of cured skins did the same for the board floor.

'Guess we'll have to wait a spell for our meal,' he said. 'It's a bigger party than Lindy was lookin' for, an'—Eddie used to give her a hand.'

Yorky stood up. 'Helpin' cooks is my strong suit,' he said.

Despite their host's protest, he grinned and vanished in search of the kitchen. Sudden laughed.

'Leave him be,' he said. 'When he had it to do, he hated it; now he don't have to, it's a treat. That's human nature.'

He proceeded to give the boy's story in brief, concluding with, 'There ain't much of him but it's good, an' he's just full o' sand. I promised him a holiday when I left the Circle Dot, an' I guess he's been livin' for it.'

'I hope runnin' into me ain't goin' to spoil things for you.'

Sudden chuckled. 'Just before we met up with yu he was complainin' we hadn't had any excitement.'

When Yorky returned to say the food was coming, and the men arrived in a bunch, Drait went to fetch his wife. His knock aroused her, and thinking Lindy had come back, she opened the door.

'Supper is ready,' he said.

'I'm not hungry,' she replied, and remembering her former use of the same words, added, 'Didn't you bring your quirt?'

The sarcasm produced no effect. 'I want to present the boys to you, an' there's a lot to discuss,' he replied evenly.

'I don't wish to meet them, and your affairs are no concern of mine,' she said stubbornly.

'Yo're wrong there. This business of pore Eddie has brought matters to a point when I gotta know how I stand. I'm puttin' my cards on the table an' givin' everyone the opportunity to duck out from here. That includes you.'

She was silent for a moment, studying him with scornful eyes. 'What happened to the women who wore this before me?'

23

In the palm of her hand was the ring he had placed on her finger.

'There was on'y one, an' she is dead.'

'You killed her?'

'A good guess. She was my mother, an' died to bring me into the world,' he replied sternly. 'Come.' And when she did not move, 'This mornin' you promised to love, honour, an' obey; I ain't insistin' on the first two, but I will have obedience.'

In the parlour seven men were sitting round the table, at one end of which were two empty seats. All stood up when Drait and his companion entered.

'Boys, this is Miss Darrell, my—guest,' the nester said.

The announcement produced surprise, mingled in one or two cases, with a half-shamed expression. Sudden surmised that the girl had been discussed in the bunkhouse, and probably allotted a less complimentary status. Quilt, the oldest, spoke for all.

'We're mighty glad to meetcha, ma'am,' he said, and a murmur of assent came from the others.

Her 'Thank you' was almost inaudible, and her frozen features failed to conjure up even the semblance of a smile.

'An' we shore hope you'll make a long stay, ma'am.' This from a tall, black-haired cowboy whose handsome face was marred by an habitual sneer.

'I'm obliged,' Drait said, and turned to his wife. 'That was Beau Lamond, the dandy o' the outfit; Quilt there is foreman, an' has the levelest head; next to him is Smoky, a good cowhand but a gamblin' fool—he'd sooner bet an' lose than not bet a-tall; the other two are the Horns, Long an' Short; they're twins— one of 'em beat his brother into the world by about twenty minutes, an' they're still arguin' which it was. Now you know 'em all, so let's eat; we can talk afterwards.'

The next half-hour was devoted almost exclusively to what, for men who have been in the open all day, is the serious business of feeding. Juicy steaks, swimming in rich brown gravy, with roast potatoes, bread, and a dried-apple pie, the whole washed down with mugs of steaming black coffee disappeared magically before the onslaught of these sons of the saddle. Sudden leaned back in his chair with a sigh of satisfaction, and smiled at his host.

'That's my best meal for many a day,' he said. 'Yu shore have a fine cook.'

'We know, but don't advertise it, Jim.'

Lindy, clearing the table, grinned delightedly.

When she had retired, Drait rapped on the table.

'I'm goin' to tell you the story o' Shadow Valley,' he began. 'Less'n a year ago, a fella named Rawlin bought the land from the State, built an' furnished this place, an' settled down with his wife an' three kids, the eldest a boy o' sixteen. Rawlin was from Kansas, a harmless critter, but with a streak o' obstinacy; he was warned he'd have trouble but wouldn't listen.

' "It's my land an' I've a right to stay on it," he argued.

'He'd fetched in some twenty head o' stock. Well, there was feed in the valley for many more'n that, an' all round for miles the range was free—but not for him. A few months went by an' nothin' happened. Then he gets an unsigned paper tellin' him to pull his freight, carries it to the sheriff, an' is advised to obey. He took no notice. Two weeks later, in broad daylight, eight masked men rode up the valley, returning in about half an hour. Rawlin asked what they wanted.

' "We've been lookin' over yore herd," one of 'em said. "Nine unbranded calves in it, an' the ear-notches show that they belong to ranches around here."

' "I ain't got no calves," Rawlin replied. "Somebody must 'a' put 'em there."

' "You bet somebody did," the fella said. "Stealin' cattle is a hangin' matter in these parts, Rawlin, but we're givin' you a chance."

'They ordered him to hook up his wagon, pack his family into it, with whatever few possessions they had room for, an' drift. While he was arguin', the boy—who had been huntin' at the end o' the valley—came runnin' up, an' one o' the skunks shot him. They escorted Rawlin' damn near to Midway, an' left him with a warnin' that if he tried any come-back, he an' his would be wiped out.

'He went to the sheriff, an' was asked if he could identify any o' the visitors? He couldn't—all of 'em had their faces covered an' rode unbranded hosses. Havin' made shore o' this, the sheriff went with Rawlin to the valley. They found the boy's body an' his rifle, which had an empty shell in it.

' "Proves he fired first an' makes it a case o' self-defence," was Camort's reasonin'. "I can't do a thing. You oughta took my advice."

'I met Rawlin in Midway; he was broke—heart an' pocket; all he had was in this venture. I bought the land, house, furniture, an' stock, at his price; the cattle went when they took away the planted calves. Now, the murderin' curs are after me, but they've another kind o' man to deal with. The unsigned warnin's have happened along, an' today—Eddie. I'm stayin' put, an' fightin' back with everythin' I got until these greedy swine have learnt their lesson.'

The harsh voice ceased. There had been no attempt at oratory; it was just a man, making a plain statement of fact, but the hard, cold eyes glinting through narrowed lids, and knotted jaw muscles, told of passion sternly controlled. Presently he went on:

'I ain't tryin' to drag you boys into my quarrel, but it's on'y fair to tell you how things are. If any or all o' you want yore time, I'll think no worse o' you. Remember, throwin' in with me may mean bein' outlawed, because the cattlemen own the Law, such as it is. If you wanta think it over, tell me in the mornin'.'

He leaned back in his chair, fashioned a fresh smoke, and waited, but not for long. Quilt was the first to speak.

'I'm stayin' with my job, Nick, an' thanks for the offer.'

'Me too,' Smoky said. Next to the foreman in point of age, he was of medium build and placid appearance. Only those who knew him well were aware that when roused he could develop all the attributes of a tiger-cat.

'I dunno what this bean-pole is aimin' to do, but I'm stickin's to you like yore skin, Nick, come hell or high water,' Shorty announced.

The bean-pole replied in kind. 'Then I gotta come in; can't have the fam'ly represented by half a man.'

'It's the useful half anyways—the rest is just dead wood,' the smaller twin snapped back.

Lamond's lazy voice interrupted. 'You can count on me.' Only the girl at the head of the table noted that his eyes were fixed meaningly, and not for the first time, on her.

Drait's relief was evident; save in one case—that of the last to speak—he knew these men well, and could rely on them.

'I'm mighty glad,' he said. 'It's a big gamble, with our lives as the stake, but with you boys backin' me, we may win out. Those killers o' children will have six men to handle 'stead o' one pore ol' pilgrim.'

Sudden had listened attentively to the story, and studied each speaker in turn. A whispered word to Yorky was answered by an emphatic nod.

'Mebbe I'm wrong, but I figure there's eight of us,' he said.

Drait looked up quickly. 'Meanin' you an' yore pal will chip in?' he asked.

'Why not?' was the cool reply. 'We're adrift, an' tired of it, but we ain't joinin' just for amusement. I'm peacable by nature, but a cowardly murder gets my dander up. So if yu'll have us . . .'

For the first time since they had returned to the valley, the nester's eyes lost their dourness. 'You'd better believe I'll have you,' he cried, and his tone said more than mere words. 'There's somethin' else I gotta mention—them five hosses I fetched in. The big one is Bull Bardoe's. I met up with the gent yestiddy afternoon; he had me covered an' meant to get me, but—I got him, though he didn't miss by much.' They could all see the livid mark on his cheek. 'The other four carry the S P iron, but Bardoe's men were usin' 'em. They ambushed, an' were about to give me a dance on nothin' when Jim an' Yorky kinda interfered. A fella named Lanty seemed to be in charge. Know him?'

'Yeah,' Quilt growled. 'He's Bull's right-hand man, an' that's the on'y right thing about him. Hope you swung the lot.'

'Shore would if I'd knowed 'bout Eddie,' Drait said heavily.

'Bardoe is no loss anyway,' Quilt shrugged. 'Just a double-crosser, workin' with the cattlemen an' robbin' 'em at the same time.' He looked at the clock. 'Time to hit the hay, fellas.'

As they filed out, with a 'So long, Nick,' and a shy 'Good-night, ma'am,' to the lady, Drait said to his foreman, 'See that Jim an' Yorky are comfortable; but for them, you'd all be ridin' the grub-line tomorrow.'

When they had gone, Drait looked at the girl, white-faced, impassive as a statue. He had said nothing about her, and though this was a relief, it had not lessened her hostility. He was saving himself, she decided; his men, rough and primitive as they were, would have despised him.

'They all stood by me,' he reflected, deep appreciation in his voice.

'To keep their jobs.'

The sneer angered him. 'Evidently loyalty means little to you. What are you goin' to do?'

The question stirred her. 'Have I any choice?' she retorted. 'Why did you bring me to this place of hatred, violence, and crime?'

'Eddie was a surprise to me too,' he said sombrely. 'I did the best I could. You are clothed, housed, have a servant to do yore work, and—I've given you my name.'

'The name of a murderer, liable to be hanged or shot as an outlaw,' she said passionately.

His face did not change, but his tone became harsh. 'You can live in Midway until my bein' shot or hanged gives you back yore freedom, or remain here,' he replied. 'An' I don't care one solitary damn which you choose.'

DRAIT breakfasted alone, and gave an instruction to Lindy. 'Miss Darrell's had a tryin' time lately so don't disturb her. She needs rest.'

The Negress nodded understandingly. 'Mighty purty gal, but she ain't lookin' too brash.'

'Take care of her,' he said.

At the bunkhouse Quilt got his orders: 'Have lead-ropes fixed to those hosses I brought in; I'm returnin' 'em this mornin'. Two men, with rifles, must guard the valley entrance —we can't afford to be caught nappin' again; the rest can continue the closing o' the other end. I'd like for you to come with me, Jim.'

By the time they had fetched their saddles from the house and reached the corral, Smoky and Shorty had done the first job. Rope in hand, the nester stepped through the gate and stood watching the circling band of nearly two dozen excited animals. Then his lariat snaked out and the loop fell over the head of a sturdy piebald. The thrower instantly dug his high heels in and flung his weight back on the rope. The tightening of the noose told the horse that resistance was useless, and it trotted demurely behind its captor.

'Neat work,' Sudden commented. 'Me, I'm a lazy devil.'

He gave a low whistle, and a great black chasing round with the others, stopped abruptly, whickered, wheeled, and came pacing to where the puncher stood. Drait studied it with the appreciative eye of an expert.

'He's a beaut,' he said. 'I'll swap any two in the corral.'

'Yu got some good ones, but I wouldn't part with Nigger for the whole bunch,' Sudden replied.

'I didn't expect you would,' Nick said. 'Hope you ain't over-tamed him, or he'll be stole.'

'Go to put a hand on him, but—watch out.'

Drait stepped forward and reached. The horse's ears flattened, the lips curled back, and the great teeth clashed within an inch of the outstretched arm. Then, with a squeal of rage, it reared; a moment and those terrible fore-hoofs would have descended on the nester's head with the force of pile-drivers.

'Steady, boy,' Sudden warned.

The effect was magical; the ears became erect again, the teeth covered, the wildness went from the eyes, and the threatening hoofs dropped softly back on the ground. Drait caught up a breath he had lost.

'Killer, huh?' he said.

28

'He could be,' the puncher admitted, and told only a half-truth. 'He knows his friends—an' mine.'

The two cowboys accompanied them to the entrance; they were taking the first spell as sentries.

'Not much for the men to do,' Drait remarked. 'I ain't got any cattle yet.'

They had reached the frowning buttresses flanking the outlet, and Sudden pulled up, his interest aroused by what he saw.

'There's plenty work here worth doin',' he said. 'Why not close the gap with a stone wall—hosses could drag the larger rocks into position—an' have heavy double doors, secured by bars, in the centre. It'd stop cattle from gettin' out, an' visitors from comin' in without permission.'

Drait slapped his thigh. 'Jupiter! that's an inspiration, Jim,' he cried. 'Shorty, fetch Quilt; we'll set about it right away.'

The foreman was soon on the scene, and Drait explained the idea. Quilt was enthusiastic.

'Bully,' he beamed. 'It's up to us to make a good job of a good notion, Jim. We'll build her plenty high, with a platform inside so we can look over,' he chuckled. 'Leave it to me, Nick; we're startin' now; t'other end can wait.'

Taking the lead horses, Drait and his companion went on their errand. They had gone less than a mile when the nester twitched the loop from the Bardoe animal, and smote it across the rump.

'Mebbe find its way home, an' if it don't, I ain't carin',' he said. 'What you think o' the outfit?'

'A fine crowd, I'd say.'

'Hand-picked—brought 'em with me.'

'Includin' Lamond?'

'Why, no, he's come recent—joined me just after I bought the valley.'

'At his suggestion, or your'n?'

'He was out of a job, an' asked for one,' Drait explained. 'Know anythin' against him?'

'Never seen or heard o' the fella,' was the careless reply. 'He just don't seem to fit in.'

'Too much of a dude for them rough-necks o' mine,' Nick laughed. 'They've been raised on raw meat.'

Sudden laughed too, and dropped the subject. He noticed they were travelling north, and asked a question.

'We'll get rid o' these broncs first off,' Drait told him. 'The *hombre* yo're goin' to see to is the foreman, an' he's runnin' the ranch till the owner can be found. Ol' Sam Pavitt passed in his checks 'bout a year ago, leavin' all his property to his on'y child—a daughter, or her issue. She ran away near twenty-five years back—he was a hard man to live with, by all accounts—an' never returned. His lawyer is tryin' to trace her.'

'Shouldn't be difficult unless she's left the State, or is dead,' Sudden remarked.

'I understand they got mighty little to go on. One letter from her was found among Sam's papers; it told that her husband—the cause o' the trouble atween 'em—had passed on, but called him by his front name only, an' mentioned a kid named "Frankie." The address had been torn off, so I guess she never had a reply. It's a fine ranch, an' I guess Gilman is featherin' his nest a-plenty.'

'Crooked, huh?'

'A corkscrew would look straight by the side of him.'

The first few miles took them over scrub-dotted plain, and no trail being visible, Sudden guessed they were making a short cut. Then they emerged upon a rough wagon-road, pitted with innumerable hoofprints. Drait jerked a thumb to the right.

'Leads to Midway,' he said. 'We'll be samplin' it later.'

They turned left, and after a while—to Sudden's surprise—the road began to improve; trees and brush had been cut down or uprooted to make it wide enough for two vehicles to pass, and attempts made, in bad spots, to level the surface, but there were signs that the wilderness was encroaching again.

'Ol' Sam had this done an' damn near lost most of his riders over it—cowboys don't cotton to road-makin',' Drait informed. 'Gilman ain't takin' risks, seemin'ly.'

A gradual rise of another mile brought them to the end of the road and a wide strip of open country covered with crisp, brown grass. In the midst of it, a group of buildings, and behind, a background of low, tree-swathed hills.

'Nice location,' Sudden commented.

'You said it,' his companion agreed. 'Good ranch-house, lashin's o' the best feed, an' plenty water,' he grinned. 'If I owned this place, damn me if I wouldn't turn honest.'

'It would certainly be a temptation,' Sudden smiled.

As they neared the ranch-house, a stocky, powerful man came out, and, leaning against one of the supports of the veranda roof, watched them ride up. There was no welcome in the button-like eyes, set too closely to a beak of a nose, and the thin lips, clamped to the butt of a black cigar, did not suggest amiability.

'What's yore errand?' he asked brusquely, as they drew rein.

'Fetched back four broncs wearin' the S P iron, an' I want a receipt for 'em,' Drait replied.

'How come they're in yore hands?'

'Four o' Bardoe's toughs were ridin' 'em, an' not bein' satisfied with their explanation, an' for another reason, I set 'em afoot.'

'What was the other reason?'

'They tried to hang me.'

The man on the veranda scowled. 'Didn't it occur to you I might 'a' loaned them hosses?'

'That didn't occur to them till it was too late to put it over,' the nester retorted. 'Besides, I figured you wouldn't be quite so all-fired friendly with the 8 B outfit.'

He got an oblique glance from the shifty eyes. 'An' that's correct,' Gilman growled. 'Back in a minute.' He went through a door, and presently returned with a slip of paper. 'I'm obliged,' he said. 'Anythin' Bardoe gits his claws on is apt to be a total loss. I'll give you a word of advice, Drait; if you've fallen foul o' Bull, hit the trail; you've no chance here, anyways. Don't forget what happened to Rawlin.'

'I ain't likely to,' Nick replied. 'Was Bardoe in that?'

'If I knew, d'you think I'd tell you—'specially in front of a witness?' Gilman asked ironically, with a measuring look at the other visitor.

'Jim Green—he's ridin' for me,' Drait introduced. 'Jim, this is Jack Gilman, foreman here.' The two men nodded 'Any news o' the missin' heir?'

'No, damn it, I wish they'd git the business settled,' was the reply. 'Got any cattle in Shadow Valley yet?'

Drait shook his head. 'What I bought from Rawlin were stolen.'

The foreman's expression of concern seemed genuine. 'Too bad,' he said. 'Come an' see me before you buy any more; mebbe I can save you some coin.'

'I'll remember that,' Drait replied. 'An' in case there's any doubts floatin' around, you can pass the word that the Valley belongs to me, an' I'm stayin' in it.'

Gilman sent an ugly look after them as they rode away. 'Stayin' in it?' he repeated. 'Mebbe yo're right; young Rawlin is doin' the same. Wonder where he picked up that two-gun *hombre*? He ain't no pilgrim, an' his hoss warn't born this side o' the Border. Needs keepin' an eye on, that fella.'

Which thought, curiously enough, was in the minds of both his visitors.

'Well, what d'you think of him?' Nick asked.

Sudden's grimace was expressive. 'I wouldn't, 'less I had to,' he answered.

'Same here, but I'll be interested to know how he's goin' to save me money, an' I'm willin' to bet I'll save more if I don't let him.'

'I ain't takin' yu,' Sudden laughed. 'Where we goin' now?'

'The licentious an' thoroughly disreputable settlement of Midway,' Drait replied. 'An' it ain't called that because it's halfway between Heaven an' the other place, for Midway is next door to Hell.'

'Sounds fierce.'

'That's how it is. Coupla years back, when the Judge was appointed, the decent citizens looked for better things, an' they built him a fine new court-house an' calaboose—hopin'. But the cattlemen got hold of him an' like the sheriff, he wants to keep his job.'

'But that depends on the Governor,' Sudden objected.

'Who wouldn't have any use for a dead judge,' was the grim retort.

'The ranchers must be pretty strong.'

'Their custom means a lot, an' they have the lawless element with 'em. How many? Well, there's the S P, north; the Big C—Cullin's, south-east; the Double V—Vic Vasco's, south-west; the 8 B—Bardoe's, due west; so I've got em all round me. It's a swell nest o' yeller-jackets you've stepped into.'

'My hide is thick,' the puncher smiled.

To the unaccustomed eye, Midway could only appear as a blot on the landscape. A few of the buildings boasted a second storey, some were false-fronted to convey that impression, and others were just cabins with sodded roofs. As they entered the town, Drait pulled up, and pointed.

'There she is,' he said. 'Midway's pride.'

It was a big building, standing back from the others. Substantially constructed of squared logs, it had a second floor, and three doors, the boards above which told that here was congregated, in the court-house, gaol, and sheriff's office, the whole machinery of the Law.

'Looks fine from here,' Sudden said. 'Seen the inside?'

'Not yet,' the nester grinned. 'There's Judge Towler.'

Sudden saw an oldish man passing on the other side of the street. Even without his battered high hat he would have been tall but for a pronounced stoop. A full-skirted shabby black coat flapped about his thighs, his boiled shirt was wrinkled and soiled, and his grey beard unkempt. Nevertheless, he still presented a kind of decayed distinction. Eyes bent, he seemed to be choosing his steps carefully, and twice they saw him stumble.

'I'm told he's hittin' the bottle pretty constant,' Drait remarked. 'Pity—he's got brains; if he on'y had courage too. . . .'

They went on to dismount at a saloon which announced itself as 'Merker's.' Underneath was the statement, 'No Fancy Names and No Funny Business.'

'An' that's no brag,' Drait said. 'If you lose here, you *have* lost, an' if you win, yo're paid.'

The company within was small—less than a dozen men were seated at the tables in front of the bar, and the various games of chance were idle. Behind a barrier of polished mahogany stood a dark-haired, smooth-chinned man whose face would not have appeared out of place above a clerical collar.

'Glad to see you, Nick,' he greeted, and when the nester presented his companion, added, 'You too, Mister Green.' He set out the inevitable bottle and glasses, and in a lowered tone, said, 'The sheriff is makin' a big talk an' is lookin' for you.'

'Now if that ain't lucky,' Drait replied. 'I came a-purpose to see him; get a bit further away, Jim; you don't know me till we hear what he has to say.'

A moment later, the swing-door was thrust aside, and the officer entered. Short, barrel-like in body, with stumpy, powerful legs, he waddled rather than walked in. Meanness was evident in his puffy cheeks, slit of a mouth, and cunning eyes, which gleamed for a moment when they rested on the nester, and then almost vanished, as though a light had been lowered inside him. He had been given—but did not rejoice in—the nickname of 'Stinker,' owing to a reputed adventure with a skunk.

Pompously throwing out his huge chest, on which his badge was prominently displayed, and hitching his gun-belt so that the butt was handy, he growled, 'Drait, I wanta see you.'

Nick turned slowly. 'Help yoreself,' he said. 'But don't come too close—my nose is a mite sensitive.'

A chuckle from an onlooker did not improve the officer's temper. 'Funny, huh?' he sneered. 'Well, laugh this one off: I'm arrestin' you.'

'Is—that—so?' the young man queried. 'I've often wondered how it felt. Seems simple. What d'you do next?'

The sheriff ignored the question—an evasion which made some of those present smile, but their faces became serious enough when he continued. 'Yo're charged with stealin' four hosses from the S P.'

The accused grinned. 'How on earth did you find that out, Stinker?' he wanted to know.

'That's my business.'

'Shore it is, but you never do it, an' didn't this time. You had yore information from a cow-thief named Lanty.'

'That amounts to a confession,' the sheriff said eagerly.

'How d'you figure it?'

'Because——' he paused, suddenly aware of an obstacle, and Drait finished the sentence:

'Lanty won't like bein' dragged into it, but he's goin' to be. Yestiddy, he an' three o' Bardoe's bullies ambushed, an' were just about to string me up when a couple o' strangers happened along an' interfered. The Bardoe men were usin' S P broncs, an' claimed to be ridin' for Gilman. I didn't believe it, an' set 'em afoot. So Lanty tries to come back at me by tellin' the sheriff he'll find stolen stock at Shadow Valley. Sent there yet, Stinker?'

'Yeah, an' if my fellas do find 'em you'll swing yet, for all yore fairy tale,' was the answer.

Drait, leaning comfortably against the bar, glanced round at the audience. 'A hard man, our unworthy sheriff,' he remarked, and passed a piece of paper to the saloon-keeper. 'Suspicious, too. Tell the company what that is, Sol.'

Merker read aloud: 'Received from Nick Drait, four S P horses he had reason to believe stolen from this ranch.' He paused a moment. 'It bears today's date, an' is signed by Jack Gilman.'

Open sniggers greeted the discomfiture of the officer, who was by no means popular with some of the townsfolk upon whom he had been forced. He glared at the offenders, but could conjure up no retort to the blow. The nester spoke, contemptuously:

'So you see, Stinker, I gotta decline yore invitation to the calaboose, but if I'm robbin' you o' one job, I'm givin' you another. When I reached home in the afternoon, I found Eddie Olsen—dead, an' hangin' from a limb. That don't seem to surprise you.'

The sheriff's unhealthy face had become a shade paler, and his attempt to depict astonishment was a poor effort. He lifted his massive shoulders.

'Nothin' that happens in Shadow Valley surprises me, 'cept that a damn fool should try to live there,' he sneered. 'Gimme the facts an' I'll look into it.'

'As you did the murder o' young Rawlin?'

'That was self-defence, an' I'll bet this was too.'

'You'd lose; Eddie was crippled, an' he didn't tote a gun. He was hanged just as a warnin' to me.'

A long-faced, bearded man at one of the tables looked up. 'Why, there wasn't no harm in Eddie,' he remarked. 'Hanged, huh?'

'Yeah, Pilch,' Drait replied. 'Nine full-growed, masked men to murder one disabled, unarmed lad.'

'Yore chaps reckernize any of 'em?' the officer asked.

'Do you think I'd be here if they had?' Nick said savagely.

The reply seemed to relieve the questioner. 'Cattle-thieves, I reckon,' he said. 'There's plenty about.'

34

'Yo're right, an' all of 'em own ranches. But these houn's warn't after cattle, but me, an' this proves it.'

He read out the notice the killers had left, and the sheriff shut his teeth on an oath; why did the cursed fools have to be so theatrical?

'What you expect me to do?'

'I ain't expectin', Camort,' Drait told him. 'You'll do what yore masters' tell you, like any other tame dawg.'

Hard-boiled as he was, the bitter taunt stung, and the sheriff's face purpled with passion. But the flinty-eyed man who had hurled it at him was an unknown quantity, and Camort had a fondness for certainties. Remembrance came that, by virtue of his office, he was a privileged person. An ugly light in his slitted eyes, he ordered a drink, and turned on his tormentor.

'That'll be all from you, Drait,' he said furiously. 'Pull yore gun, you——'

As the last word left his lips, he grabbed the glass on the bar, flung the contents full in the nester's face, and reached for his hip. Drait was helpless, blinded by the fiery spirit, and it seemed the dastard design must succeed. Camort's gun was out, and his finger actually pressing the trigger when flame jetted from the left hip of the strange puncher, now standing clear of the bar; the threatening weapon clattered on the floor, and with a yelped oath, its owner clutched a ripped fore-arm. Before he could move, iron hands gripped his throat, shook him like a rat, and flung him away. Against the power in those long, muscular arms the sheriff's bulk availed him not at all. The astounded spectators saw him stagger backwards, crash into a table, and lie prone amidst the ruins. The puncher stepped towards him.

'Stinker is correct,' he said. 'Of all the rotten skunks I ever met—an' that's quite a few—yo're the meanest. I oughta blowed yore light out; if yu get in my way again, I'll do it—that star yu disgrace ain't a circumstance to me.'

Camort, understanding that he was safe for the time, ventured a threat : 'I'll git you both for this.'

Sudden laughed, and looked at the company. 'Make a note o' that, gents. If we're found shot from behind, yu'll know who did it.'

'You betcha,' Pilch replied. 'An' don't judge this town by that fella, Mister—he warn't no pop'lar selection. If he'd downed Drait by that trick I'd 'a' laid him out too, an' that's whatever.'

'Good for yu,' the puncher smiled, and seeing that his friend now had the use of his eyes again, added, 'Comin', Nick?'

When they were in the saddle again, the nester said, 'That's the second time in twenty-four hours you've saved my life. Hell,

I'll be scared to go about without you soon, but if the ante is too big, I ain't holdin' you.'

'Shucks!' the other said. 'Why, that two-bit imitation peace-officer would say I'd run away from him. No, sir, I'm seein' this game through to my last chip.'

'I'm shore obliged,' Drait said, and meant much more.

CHAPTER IV

A WEEK passed uneventfully. Every morning Mary rode up the valley with her husband for a lesson in shooting, only to come back with a sense of frustration. He was a considerate, attentive companion and nothing more; all her advances failed to penetrate the armour of bluff good-fellowship in which he seemed to have encased himself. At times, she wondered if he suspected her design and was also playing a part—a thought which only stiffened her resolve to punish him. But nevertheless, she enjoyed the jaunts, the valley had an endless variety of interest. So she was conscious of real disappointment when Nick announced he could not accompany her.

'Gotta go into town,' he explained. 'O' course, you could take Beau.'

The suggestion was casually made, but there was an expression on his face she could not read. 'I shall be quite all right by myself,' she replied.

'I dunno—that end ain't plugged yet,' he said doubtfully. 'Have yore gun along.'

She promised, and then remarked, 'The sheriff of Midway doesn't think much of you, does he?'

This brought the ghost of a grin. 'I wouldn't wonder if he's thinkin' quite a lot o' me,' he drawled.

'Are you taking Mister Green?'

This time there could be no evasion. 'Who's been talkin' outa turn?' he asked.

'I don't know,' she told him, adding softly, 'I only want you to be careful.'

In the case of nine men out of ten, her apparent solicitude would have produced some sign, but the nester's face remained unchanged. Muttering something about chattering chumps, he went out. At the corral he met Yorky and gave him instructions, concluding with, 'Don't show yoreself 'less you have to; guess there ain't any real risk, but till that far end is corked up . . .'

Yorky nodded; he would have liked to ask a question, but had been well-schooled by Sudden, and knew when to keep his mouth shut. As Drait rode away, the boy's approving eyes followed him.

'Two of a kind—Jim an' him,' he informed the air. 'Gosh! Glad I'm on their side.'

Nick found the rest of his outfit busy at the wall, which was now a formidable obstacle. Calling Quilt aside, he explained about Yorky, and added a word of praise.

'We'll finish her today, an' she ain't no slouch of a job,' the foreman said. 'If yo're needin' Jim. . . .'

'Why should I be?'

'Headin' for town, ain't you?'

'Well?' Sharply.

'The sheriff is shootin' off his mouth quite a bit. Shore, he's still crippled, but he has friends.'

Drait frowned. 'Who's been yappin' around here?'

'I can tell you one who ain't an' that's the fella what knowed all about it—reckon he was raised among Injuns,' the little man grinned. 'Was you expectin' to keep it secret?'

'Beats hell how the news gets about in this country,' the nester grumbled.

'Little birds certainly ain't scarce,' Quilt agreed, and when the other was out of hearing, added, 'Nick, if you wasn't more generous with yore dollars than yore words nobody'd work for you 'cept damn fools like me.' He pondered a moment. 'An' I shore am one; if I hadn't mentioned Jim, mebbe you wouldn't 'a' gone alone; I oughta be booted.'

Mary, riding slowly along the valley, was thinking much the same thing. The rebuff she had received still brought the colour to her cheeks. She had learned from Lindy of the bearding of the sheriff. Brutal, unscrupulous the nester might be, but she had to admit that he had the quality most esteemed in the West—courage. Fight—that was Nature's universal law. . . .

An amused voice broke in on her meditations. 'You didn't oughta be all alone this bright mornin'.'

She turned to find Beau Lamond pacing just behind, hat in hand, a confident gleam in his dark eyes. She drew rein.

'Did Mister Drait ask you to ride with me?' she enquired.

'Why, no, must 'a' forgot,' he smiled.

'On the contrary, he offered me your company, but I told him I preferred my own.'

His conceit would not accept this. 'Say, but that was real cute of you,' he complimented.

'Not at all, it was true,' she returned icily, and rode on.

He made no attempt to follow her, save with his furious gaze.

'So that's the way of it, huh?' he growled. 'Well, it takes two to make a game, an' I can wait.'

Savagely he wrenched his horse about and spurred to the gate. Smoky read the flushed features aright.

'Sorta took the wrong turnin', Beau?' he queried.

'Mind yore own damn business,' the other snapped.

'Somebody just bin tellin' you that?'

Before the incipient quarrel developed, Quilt crushed it. 'Better both try it,' he said sharply. 'Git busy.'

The girl did not look round. Her anger was not all caused by the cowboy's presumption, some of it being due to the unwelcome feeling that she was missing the big, taciturn man who had been her daily companion. Resentfully, she told herself that it was absurd, but nevertheless, the valley did not seem quite the same. She passed the pool, almost without a glance, dismounted and fired twelve shots at the tree, hitting it twice. This would please Nick, at which thought she straightway resolved not to tell him.

On reaching the end, she faced round and sat drinking in the scene. The green oval, with its mirror-like pool and frame of grey, toothed rock, seemed utterly peaceful. The bulge in the cliffs prevented her from seeing the ranch-house, or the entrance where the men would be working. The sun's rays, growing stronger, were licking the diamond drops from the grass. Mary breathed deeply.

'Brownie, it's—just—Eden,' she told her pony.

'Needs an Adam though,' chuckled a gruff voice.

She turned her head; a big man on a horse was just at her shoulder; it was Bardoe. Her cry of astonishment and attempt to back away brought suspicion. Grabbing her rein, he bent and peered closely; recognition dawned in his eyes.

'So it's you? Well by Gawd, that's luck I warn't lookin' for,' he cried. His gaze travelled over the trim figure gloatingly. 'I knowed you was a pretty piece, but duds shore do make a difference.'

He leaned nearer and she tried to sway away. 'I thought you were killed,' she said.

'Near thing,' he replied, tapping the soiled rag twisted about his head. 'Creased me, that's all. I was out for a coupla days, an' them cussed idjuts o' mine had me all ready for plantin'. Funny to come to life in yore coffin. You don't seem overjoyed.'

'Why should I be?' she retorted. 'I'm glad you escaped, but——'

'One man's as good as another, huh?' he sneered. 'Mebbe better, if he buys you fine fixin's. Allasame, yo're wrong—Drait ain't goin' to last ten flicks of a cow's tail. He makes mistakes;

the man who steals my hoss, money, an' woman, has gotta take my life too.'

'I was not your woman,' Mary said furiously. 'And——'

'Don't say it,' he grated. 'We're startin' for the 8/B right now.'

He dragged her pony's head round. Suddenly she remembered, drew her revolver from the holster, and levelled it at his head. 'Get away from me or I'll fire,' she threatened.

For an instant he paused, staring, and then, with a grin, came closer. She pulled the trigger, but only a click resulted; she had neglected Drait's instruction to always reload at once. In anger and disgust she flung the weapon to the ground. Bardoe's laugh was torture.

'I like 'em with guts,' he said. 'Yore man should 'a' told you that an empty gun is more dangerous than no gun a-tall.'

'He did,' she muttered miserably. 'I forgot.'

'Well, well, you'll know better next time—mebbe,' he jeered, and jerked at the rein of the unwilling Brownie. 'C'mon, lift yore damn legs, you.'

'Lift yore damn paws, you,' echoed a rather high-pitched but very steady voice.

Bardoe dared not disobey; one glance at the girl's face told him he was trapped. As he made the movement, he risked a lightning peep over his shoulder but got no satisfaction. The newcomer was young, little more than a boy, but there was nothing juvenile about the Winchester he held, finger tight against the trigger; the slightest increase of pressure.... Like most of his kidney, Bardoe was a willing gambler, but here he had no chance; long before he could start anything, hot lead would be boring his body.

'Shuck yore shootin'-irons—all of 'em,' came the curt order. 'An' make it snappy.'

The ruffian obeyed; with the enemy behind him, even a gun in his hand was of no use. A pair of revolvers and a rifle dropped to the ground. Lynx-eyed, Yorky watched the operation.

'You all right, ma'am?' he asked.

'Yes,' she replied. 'Please let him go.'

Yorky did not approve of this—he wanted to hand the fellow over to Quilt—but the girl was obdurate, and he gave in.

'Yo're playin' in luck, *hombre*, but don't figure on it,' he said. 'Next time you'll be shot on sight. Now fade.'

'Yore turn today, mebbe mine tomorrow,' Bardoe retorted, with a black scowl.

The boy waited until he disappeared, and then, having fetched his horse and collected the forfeited arms, they set out for the house. After she had thanked him warmly—to his great discomfort—she wanted to know how he happened to be at that end of the valley.

'I was lookin' for another way out, an' stickin' close to the cliff,' he explained.

'Did you find one?'

He shook his head. 'Ain't finished searchin'.'

She suspected this to be a mere excuse but did not pursue the subject. Yorky, she learned, had come upon the scene only a moment before he intervened and did not know the intruder's identity.

'That was Bardoe,' she told him.

'Hell's gates!' Yorky swore, apologised, and added bitterly. 'I savvied we was wrong to turn him loose.'

'That was my doing,' she said.

The reappearance of the man was a shock, and his parting threat told her that she had not seen the last of him. The remembrance of the unconcealed lust in his gaze made her shiver. Odd that she might yet come to regard Drait as ... She drove away the thought impatiently; at the best, he could be no more than the lesser of two evils.

*   *   *

The foreman of the S P watched the approaching horseman and grinned crookedly when he recognised him. 'Boy, you got a nibble, but you need to play him afore you strike,' he told himself. 'He ain't no sucker.' And when the visitor reached the ranch-house, "Lo, Drait, take the weight off'n yore saddle.'

The nester complied, and sat rolling a cigarette, waiting for the other to open the ball.

'How's thing's at Shadow Valley?' Gilman began.

'Fine as silk,' Nick replied easily.

'Been to town lately?'

'Any good reason why I should?'

'No, but there may be one for keepin' away.'

'You ain't referrin' to that bum sheriff, are you?' Drait asked scornfully.

'Not as a good reason,' Gilman laughed. 'Allasame, if you do have to go, take yore friend along, an' tell him to be more careful where he plants the pills; shootin' the buttons off'n a rattler may be fine marksmanship but it's pore judgment. Still figure on stayin' in our midst?'

'Shore do—there's plenty room for another range without crowdin' anybody,' Drait replied.

'Well, it ain't worryin' me none,' the foreman said carelessly.

'Mebbe if I owned the S P I'd talk different, but . . .' He finished with a shrug.

'You should have a good job here.'

'Don't think it; that law-sharp at Rideout keeps me mighty close-hauled—you'd fancy the damn place belonged to him. I'm runnin' the whole shootin' match an' drawin' a foreman's pay. Is that fair?'

'I'll say it ain't,' the other agreed. 'Mebbe the new owner'll make it up to you, when they find him.'

'More likely to turf me out, figurin' to do it better hisself,' Gilman said gloomily. 'Started yore herd yet?'

'You said you might do somethin' about that.'

'How about sixty yearlin's an' forty calves at eight bucks per head all round?'

'Sounds cheap.'

'It is, but the ranch is short o' ready coin. It'll be unbranded stock, mostly our'n—my fellas ain't too careful—with mebbe a sprinklin' o' strays, but when yore iron's on 'em it'll be nobody's business.'

His slitted eyes watched the nester closely as he made this proposition, but he saw only what seemed to be appreciation of a real bargain.

'I'm obliged,' Drait said. 'I'll certainly chew on that.'

'Let me know, an' the beasts'll be ready. You can collect at daylight—I don't want it knowed that the S P is pushed for money.'

Drait came away in a thoughtful frame of mind. Either Gilman was deliberately robbing his employers, or he was setting a trap, and it was more than possible he was doing both. Dealing with a lawyer who knew nothing of the cattle business the former would be easy, but the alternative required serious consideration. Probably the foreman was working with the other ranchers, and Drait had no desire to hand them a weapon against himself.

When he arrived at Shadow Valley he found the wall completed, and he had to wait while a grinning Smoky unfastened and flung open a half of the massive gates.

'Well, Boss, here she is,' he said. 'Strong enough to stop a stampede, an' six fellas what can shoot'll hold her agin a regiment.'

Drait nodded. 'Shouldn't have no more surprises.'

But there was one waiting for him at the house. Mary was at the door, and he almost fancied she was relieved to see him.

'There is something you have to know,' she began. 'Bardoe is alive.'

With a frown which grew heavier he listened to her story.

41

Only when she had finished did he make the comment. 'You let him go?'

'I was to blame,' she replied. 'Yorky wanted to hold him.'

'Yorky was right.' He looked at her ironically. 'You tried to shoot the man, an' then . . .'

'I can't explain,' she interrupted passionately.

'I s'pose you thought I'd finish what I'd bungled,' he said, and when she did not deny, 'I don't shoot unarmed men—he'd have had an even break, which is more than he gave me. Well, that job's still to do, but there's another I must be seein' to.'

He strode to the bunkhouse, where he found the outfit, all save Smoky. The foreman asked a question.

'Good work,' Drait replied. 'But there's a rat-hole at the other end that's gotta be stopped complete an' *pronto*. Yorky, I'm right obliged to you.'

The boy squirmed uneasily. 'Ain't worth mentionin',' he said. 'If I'd knowed who he was . . .'

'Shore, I understand,' the nester smiled. 'Jim, there's somethin' I wanta ask you.'

When they were outside the bunkhouse, Drait told of the offer he had received. 'O' course, he'll put the dollars in his own pocket—after squarin' his men,' he concluded. 'I don't care none about that; what I'm wonderin', is he diggin' a hole for me?'

'If the critters ain't marked, I don't see how he could do anythin',' Sudden said. 'There's one precaution yu might take; where does he bank?'

'With the Western Union; it's the on'y one in Midway; we all use it.'

'Good. Draw the money out in big bills, have the manager make a note o' the date an' numbers, an' tell him you might need to know who pays 'em in again. If Gilman tries any tricks, he may get tangled in his own rope.'

'I want those beasts, an' I figure he'll play straight, anyway till he's got some more o' my dollars. But I'll do as you say—fix it in town tomorrow. Oh, there won't be no trouble, but come if you like an' fetch Yorky along; I owe him a break.'

So the morning found the three of them outside the bank premises in Midway. The nester went in to transact his business, and his companions waited, looking at an all too familiar scene. Heavy freight wagons, drawn by plodding mules, churned up the dust, distributing it impartially on passing pedestrians. In front of the saloons stood lines of patient ponies, their flicking tails waging the unending war against the flies. The passers-by afforded a wide choice in race and colour; roughly-dressed, craggy-faced whites, yellow-skinned Mexicans, slit-eyed, smiling Chinamen, and Negroes. Sudden, sitting carelessly in his saddle, appeared indifferent, but his keen eyes missed nothing, and he at once noticed that the nester's arrival had aroused interest.

'Somethin' in the wind,' he said to Yorky. 'Where's that lousy sheriff off to, an' what's he so pleased about?'

Camort had passed on the other side of the street, his arm still in a sling, and his face alive with malignant satisfaction. Yorky studied the stumpy figure.

'If he smells as bad as he looks they've christened him correct,' he decided. 'How do things like that git their jobs?'

'Just because they are things like that,' Sudden said caustically. 'Comin' from where yu do, yu oughta know. The big men have the whip-hand. The election is a farce; the outfits have to vote as they're told, an' the tradesmen daren't offend large customers. The ballot ain't secret, an' Heaven help the fella who supports the wrong side.'

Drait rejoined them. 'All fixed,' he said. 'Williams, the manager, is a good chap; he don't admire the way the town is run, but like plenty others, he has to play his cards close. I hear the sheriff is on the warpath again; seen anythin' of him?'

'He watched yu go into the bank, an' it shore looked like the answer to a prayer. Then he seemed to remember somethin' important.'

'You don't say,' Nick grinned. 'What we goin' to do?'

A man slouching slowly by answered the question: 'Scatter dust if yo're wise. Camort reckons he's got you cinched.'

'Thanks, friend, but he's a pore reckoner—lack of schoolin' I expect. We'll go find him.'

The unknown shrugged. 'It's yore funeral,' he said.

'Oh, I guess not,' Nick replied. 'On'y the good die young an' I'm bad—terrible bad.'

They proceeded to Merker's, the owner of which greeted them with, 'Nick, you can crowd yore luck too close.'

The warning of a well-wisher, an explanation was due. 'I came into town on my own affairs,' the nester replied quietly. 'Then I hear a man is anxious to see me. I don't like disappointin' folks.'

'He thinks he has you,' Merker said.

'He's thought that before,' Nick smiled, and glanced about him. 'Midway 'pears to be thirsty.'

'No—curious,' was the meaning answer.

So that was it; those present knew what was afoot, and had gathered to see the fun—if any. A stirring apprised him that something was happening. He turned his head. The sheriff marched in, followed by a lanky, hawk-faced fellow carrying a sawed-off shot-gun, which, spraying its load of buckshot, made missing, at short range, well-nigh impossible. This individual, whose eyes seemed to have a permanent difference of opinion, and in consequence, was generally known as 'Wall-eye,' was the newly-appointed deputy to the peace-officer. The pair halted in front of the nester and his companions. Drait broke the silence:

'Hired yoreself a bodyguard, Stinker?'

The sheriff's reply was addressed to his assistant. 'If any o' them guys makes a move, let fly.'

'If he does, you'll wake in the next world, Camort.' This from the saloon-keeper, who leaning forward on the bar, had a forty-five in his fist, trained directly on the man he warned. 'An' I don't mean—mebbe,' he added.

The sheriff glared. Merker was a quiet man who minded his business, but was known to be impatient of interference, as more than one obstreperous customer had discovered; he did not waste breath on empty threats.

'Yo're obstructin' me in the execution o' my dooty,' Camort blustered. 'I represent the Law.'

'Mebbe—it's usually described as an ass,' Merker replied coolly. 'Anyway, you don't turn a riot-gun loose on my premises. I'm rememberin' that time when you blinded a man, an' then tried to down him.'

The other's face was venomous. 'I ain't forgettin' this, Merker.'

'Which you'd better not. Now, spit yore poison, an' fade.'

'Suits me. I got a warrant, signed by the Judge, for the arrest o' this jasper, Drait.'

The jasper in question received the news with a sober nod. 'On what charge?' he asked.

'Waylayin' an' murderin' Bull Bardoe,' Camort exulted.

'Is that all?'

'You'll find it a-plenty.' He addressed the audience. 'Bull was found over a week back by some of his own men up on the Table Mesa trail, shot through the head.'

'Very sad,' Nick murmured. 'Did he say I killed him?'

'How——?' the sheriff began, and then saw the twinkle in the nester's eyes. 'Funny man, huh? Well, have yore laugh while you can. The Judge will hold the trial this afternoon, an' by sunset you'll be swingin' high an' dry.'

'Fast work, Stinker,' the accused retorted. 'What are you afraid of?' Getting no answer, he went on, 'You gotta give me time to prepare my defence an' call a witness.'

'On'y one?' Camort sneered. 'Twenty won't help you.'

44

'Got it all planned out, huh?' Drait smiled. 'Yeah, just one—Bull Bardoe hisself.'

He saw the flicker of fear in the man's eyes, and then came a guffaw, too forced to be natural. 'I doubt if you'll have time to dig him up.'

Someone thrust aside the door of the saloon, and stood there. 'Hi, Stinker, look what's blown into town,' he cried.

Every eye was turned to door or window, to see the familiar figure of Bull Bardoe pace slowly along the street, quite unconscious of the sensation he was causing. The occupants of the saloon gazed in bewilderment, the sheriff's expression was one of rage, and his utterance anything but pious, and Nick Drait grinned. Merker spoke:

'Bull certainly is the most active corpse I ever saw; it don't seem proper for a murdered man to go cavortin' about like that.'

The laughter which followed the irony had little of amusement in it, and Camort realised that he was the recipient of sinister looks; he must do something.

'I've bin misinformed—made a fool of,' he said indignantly.

'Then somebody's wastin' time,' Drait said caustically. 'It's a plain enough frame-up, an' that's why you were rushin' things. Bull was to keep under cover until you'd jerked me into the next world. One o' you seems to have slipped up.' He turned to the spectators. 'I hope yo're proud o' this dawg you made a sheriff.'

'We ain't, not none,' Pilch growled. 'We'd like to hang him a whole lot.'

'It's all a lie,' Camort asserted. 'I was told he was dead, an' that the hoss he allus rode was in Drait's corral.'

'Bull's forkin' that same hoss right now,' someone pointed out. 'I ain't shore we didn't oughta do what Pilch sez.'

The ring of threatening faces made the sheriff's heart skip a beat; Western mobs were easily inflamed, and his friends the cattlemen and their outfits were far away.

'I was on'y tryin' to do my dooty,' he protested lamely.

Jeers greeted the statement. The nester stepped forward and took the warrant from the officer's nerveless fingers.

'I'll see Towler myself about this,' he said. 'Twice you've planned to put somethin' over on me; the third time won't be lucky—for you. Now, get out.'

'An' stay out,' the saloon-keeper added.

The sheriff and his deputy slouched through the door, and the latter made no secret of his feelings. 'It ain't offen I'm glad to leave a saloon, but I'm admittin' this is one o' the times,' he said. 'We wasn't a bit pop'lar in there.'

'If it's popularity yo're after you got the wrong job,' his boss told him. 'As for them sots, they jaw plenty but dasn't do anythin'. I'd like to give Bull my candid opinion.'

'Shall I find him for you?' Wall-eye offered.

'I can do that for myself—if I want him,' the sheriff said, knowing perfectly well that he would not. He had courage of a kind, but it was not of the quality necessary to bully Bardoe.

The nester and his friends followed soon after, making their way to the Judge's office, which adjoined the court-room, and was part of the gaol building. An unceremonious entrance brought the judicial feet from the desk-top to the ground, and a look of astonishment from their owner as he recognised the leading visitor.

'What are you doing here?' he asked, with as much dignity as a man caught napping might immediately muster.

'Not expectin' me, Towler, huh?'

'Hardly—in this part of the premises,' the Judge retorted.

Drait threw the warrant on the desk. 'Did you sign that?'

'Certainly, it is one of my duties.'

'Do you require proof that the person named may be guilty?'

'Evidence is the sheriff's affair; I deal with it when I try the case.'

'Are you aware that Bardoe—the man that paper accuses me of killin'—rode into town, alive an' well, less'n half an hour ago?'

The Judge sat up straight. 'Are you insinuating——?'

'No, I'm just tellin' you,' Drait cut in harshly. 'In front of twenty others, Camort said I was to be tried an' hanged before sunset—that I hadn't a chance. An' this for a crime which existed on'y in his—an' yore—imagination.'

'This is an outrage,' Towler spluttered, but his watery eyes dropped before the fierce gaze of the nester.

'Shore is,' the latter agreed drily. 'What you goin' to do about it?'

The Judge re-lighted the stub of a cigar, and remembered that he was an important personage. 'I was referring to the insult directed against myself,' he replied. 'Any difference you have with the sheriff is no concern of mine.' He was rather proud of this effort.

'An' the recent murder of two men in Shadow Valley is also no concern o' yores?' Drait asked cynically.

'I am not here to discover or arrest malefactors,' Towler said disdainfully. 'I am answerable only to the Law——'

'An' the Governor who appointed yu,' Sudden reminded.

The Judge looked at this hard-featured man whose cold, level voice he heard for the first time. This must be the fellow who had crippled the sheriff. He decided not to reply.

'Yo're forgettin' Stinker an' the cattlemen,' Drait said.

The taunt stung like a whip-lash. Quivering with rage, the badgered jurist cried, 'I won't put up with this; I'll have you charged with contempt of court, and——'

'I'll plead guilty to that,' was the biting reply. 'Listen, Towler; I came here to find out whether you were fool or crook. Yo're both, but you haven't the guts to be real bad, or to run with the rats who are usin' you. Yo're on the wrong trail, an' it'll land you in the pen—if you live. *Adios.*'

With which ironical farewell, the visitors filed out. Towler sat staring at the closed door for some moments, and then opened a drawer, produced a flask, and took a hearty pull at it.

'Damn Bardoe,' he said fervently.

CHAPTER V

'Where we bound for, Jim?' Yorky wanted to know when they set off on the following morning.

'Payin' a visit to Mister Bardoe,' Sudden said. 'But we ain't intendin' to intrude, in fact, we're goin' to be real shy. What's yore opinion o' Nick?'

The boy thought for a moment. 'A mighty good friend and a damn bad enemy,' he replied. 'If th' other man fights dirty, he'll do th' same, or wuss.'

Sudden nodded. 'That's how I figure him.' He glanced slyly at his companion. 'I dunno how things'll break, but backin' his play won't exactly be a pleasure trip.'

'If yo're worryin' about me, forget it,' Yorky said. 'Think I wanta ride around gazin' at scenery? I like action.'

They were headed west, through a jumbled mess of country—open plain, forested slopes, stony, dry ravines, all of which led to higher ground. In front, but miles distant, rose a wide, flat-topped bluff.

'That'll be Table Mesa,' Sudden remarked. 'Somewhere around there is Mister Bardoe's hang-out. If we run into him, keep yore hat pulled down; he's had a look at yu.'

'Not much o' one, 'less he's got eyes in th' back of his head,' the boy laughed. 'Allasame, there's times I like to be forgotten.'

As they drew nearer to the Mesa the surface of the country became less irregular; stretches of good grazing studded with mottes of scrub-oak, thorn, and cactus were frequent, and in the distance, moving spots which could only be cattle. Not wishing to be seen, the intruders were forced to skirt the edges of these open spaces, where the brush afforded cover. Presently, in a secluded grassy hollow, they came upon a dozen or more steers. The animals appeared to be disturbed, restless, and now and again one would turn to lick its haunch. There was a lingering odour of burnt hair, and on one side of the hollow a tiny curl of blue smoke from the remains of a fire.

'Fresh brands,' Sudden remarked. 'If they're 8 B it's none of our business.'

They edged their horses slowly forward until the tell-tale marks could be read. 'Double X an' the bottom halves is new— put on within the hour,' the puncher commented. 'Up to then they were owned by the Double V. This is gettin' interestin'.'

They went on, discovering more Double X cattle, these with the alterations partly healed, and then lighted on a bunch bearing the brand 8 B.

'That's his own, same as on th' hoss he rode into th' valley,' Yorky said.

'Take another squint, son,' the elder man advised. ' 'Bout a coupla weeks back, these were S P steers. See where the S has been turned into the figure, an' a lower loop added to the P?'

'Yo're right, Jim,' Yorky agreed. 'I don't know it all yet.'

'An' that's allus worth findin' out,' Sudden smiled. 'Wonder why he's keepin' off Cullin?'

'Mebbe he ain't; we just don't happen to 'a' found 'em.'

They continued the search, but a broad expanse of open range compelled them to stay in the shelter of the undergrowth, and they found no more cattle. On the edge of a small clearing they halted; in it stood a largish log building, one-storied, and of uncared-for appearance. This, they guessed, must be the 8 B ranch-house. Screened by the trees, they waited, and presently a rider, coming from the east, loped across the plain and pulled up. They saw him pass, heard his hail, 'Hello, the house,' and a gruff greeting.

'Gilman, of the S P, by thunder!' Sudden muttered, and slid from his saddle. 'I'm goin' to take a chance; stay put—yo're my ace in the hole.'

There was a window facing them, and it was partly open. Stooping and moving swiftly, Sudden reached and crouched beneath it. Two men were within, evidently the host and his visitor, for there was a clink of bottle against glass.

'Here's how, Jack,' the gruff voice said. 'An' what brought you this way?'

'Well, I hears yo're dead, an' then that you ain't,' Gilman replied. 'Figured I'd better come over an' find out my chances o' collectin' for that hundred head I let you lift.'

'You'll have to wait till I've sold 'em,' came the reply. 'I was comin' to settle when I run into that blasted nester.' He gave

48

his own version of the encounter, ending, 'He took my money, hoss, an'—all.'

'You returned to this yer world o' sin a day too soon; by what I hear,' the other chuckled.

Bardoe's burst of profanity betrayed his soreness. 'Made me a laughin'-stock,' he added. 'Camort's a blunderin' idjut. 'Bout time we had a sheriff whose head ain't full of sawdust. Drait has gotta go.'

The foreman's voice sounded indifferent. 'Not ownin' the S P, I dunno as I care much.'

'Why shouldn't you own it? If you work things right, by the time they find Pavitt's kid you'll have the cash to buy, an' the ranch that poor, he'll be glad to sell.'

'Shore is an idea.'

'Skittles! Don't pretend I'm tellin' you anythin'. Count me on yore side, an' I reckon that goes for Cullin an' Vasco, none of us wants a stranger buttin' in here.'

'I'm obliged,' Gilman replied. 'Well, I'll be taggin' along.'

The eavesdropper at the window took the hint and regained cover without delay. He grinned when he saw that Yorky had his rifle out. They watched the visitor depart, and then followed suit, taking a more southerly line.

'If we can find the Double V ranch-house we'll mebbe put a kink in Mister Bardoe's rope,' Sudden explained.

They covered some half-dozen miles and then the scattered cattle they encountered advised them that they were on the right range. Suddenly a horseman emerged from a clump of brush. He had a rifle across his knees, and his face, though hard and suspicious, was not aggressive. Apparently their interest in the grazing cows had aroused his curiosity.

'You fellas lookin' for anythin'?' he asked mildly.

'Why, we're kind o' searchin' for the Double V ranch-house,' Sudden replied.

'Three mile further on. If yo're wantin' Vasco, you've found him. What's yore trouble?'

'It ain't our'n, but I'll explain,' the puncher said. Getting down, he trod a bit of sand level, and with his finger drew on it the Double X brand. 'Who owns that iron about here?'

'Nobody as I knows of. Why?'

'We've seen cows wearin' it,' Sudden told him. 'The odd thing was that the upper half o' the brand was old, an' the lower added today.' He swept a toe over the latter, and stepped back. 'Easy done' ain' it?'

The rancher swore. 'Where'd you see them cattle?'

' 'Bout six mile o' here, bearin' north; they was mixed with some 8 B steers.'

Vasco swore again. 'I'll git some o' the boys an' we'll look into this straightaway.'

Sudden hoisted himself into his saddle. 'Yo're playin' the wrong card,' he suggested. 'He'll plead ignorance; you know, we could have done the blottin, for reasons of our own. No, sir, yore game is to keep cases an' catch him red-handed.'

The rancher considered this for a moment; something he had heard recurred to him; he studied the pair more closely, and suspicion grew in his eyes. 'You ridin' for Drait?' he asked, and when Sudden nodded, went on. 'Mebbe yo're right—I'd better hold off an' collect evidence my own self.'

'Shore,' the puncher smiled. 'An' don't forget I've been tellin' yo to do that very thing. Yore friend in the scrub is gettin' impatient. What's the matter with him? Modest—or somethin'?'

The red crept up under the tan on Vasco's face; he had been outplayed. 'It's my foreman—he ain't usually careless,' he said. 'Hi, Pawley!'

A tall, lean rider came out of the bushes, a somewhat sheepish expression on his craggy countenance; no man likes being caught in an undignified position. Sudden noted the long nose, high cheek-bones, and steady eyes; they told him something.

'Meet two o' the Shadow Valley boys,' Vasco said, and looked a question. Sudden supplied their names, and the foreman shook hands.

'You got a keen eye, Mister,' he complimented.

'Mostly guess-work,' Sudden replied. 'I figured yore boss wouldn't tackle two armed strangers 'less he had help handy.'

'Huh! You don't know him,' Pawley grunted. 'Takes too many damn chances.' Then he grinned. 'We Texans do git around, don't we?'

Sudden returned the grin. 'Brother, yu said it; we follow the longhorns.'

'When you've finished slammin' me an' swappin' childhood memories, Pawley, you might as well hear the news,' Vasco chimed in.

The foreman's face lengthened as he listened. 'Well, we're losin' 'em—a steady leak,' he admitted. 'I'd say Green has the right notion—we gotta be shore. I've allus told you, Vic, that iron o' yores is a rank temptation—Double M, Two Diamond; oh, hell it's as easy as turnin' over.'

'I put it on the first cow I ever owned,' the rancher said stubbornly.

'An' it'll go on the last if you ain't careful,' was the sardonic retort.

'Cheerful cuss, ain't he?' Vasco smiled. 'Well, gents, I'm shorely obliged, an' I'll be pleased to see you any time.'

On their way home Yorky was silent for a while, and then, 'Ain't you sort o' helpin' th' enemy, Jim?'

'I guess not. Look it over. If Bardoe is found to be robbin' other ranches, that's his finish. If it's owin' to us, Vasco, anyway, would be grateful; he's a straight man, if I'm any judge. Bet yu a dollar Nick'll be pleased.'

'Tiny sez betting is sinful 'less yo're certain o' winnin',' Yorky fenced. 'Me, I'm aimin' to be good—this time.'

This decision was amply justified when they reported the day's happenings; Nick was patently delighted. 'You done noble,' he said. 'Puttin' the Double V wise was one smart move, Jim, an' is goin' to help me a lot. I ain't met Vasco, but it's possible he's been misled.'

'By the way, Nick, not a whisper o' this to anyone—even Quilt,' Sudden warned. 'If Bardoe gets wind of it, we're sunk.'

'As you say, Jim, but I'd trust Quilt with all I got.'

'Mebbe, but a careless word could be enough for one who's waitin' to hear it. Better be safe than sorry.'

Drait nodded. 'So Gilman is after the S P, an' lettin' Bull steal stock, at a price; I sorta suspicioned that. You didn't get to Cullin?'

'No, I reckoned we'd had all the luck due to us for one day.'

'He's a bad egg,' Drait went on. 'The king-pin of what's wrong around here, I figure, but he's mighty careful not to show his hand.'

CHAPTER VI

In an early morning drive, the cattle purchased from the S P had been brought to Shadow Valley, and by the end of the day, bearing the brand of the new owner, were turned loose; they could not get out, for the exit at the upper end had been blocked by a solid wall of stone. Drait smacked the last bawling victim of the iron on the rump as it lumbered past, and grinned at his perspiring crew.

'Good goin', boys,' he complimented. 'Thanks.' And because he had himself worked as hard as any this brief approval satisfied them. 'Pie tonight, if them dried apple-rings came with the other stuff I ordered.'

'They shore did,' Long told him. 'An' I hope Lindy had made a-plenty.'

'You should worry,' his brother said. 'She allus counts you as three, anyways.'

Yelling like madmen they raced for the bunkhouse and first

use of the towel. Sudden and the nester followed more soberly.

'Glad that's done,' the former remarked. 'But I ain't altogether easy.'

'I'm suspectin' a snag my own self,' Nick admitted.

At the bunkhouse door they parted; the uproar within told that the food was not yet on the table. At the house, Drait, having made himself presentable, went into the parlour, where his wife was awaiting him. Her smile was a surprise.

'A tiring day, but I can see, a satisfactory one,' she said.

'I'll have to be careful,' he replied. 'A face that tells tales is a considerable drawback in these parts. Brandin' is hard work, but when it's yore own beasts it lightens the job. I've got a hundred head carryin' my iron, an' that's a good foundation for a herd if——' He lifted his shoulders.

'You think the ranchers may interfere?'

'Interfere is good.' His grin revealed the strong white teeth and she noticed—not for the first time—the difference his infrequent smile made. 'Oh, I guess they'll try again. Does that scare you?'

She shook her head. 'I'm gettin' fond of this place,' she said, and there was warmth in voice and look.

'That's fine; any time you feel different, just mention it.'

She was disappointed. Again the thought came that he had divined her desire to enslave and punish him. So far, his response had been entirely negative. It annoyed, but did not decrease her determination.

* * *

'What for sort of a burg is Rideout?' Sudden enquired of Drait early on the next day.

'Bigger edition o' Midway, with a branch railroad throwed in. Wanta pay her a visit?'

'If yu ain't anythin' special for me an' Yorky to do . . .'

'Help yoreself, Jim; we're all likely to be lazy for a day or so now the brandin's done.'

The news of the projected trip brought a solemn warning from Smoky: 'It's the gosh-dangest town in the State,' he said. 'Cowboys is the natural prey o' the varmints what live there. First they take yore guns, an' then the rest.'

'When they've got my guns they'll be needin' the rest.' Sudden laughed. 'An' Yorky ain't so Sunday-school as he might appear.' He looked round. 'C'mon, son. Two breakfasts is aplenty; we ain't goin' to a famine-struck land.'

The first few miles were traversed in a silence which Yorky forbore to break.

'I've been holdin' out on yu,' the puncher said at length. 'It ain't accident that we're in this part o' the country. Fact is, I got somethin' to do, an' I oughta told yu it couldn't be just holiday.'

The boy's eyes glistened. 'But, Jim, that's th' best news yet,' he cried. 'If you'll let me do somethin'.'

'Shucks, why d'yu s'pose I fetched yu?'

'Is Nick mixed up in it?'

'I dunno—yet. Meetin' him was just plain luck—I was needin' an excuse for stayin' in the district. Yu can add too that I like him, an' reckon he's bein' treated mighty mean.'

Yorky nodded sagely. 'What we gotta do?'

'Discover the rightful owner o' the S P first off,' Sudden said. 'That'll put Mister Gilman's li'l scheme in the discard, an' some other noses outa joint too, I wouldn't wonder.'

'In fact, we're goin' to make ourselves real unpop'lar, huh?' Yorky grinned. 'Well, I don't give a damn.'

Rideout proved to be what they had been led to expect, a bigger and busier Midway, but equally sordid and unpleasing to the eye. They found an eating-house and devoured a meal which evoked a philosophic reflection from Yorky: 'To 'preci-ate good cookin' you gotta get away from it.' As he paid the bill, Sudden asked a question.

'Seale, the lawyer? You'll see his shingle down to the deepo. Will you find him in? I dunno, but I'm damn shore you won't *find him out*—nobody's done that yet. He's cute, is the "Weasel."'

They left the fellow still chuckling over his witticism, and went in search of its subject. The lawyer's office appeared to consist of one room over an empty shop, and was reached by a stairway at the side. Sudden rapped, and a squeaky voice invited them to enter. The Westerner has a happy knack in the matter of nick-names, and one glance at the receding forehead, long nose, pinched-in mouth, and small, suspicious eyes told the visitors that the man behind the desk in the centre of the room was he they had come to see. Soiled linen, and a shiny black coat which hung sack-fashion on the narrow shoulders only added to the rodent-like impression. The office itself was equally shabby: a rag of carpet, a table upon which were law-books, a filing cabinet, an old-style safe, and two hard chairs comprised the rest of the furniture.

'Temporary premises, gentlemen, just temporary premises,' the lawyer excused, and it was evident that the words and the gesture accompanying them had become automatic. 'Find seats and let me know what I can do for you.'

Sudden leaned forward; he had taken his man's measure. 'To begin,' he said, 'I want yu to savvy I ain't here to waste yore time, which, to a legal gent, is the same as money.'

Seale's beady eyes lighted up a little. 'It is true my profession requires that certain charges be made,' he replied. 'Strictly in accordance with the service I am able to render, Mister——'

'My name wouldn't mean a thing to yu,' Sudden said. 'I'm from down South, near the Border, on a kind o' vacation. Yes, sir, I was shorely tired o' lookin' at cows' hind-ends. When Eli Dean—fella I was ridin' for—heard I was headin' for these parts, he sez would I do him a service? Well, I agreed, for Eli is one white man, an' here I am, yu see.'

'Quite, but you haven't told me why.'

Sudden slapped his leg. 'If I ain't the chucklehead. It's this-away: Eli wanted me to search out an old friend, man he'd punched cattle with from hell to anywhere an' back again in the days when they was both a deal younger. The name was Pavitt —Sam Pavitt, an' I hear he's been under the turf for 'bout a year.'

'That is true, I am sorry to say.'

'We all gotta go, an' I reckon Eli was expectin' that—Pavitt bein' older'n him, an' he ain't no yearlin'—for he said there was a daughter he'd welcome news of; it was when I asked 'bout her, I got sent to yu.'

'Naturally, since the estate is in my hands,' the lawyer said importantly. 'As regards the daughter, I am afraid I cannot help you. She ran away, more than twenty years ago, to marry a man her father disapproved of, and I am still trying to discover her whereabouts; she owns the S P ranch now. You see, I've no information; neither the name of the husband, nor that of the place where they lived. The old man never spoke of her.'

'No letters?'

'One only, with the address missing, saying that her husband had died, and mentioning a child, "Frankie". It was signed, "Mary". I have advertised, and have a man out now, making enquiries, all to no purpose. It is very discouraging and expensive. The property is a good one, but is losing value, and I've written to the Governor of the State suggesting he authorise me to sell it and hold the proceeds on trust for the missing heir.'

' 'Pears to be a sound idea,' Sudden said.

'I think so,' Seale said complacently. 'I've had a generous offer and am only waiting for permission to close the deal. I fear that is all I can tell you, and as I have a conference . . .'

This was dismissal, but Yorky had been whispering. 'My friend suggests yu might let us look at that letter yu spoke of,' Sudden said. 'We fellas are used to followin' trails, an' might spot a pointer.'

'Why, certainly,' the lawyer agreed. After all, he must make some sort of a show for the 'easy money' these greenhorns would pay him. Taking out a bunch of keys, he opened the safe, selected a paper from several others, and, with satirical smile, watched them study it.

'Nothin' there,' Sudden declared, as he handed it back. 'It was just a chance; I wouldn't like Eli to think I'd overlooked a bet.' He laid a bill on the desk, and stood up. 'Talkin' allus makes me dry; mebbe yu'll join us?'

This was an invitation Seale never refused, especially from one who had paid handsomely for nothing. He locked the safe, then the door, and preceded them down the stairway. Yorky followed, and they were nearly at the bottom when the boy slipped, clutched at the lawyer to save himself, and they finished in a heap on the floor. No damage resulted, and the culprit was profuse in his apologies.

'These damned high heels ain't made for steps,' he lamented, and when they reached the street, 'Jim, I ain't much on liquor, an' I want smokin' an' feed for my gun. You goin' across th' road? Right, I'll be along.'

Sudden nodded, and followed the lawyer into the saloon. 'A good kid, but kind o' young,' he excused.

'Plenty of us would like to suffer from his complaint,' the man of law smirked, and raised his glass. 'Here's how, and I'm sorry your errand has ended in failure.'

The puncher shrugged. 'Fella can't allus score, specially with long shots,' he said. 'I expect yu've lost cases yoreself.'

'A few—long shots,' Seale admitted. 'Staying in town?'

'I guess we'll mosey along,' Sudden replied, as he called for a second round. 'That boy should show up soon.'

'He'll be all right—the place is quiet at this time of the day. Why, there he is, at the door.'

Yorky was outside, with the horses, and having parted from the lawyer, they mounted and rode out of the town. Sudden asked no questions until they were clear, and then: 'What's the hurry, son?' For Yorky was casting an anxious eye to the rear from time to time.

'That fella was lyin', Jim.'

'Yo're tellin' me. Why did yu wanta see that fool letter?'

'I didn't, but I wanted to know where he kept his keys,' was the surprising answer.

Sudden looked at him severely. 'Yu been drinkin'?'

'No—thinkin',' Yorky replied. 'You see, Jim, I had a hunch there was somethin' in th' safe he wouldn't show us, an' I figured if I could get at th' right pocket. . . .'

He paused, furtively scanning his companion's face, but it told him nothing. Sudden was remembering that slip on the stairs, the long, slim fingers of this waif from the underworld of a big city—fingers which could manipulate cards with the dexterity of a magician. But he was not one to probe into the murky past of a friend; there had been episodes in his own. . . .

'I was a pretty good "dip" but I give it up after I run into Clancy,' the boy went on, rather shamedly. 'I could 'a' cleaned him, but honest, Jim, I on'y borried th' keys.' He was obviously scared that the man he most admired in all the world would not approve.

Sudden's slow smile was back again. 'Shucks, I ain't blamin' yu. Anythin' goes, when yo're fightin' a rogue. What did yu find?'

'A letter from a woman livin' at Deepridge, offerin' information 'bout Mary Pavitt; 'peared to be in answer to an advertisement. It was signed "Sarah Wilson".'

'Thought he warn't exactly emptyin' his bag,' was Sudden's comment. 'Yu left the letter?'

'Figured it was wiser. But here's one I fetched away.'

The document was brief and to the point. Sudden whistled softly as he read it:

'Dear Seale,
    Confirming our conversation this morning, I am prepared to pay five thousand dollars for the S P ranch, and to take the stock at eight dollars per head. If you can arrange this your fee will be one thousand, cash. This is my final offer.
                                        Gregory Cullin.'

The puncher folded the letter and stowed it away. 'Great work, son,' he complimented. 'I'd give somethin' to see Seale's face when he discovers his keys is missin'. What you do with 'em?'

'Left 'em on th' stairs where we tumbled; he may think they just dropped out'n his pocket.'

'Mebbe, if he don't search his safe too careful. Anyway, the sooner we get this in a good hiding-place, the better. I've a notion it'll come in mighty useful, but for the present we'll keep it under our hats; it's sound policy sometimes to let the other fella move first.'

'I saw somebody we know in Rideout, an' he didn't wanta be seen,' Yorky said. 'Beau Lamond.'

'The devil yu did?'

'Yeah, just after I left Seale's place; he was comin' towards it an' a'most jumped into a store when he catched sight o' me.'

'Didn't strike me as sufferin' from modesty,' Sudden said. 'If he don't mention it, we won't neither.'

CHAPTER VII

THE Big C ranch was the most important of those in the neighbourhood of Midway. This was due, not to its size, but to the forceful personality of its owner. Gregory Cullin, not yet forty, and unmarried, possessed a profound contempt for humanity, and an equally deep belief that everything comes to he who takes. His tall, compactly-built, powerful frame, frowning brows and thick, pouting lips gave him an aggressive appearance. He was subject to violent fits of rage, but few suspected he used them as a weapon to gain an end, and that beneath the wildest was a cold calculating brain, functioning as usual.

The ranch-house resembled the man, roughly but strongly fashioned. It was not large, but roomy inside, and the plain furniture was comfortable, but only that. It was said that Cullin, asked why he did not indulge in a more luxurious home, replied: 'This ain't a home, on'y the workshop in which to make my pile.'

On the evening of the day after Sudden's visit to Rideout, a meeting took place at the Big C. Gilman, Bardoe, and the sheriff had arrived, and they awaited one other. Despite the blazing fire, whisky and cigars on the table, the guests did not seem to be at ease, and Cullin's face had an expression little like that of a genial host.

'Where in hell's Vic?' he asked petulantly.

This being the third time he had put the question, no one had any answer to offer. A moment later came the tramp of a horse outside, a heavy step in the passage, and the owner of the Double V entered, flung his hat and quirt into one chair, and seated himself in another.

'Howdy, fellas,' he greeted, poured himself a drink, and reached for a smoke.

'What's been keepin' you?' Cullin demanded.

'Business—*my* business,' Vasco replied curtly. 'Why are we meetin'?'

'Somethin' has to be done about that fella Drait.'

'Is he doin' any harm?'

'He's a nester, an' therefore a cattle-thief,' Bardoe put in.

'You say so,' Vasco retorted. 'But all cattle-thieves ain't nesters.'

Bardoe scowled but was silent, and Cullin's impatient voice dismissed the argument: 'What he is or does don't matter, he's been told to go, an' has gotta go. Any suggestions Vic?'

'Yeah, leave him alone. He's bought the land an' is entitled to

57

live on it, so long as he don't interfere. How much o' yore range do you own, Greg?'

The Big C man flushed at this home-thrust, for, as Vasco well knew, he had no title even to the ground his buildings occupied. 'What's that gotta do with it, an' is it any o' yore affair what I own?' he snarled. 'God damn yore impudence, I've a mind——'

Vasco's eyes narrowed. 'Then use it, an' keep yore temper,' he said. 'These fits o' yores may impress the scum on yore pay-roll, but I ain't ridin' for you an' you can't ride me. As for drivin' Drait out, hangin' a crippled cowboy ain't the way.'

'That was a mistake,' Cullin said, aware that he had gone too far. 'The men exceeded their instructions.'

Vasco's laugh was contemptuous. 'Don't try to tell me you weren't there, because I know different. You an' the same brave fellas who shot down the Rawlin kid. You ain't listenin', o' course, Camort.'

'I ain't believin' it,' the sheriff said doggedly.

'I take it you ain't helpin' us in this,' Bardoe remarked.

'You take it correct,' was the quiet reply. 'Prove to me that Drait is stealing my cows an' mebbe I'll take another view.'

'He has a hundred head, calves an' yearlin's, in the Valley. Any o' you know where he got 'em?' Cullin asked, and getting no reply, went on, 'There's a gal, too; know anythin' about that?' Bardoe looked black and Gilman laughed meaningly, but no one answered. 'Hell,' Cullin continued, 'Do I have to gather news as well as think for you all?'

'Don't trouble on my account,' Vasco said bluntly. 'For the rest, I'm with you in any move which doesn't break the Law.'

'We got the Law—such as it is—on our side,' Gilman pointed out, with a jeering grin at the sheriff.

'Which is one damned good thing for some o' you,' that worthy summoned up courage to say.

The Big C man's brows came together. 'Camort,' he said, and there was the rasp of a file in his tone. 'who do you think would be the best man to fill yore place?'

Camort collapsed like a punctured bladder. 'Why, Mister Cullin, I ain't done nothin'.' he stammered.

'You said it,' the rancher snapped. 'An' a man who does nothin' is no use to us; we want results.'

'I had it all fixed,' the sheriff protested, with a malevolent glare at Bardoe.

'You made a sad error,' Vasco laughed. 'When you wanta hang a man for murder it's usual to have a corpse; you should 'a' killed Bull first, an' made yore case good.'

Cullin, satisfied with the crushing of Camort, applied himself

58

to the more important rebel. 'Quit foolin', Vic,' he said testily. 'This ain't a laughin' matter.'

'I think it is, an' Midway agrees,' Vasco retorted, as he got up. 'Take my advice—go slow with Drait; he's an awkward mouthful an' has useful help. So long.'

'Now what's he mean by that?' Bardoe questioned, when the Double V rancher had gone.

'I dunno, but Vic droppin' out thisaway makes a difference,' Cullin admitted. 'He's right in one thing—we'll have to take our time an' plan careful.'

'It shouldn't be difficult to plant some Double V cows in Shadow Valley,' Bardoe suggested.

'Too obvious,' Cullin decided bluntly.

It was his way, and Bardoe did not take offence. He despised them all, but a seeming comradeship made it less likely they would suspect him when stock was missing, and he would have made friends with the Devil himself if it would put anything in his pocket.

*　　*　　*

So, for the time being, Shadow Valley suffered no molestation from without. Sudden and Yorky had journeyed forth again, ostensibly to see some more of the country, but actually to follow up the clue obtained in Rideout. The rest of the outfit, having little to do save guard the gate, smoked, lazed, and played one-cent poker.

The nester and his wife took daily rides together, and the girl used them for her purpose, only to realise that she was making no impression on her companion; considerate, mildly-humorous, his attitude was that of a good-natured brother, and it made her furious. She would have preferred his former harsh, dominating manner. Once or twice she deliberately endeavoured to anger him, but she might have been trying to inflame an iceberg.

In desperation, she resolved on a final test—to make him jealous; if this failed, she had lost, for it would mean that his indifference was real. She began to look a little more kindly upon Lamond when they chanced to meet, and it was not long before the cowboy made an excuse to call at the house—when she was on the veranda—and asked for Drait.

'I am waiting for him now,' she replied.

His grin was impudent. 'That's all wrong,' he said. 'The fella oughta do the waitin'.'

'Perhaps that doesn't apply in this wild land,' she smiled.

'Why not—we ain't savages, but I hope he don't hurry. Ain't seen much o' you lately.'

Before she could reply, Nick appeared. 'Lookin' for me, Beau?' he asked.

'Like to visit town, if I ain't needed here,' Lamond explained.

'Quilt is foreman,' the nester reminded. 'If he doesn't want you, it's all right with me.'

The cowboy nodded and rode away. 'Wasn't that a little severe?' Mary questioned.

'He knew damn well he was wrong,' Nick returned. 'When I make a fella foreman I mean him to be just that.'

She understood; he was only annoyed because the man was offering a slight to his immediate boss.

'I don't suppose he meant any disrespect to Quilt.'

'I know the breed; puttin' one over on the foreman is just pie to them, but none o' the others would 'a' tried it.'

'You don't like him, do you?'

'No,' he replied, with disconcerting candour, and went out.

He left early on the following morning, and she rode alone up the valley. Ere she had gone far, however, Lamond caught her up, and swept off his hat in a theatrical bow. She ignored his greeting.

'Seein' the Guardian Angel ain't ridin' herd on you today, I guessed I might be welcome,' he explained, with an engaging smile.

'Haven't you any work to do?' she asked.

'Shore, Quilt sent me to look over our han'ful o' beasts, so we're goin' the same way. You can help me round 'em up.'

She gave in, and as he could be quite entertaining when he chose, she was soon glad of his company. The excitement of routing the cattle out of the brush brought a sparkle to her eyes, colour to her cheeks, and the cowboy forgot his caution.

'My, if you were married, you'd make a bonny widow,' he said, with a look she could not interpret.

Instantly her face froze, and she turned her pony. 'I must get back to the house; Lindy will be waiting for me.'

'Hey, what's yore hurry?' he cried, but she had gone, and he swore at himself for a clumsy fool. 'She ain't a biscuit-shooter, but what made her take it thataway? I wonder if . . .'

The girl returned home, angry with herself and the cowboy. She had no particular liking for the man, and had merely designed to use him as a weapon, but his remark had sent a shiver down her spine. Did he suspect anything? She told herself that was impossible, but nevertheless, she was frightened; playing with fire in a lawless land was a dangerous game.

That same evening, Drait—on his way to the bunkhouse—observed a tall, furtive figure slip out and disappear in the direction of the upper end of the valley. Wondering what was taking Lamond there at such a time, he followed, the darkness making it easy to do so undetected. Like two shadows they moved soundlessly over the turf until they reached the newly-erected barrier, where the leader uttered a low owl-hoot. Drait effaced himself behind a handy bush. The call was answered by another, and then Lamond said:

'That you, Greg?'

'Shore,' was the reply. 'Any news for me?'

'Yeah, the cattle came from the S P.'

'How d'you know?'

'Overheard two o' the boys talkin'. Also, one yearlin' had the S P brand; we're still eatin' it, an' the hide was burned.'

'Rustled, huh?'

'What d'you guess? Unbranded stock, smuggled in here at dawn,' Beau returned ironically.

The Big C man swore. 'So that's his game, huh? Goin' to bleed us one at a time, takin' stuff that can't be traced. It's a good plan, Mister Drait, so long as you keep it dark. Anythin' else?'

'Well, I dunno as it'll interest you, but them new fellas, Green an' Yorky, paid a visit to Rideout an' went to see the Weasel.'

'The hell they did. What about?'

'Yore guess is as good as mine,' the cowboy replied. 'No, Cullin, the bag is empty—like my pocket.'

'Which is allus empty,' the rancher grumbled. 'Here's a fifty for you.'

'It'll be as welcome as a pretty woman, which reminds me, Drait has certainly picked a Lulu; you oughta see her.'

'Women—pretty or otherwise—don't attract me,' Cullin said. 'So long.'

The nester waited until the cowboy was well on his way, and then returned to the ranch-house. So Green's instinct had served him truly—Lamond was a spy, and had come to him for that purpose. He glared grimly into the velvet blackness of the night; in the morning he would deal with the matter.

He rose early, breakfasted, and went to the bunkhouse; Beau was not there. Re-entering the house, he became aware of a wheedling voice from the parlour:

'Aw, honey, why don't you come away with me? I can make plenty coin, an' we'll go places, an' see life. I'll treat you right. Drait's finished here. . . .'

Lamond had his back to the door, and was facing the girl across the table. Her widened eyes warned him, and he turned to find the man of whom he was speaking. For a moment both were silent, then the nester said quietly:

'Did you wanta see me, Beau?'

61

The cowboy's expression showed relief—he had not been overheard. 'Why, yeah, I'd like to go into town.'

'To spend that fifty-dollar bill?'

The man's eyes narrowed, but he said jauntily, 'I don't get you; fifties an' me has bin strangers quite a while.'

'When I took you on, yore tale was that Cullin had acted mean,' Drait said slowly. 'It was all a lie, part of a plot to betray me. Don't trouble to deny it; I heard every word you told Cullin, an' watched you receive the price of yore treachery, you dirty Judas.'

Lamond tried to brazen it out. 'Anythin' goes agin a cow-thief,' he sneered. 'Cullin will smash you.'

Drait was pondering. 'If I told the boys there'd be another grave in the Valley. I don't wanta pollute it with muck, but you deserve to die.'

Mary, who had watched the scene as though petrified, now found her tongue: 'No, not that,' she cried. 'Please let him go.'

Drait's hard, inscrutable gaze struck her like a blow. 'You wish it?' he asked, and when she nodded dumbly, turned to the traitor. 'Clear out, with yore belongin's,' he grated. 'An' if this woman is one of 'em, take her.'

The implied insult roused the girl's spirit. 'This woman is no man's belonging,' she flamed.

Her words wiped the dawning grin from Lamond's lips. Matters had gone well for him, but his malicious desire to hurt would not allow him to leave well alone.

'Aw, honey, after the good times we've had,' he protested. 'Take him up on that——'

He got no further; the nester took one stride; his fist shot out, and with all the urge of the body-movement behind it, caught the traducer full on the jaw. The terrific force and precision of the blow sent the cowboy tottering back on his heels to slump with a crash to the floor. For a long moment he lay there, dazed, and then looked up into merciless eyes and the muzzle of a six-shooter.

'Take that back, or by God——'

The speaker's face was instinct with the desire to kill, his finger nudging the trigger. Lamond did not hesitate. 'I was lyin',' he said sullenly.

Drait pointed to the door. 'I'm givin' you fifteen minutes,' he said harshly, and looked at the girl. 'It's for you to choose.'

She drew herself up. 'In a choice of evils I prefer the brute to the liar,' she replied, and with a scathing glance, went out.

'Settles that,' the nester said. 'Yore time's tickin' away.'

The cowboy climbed to his feet, and as he staggered out of

the house got a final warning: 'Find another stampin'-ground; I don't let a man off twice.'

Dry-eyed, Mary sat in her bedroom, torn by emotions among which hatred of the opposite sex easily predominated. She was further from her purpose than ever; any regard her husband might have had for her must now have vanished, leaving contempt in its place. But if defeat was bitter, it did not bring despair. Through clenched teeth, she muttered, 'You're only adding to the bill, Nicholas Drait.'

The afternoon brought another surprise. Quilt was talking with Shorty at the entrance to the valley when a hail from outside announced the advent of a visitor. The foreman mounted the fire-step; Cullin and three of his men were awaiting admittance.

'What's the meanin' o' this?' the cattlemen demanded, pointing to the obstruction.

'Speaks for itself, I'd say,' was the answer. 'But its main purpose is to keep out coyotes—'specially the two-legged variety what cover their faces an' come a-ridin'.'

'Don't be insolent, my man,' Cullin frowned.

'I ain't yore man, an' glad of it,' the foreman retorted 'What you wantin'?'

'To see Drait.'

'Well, you can come in, Cullin—alone.'

The rancher's face reddened. 'It's all or none,' he snapped.

'None it is,' was the indifferent reply.

The Big C man swore impatiently and turned to his followers. 'Wait for me,' he said, and the gate having opened rode through.

'Nick's up at the house,' the foreman said. 'You know the way—I reckon.'

The jeer in the last two words deepened the cattleman's scowl, but he did not reply.

A young woman, seated in a rocking-chair on the veranda, looked up from the book she was reading as he drew rein. She saw a man staring at her, apparently dumb with amazement. And so it was. Cullin knew she must be the girl he had heard about, but her unexpected charm made it hard to believe. She was a revelation, and for a moment or two he could but gaze avidly. Only when he saw a smile, trembling on her lips, and realised that he was acting foolishly, did he snatch off his hat, and find words.

'I take it yo're Mister Drait's—friend, ma'am,' he said. 'I wanted to see him.'

'He is at the bunkhouse,' she replied. 'Won't you sit down and wait?'

Eagerly enough, the caller accepted the invitation, taking the chair to which she pointed. Usually self-possessed in any company, he was astonished to find his brain fumbling for something to say.

'I reckon you find time hangs some on yore hands here, ma'am,' he managed at last.

She smiled, showing even, white teeth. 'Not for a moment; the valley is charming, I have books, and with eight hungry men to provide for there is plenty to do. You wouldn't believe how they eat.'

'I would, seein' I have to foot the bill for near twice that number,' he replied, and with a glance at her slim hands, 'but shorely you don't have all of it to do.'

'No, Lindy—our cook—does most,' she admitted. 'I just potter about, trying to help.'

His murmur of 'Lucky Lindy' brought a dimple into evidence, and then she said, rather hurriedly. 'Here is Mister Drait.'

The nester's brows came together when he recognised his visitor. 'What are you doin' here, Cullin?' he asked.

With a man to deal with, the owner of the Big C recovered his poise. 'Passin' my time very pleasantly,' he replied, with a smile at the girl. 'I wanta talk with you.'

'Come inside,' Nick said brusquely, and led the way to the parlour. When they were seated, he added, 'Well?'

'See you've walled up the entrance.'

'Anythin' against a man fencin' his own property?'

'S'pose not, but it ain't a neighbourly act.'

'I can show you a couple o' mounds due to acts that warn't neighbourly neither,' Nick reminded.

This was a bad beginning, and Cullin did not reply at once. He had come there to deliver an ultimatum—the nester must take what the cattlemen chose to offer, or be driven out by force. But that slender figure on the veranda, with its crown of curls which the sunlight turned to reddish gold, had changed all that. Why, he did not yet comprehend, only that so it was.

'What's done is done,' he said heavily. 'Mistakes happen. No use in lookin' back—it's the present an' future need takin' care of. You expect to raise cattle here?' And when Drait nodded. 'You ain't got grazin' for more'n five or six score.'

'Plenty feed outside the valley.'

'An' plenty usin' it, north, south, an' west, all of us here before you. Where's yore right to come crowdin'?'

'It's free range—not one o' you own a foot of it, an' if you trebled yore herds there'd be grass enough. I'm a cattleman, an' know what I'm talkin' about. Further, you can leave Bardoe out—he on'y raises cows when the owners ain't on the watch.'

64

'Can you prove that?'

'I don't have to; if you ain't wise to it a'ready, you soon will be.'

Cullin laughed unpleasantly. 'I hear you've a hundred head in the valley now,' he said. 'Rustled from the S P.'

'The first half is correct, the second a lie,' Drait returned curtly. 'I threw the man who told you out on his ear this mornin'. You didn't get value for yore fifty, Cullin.'

The blow was a shrewd one, and the Big C owner felt a gust of passion surging within him. But a violent quarrel would not further the vague scheme already milling in his tortuous mind; cunning was the card for the moment.

'Mebbe I've gone the wrong way to work 'bout you, Drait,' he said. 'We should have had this pow-wow when you first came. Still, better late than never, they say, an' I guess we can fix somethin' up.' He was silent for a space, apparently deep in thought, and when he looked up again it was with the air of one who has come to a momentous decision. 'What I'm goin' to tell you is known on'y to myself an' one other; you must keep it tight behind yore teeth.'

'I won't chatter, but please yoreself,' the nester replied indifferently.

'The S P will shortly be in the market,' Cullin confided. 'It's a fair range, but has been let go to seed. I intend to buy it, an' I'll need a capable man to take charge—the Big C is a full-time job for me—an' I wouldn't trust Gilman. What about you takin' it on? Shadow Valley'd be a useful link between the ranches.'

Drait was in no hurry to reply; he was trying to plumb the deeps of this amazing and utterly unlooked-for proposition, in which he felt sure there was a catch. 'I'll think it over,' he said at last. 'Time enough to decide when you get the S P.'

Cullin professed himself satisfied; he had postponed an immediate settlement of his difference with the nester, and provided an excuse for visiting the valley. Mary was still on the veranda when they came out, and the half smile she gave him as he bowed to her, mounted, and rode off, quickened his pulses. He would have liked to delay departure but caution dictated otherwise.

'An' there goes the slimiest reptile in the State,' was Drait's valedictory utterance.

'At least he knew how to behave,' the girl said.

'Oh, he can ape the gentleman for his own purpose,' Nick sneered. 'It may interest you to know that he's a confirmed hater o' yore sex.'

'It does not interest me at all,' she replied coldly.

An hour later, the 'reptile' was standing in his own parlour disgustedly surveying the unswept floor, dusty, littered furniture, and torn curtains, so different from the one he had left, spotlessly clean, neatly arranged, and brightened with freshly-picked flowers. Angrily he summoned his Mexican cook and barked orders which promised the man a busy day for the morrow.

CHAPTER VIII

AFTER being absent for three days, Sudden and Yorky returned. Drait was clearly relieved to see them; he had a great liking for both, and unbounded faith in the judgment of the elder of the pair.

'Come up to the house tonight, Jim,' he invited. 'I'm needin' yore advice.'

Mary had retired to her own room when the puncher arrived, and the two men had the parlour to themselves.

'So yu've lost Lamond?' Sudden opened. He had heard as much in the bunkhouse.

'Yeah, but I wouldn't call it a loss,' Nick corrected. 'You had him sized up about right. How do you do it, Jim?'

'Oh, I dunno,' Sudden smiled. 'I was raised among hosses an' used to study 'em, lookin' for danger-signals a wrong-minded one allus gives sooner or later. I s'pose I got into the habit o' treatin' humans the same; I don't claim it'll work every time.'

'It did this,' the nester said. 'I won't trouble you to try it on Cullin—it ain't necessary, but mebbe you can give a guess at the game he's a playin'. He came here, an' instead o' bluster an' threats offered me a share in a deal he has in view. Can't tell you what it is, I promised to stay mum; on'y Cullin an' one other knows of it.'

Sudden grinned. 'It wouldn't be the buyin' o' the S P, by any chance?'

Nick straightened in his chair. 'Hell's bells!' he cried. 'Either yo're that one other, or a wizard.'

'I ain't neither,' the puncher denied. 'Take a squint at this.'

He passed over Cullin's letter to the lawyer, the reading of which did not lessen Nick's astonishment. 'How in blazes did you come by it?' he wanted to know.

'Before I tell yu that, I gotta own up that I've been keepin' somethin' back,' Sudden replied. 'I let on that me an' Yorky were just sorta sight-seein'. That's true in his case, but I was in these parts for a purpose, an' I teamed up with yu because it suited my plans. Also I guess I kind o' took to you,' he finished awkwardly.

66

'Didn't find too many o' them danger-signals, huh?' Nick asked slyly.

Sudden laughed. 'I'm here, ain't I?'

'Yeah, an' I'm damn glad. The rest don't matter nohow; yore business is no concern o' mine.'

'Don't be too shore; my job was to find the owner o' the S P.'

'Well, it ain't likely to be me,' the nester chuckled, and then, '*Was* to find him, you said. Does that mean——?'

'Here's the story,' the puncher replied, and told of the visit to Rideout; the interview with the lawyer, and subsequent proceedings. 'It was pretty clear that Seale didn't want to find the heir, an' the letter from Cullin made it a shore thing; he was after that thousand bucks, an' with the price o' the ranch an' cattle left in his hands, it must 'a' looked like a dream come true. Thanks to Yorky, he'll have to think some more—an' think hard.'

'I figured that boy had brains,' the nester said.

Sudden smiled agreement. 'Well, we picked up the trail where Seale dropped it, at Deepridge. Mary Pavitt an' her husband had married, lived, an' died there. The child, a girl, was sent to a sort o' home for orphans at Redstone, with what money there was to pay for her keep an' education. When she was about sixteen, she went as a mother's help to a small farm in the district. Nearly four years later, these folk moved East, an' she got another job at Shanton. Know it?'

'Passed through once, an' that was a-plenty,' Drait replied. 'It's a bit south o' Table Mesa.'

'That's so,' Sudden agreed. 'We found the house—if yu could call it that—owned by a mighty craggy couple, the woman a virago an' the man a shifty-eyed sneak. They denied all knowledge o' the girl at first, but when they found that wouldn't get 'em anywhere but into trouble, they admitted she had been there, but had disappeared, somethin' short o' two months ago. Her name was Mary Frances Darrell. Mebbe yu can finish the tale.'

The nester looked up. 'It's an amazin' one, for shore, an' there ain't much I can add to it,' he began. 'I found her wanderin' in the woods the afternoon afore I met you. She admitted she had run away, had no folks, an' nowhere to go; I fetched her here. O' course, I never dreamed o' connectin' her with Pavitt; she didn't mention him, an' they were searchin' for a woman twice her age or a young man.'

'She may not have heard the name till she came to the valley,' Sudden suggested. 'I'd like a word with her if it ain't too late.'

'I'll find out,' Nick replied.

He returned in a few moments. 'She's comin' along,' he said. 'Mebbe it'll be easier for her if I ain't here. Back soon.'

Before the other had time to protest, he had gone, and almost immediately, the girl came in, seated herself in the chair Nick had vacated, and looked enquiringly at the puncher.

'You have something to tell me?'

'Somethin' to ask yu first,' he smiled. 'An' it ain't just curiosity. Yu were born at——?'

'A town called Deepridge, but as I left there when I was eight—having lost both my parents—I remember little of it.'

Further questions brought confirmation of his own discoveries concerning her movements. There was one more test.

'What did yore parents call yu?'

'Frankie. You see, I was a disappointment; both of them had wanted a boy.'

Sudden, conscious that he was reviving sad memories, grinned and said consolingly, 'Shucks! boys ain't so much.'

This brought a smile, wistful, maybe, but still, a smile.

'Can you tell me yore mother's maiden name?' Sudden went on.

She shook her head. 'I cannot recall ever having heard it.'

'Well, I guess yu've told me all I need to know,' he said. 'I'm obliged to yu, ma'am.'

'May I put a question?' she asked, and when he agreed that it was certainly her turn, added, 'Why do you want this information?'

He told the history of Mary Pavitt, her flight from home, and the old man's bequest. 'I've been lookin' for her child, who is the rightful owner of the S P ranch; I reckon I've found her,' he ended.

'It seems—incredible,' she breathed.

'The incredible part is that yu weren't unearthed a while ago,' Sudden said drily. 'That lawyer fella must be dumb, or. . . .' He left her to supply the alternative. 'One thing more : I wouldn't speak of it, even to Lindy; there might be a snag somewheres.'

'Does Mister Drait know?' she asked.

'Naturally, I told him. He won't talk.'

She rose and began to stammer thanks, but he waved them aside. 'Nothin' to that,' he said hastily. 'I'm on'y doin' what I came to do.'

In the semi-darkness of her room, Mary strove to school her excited brain into a calm consideration of this seeming inevitable change in her life. What would it mean? Wealth, independence, freedom? Not the latter, for she would still be tied to the harsh, inscrutable man she had married. She wondered whether Drait would be glad, or sorry? He would never let her know, but she shut her teeth on the determination that it should be which she chose. She would be leaving Shadow Valley, and to her surprise, this thought produced a pang of regret.

While the girl was wrestling with her problem, her husband returned to the parlour, dropped into a chair, and looked enquiringly at his companion.

'It's as certain as the Day o' Judgment,' the puncher told him, adding meditatively, 'It busts up Cullin's game—yu won't need to consider that offer now.'

'I never intended to,' Drait said.

'If she decides to keep the ranch, she'll want a good man to run it; Gilman would steal the floor from under her feet.'

'Yeah, it'll be a jolt for him, too. Bardoe won't like it, an' the sheriff'll be peeved. Take it all round, Jim, you ain't goin' to be the best-liked man hereabouts.'

'That's happened before,' Sudden replied, a twinkle in his eyes. 'I never let it lose me any sleep. If some o' the folks I've met up with in this world o' sin had liked me, I'd 'a' hated myself.'

'I got fifty more critters from the S P while you were away. Yeah, I took the numbers o' the bills. What you meanin' to do about Seale?'

'Invite him to come over, mentionin' why. I'll bet he will too, a-runnin', an' I'll double the bet that from here he'll head straight for the Big C, in the hope o' still bein' able to corral that thousand bucks.'

'Well, I'm mightly glad you've turned the trick, Jim, both for the gal's sake an' yore own. With the job practically finished, I s'pose you'll be hittin' the trail soon?' Drait said moodily.

Sudden shook his head. 'There's a lot to be done yet.'

'Good,' was the hearty reply, but as he returned to the bunkhouse the puncher had a feeling that his latest exploit had not quite pleased the nester, and he wondered why.

CHAPTER IX

THE letter announcing the bare fact that an heir to the S P had been brought to light produced a galvanic effect upon the Weasel. Though he tried to persuade himself that it must be a spurious claim which could be easily disproved, he lost no time in looking into the matter. The weekly coach carried him to Midway, and there he hired a buckboard to complete the journey, consoling himself with the reflection that the estate would pay his expenses.

He was conversant with the sinister history of Shadow Valley, and knew it was at present in the possession of an undesirable named Drait. But the letter he had received was signed 'James Green' and this told him nothing. So, when ushered by Lindy into the parlour, it was quite a surprise to find a familiar face—that of the cowboy from the Border, who had visited him in Rideout.

'So it's you?' he said.

'Li'l ol' me,' the other smiled. 'Couldn't go back to pore Eli empty-handed, yu know. Help yoreself to a seat.' He turned to the young girl, who, sitting rather in the shadow was the only other occupant of the room. 'This is Luke Seale, ma'am; he's been tryin' to find yu for a goodish bit.'

'My search was for a much older woman or a youth called "Frank,"' the lawyer said sharply. 'If this is a joke. . . .'

'Do I look that sort o' fool?' Sudden demanded. 'Now, pay close attention to what I'm goin' to tell yu. My enquiries started at Deepridge, where your'n left off.' The Weasel blinked at this, and then listened in glum silence while Sudden, step by step, related the tale of his investigation.

'Sounds all right,' he said sourly, when the puncher ended, 'but it's no more than hearsay, so to speak; the Law demands documentary evidence.' At the back of his mind, however, a four-figure sum of money was receding into the distance.

'We aim to please,' Sudden smiled, and dived into a pocket. 'I got on the trail o' the preacher who married Mary Pavitt an' Francis Darrell—fella named "Josiah Jones."' Neither of the men noticed the girl's start of surprise. 'He ain't at Deepridge no more, but I can tell yu where to locate him. He dug up an old register an' here's a copy o' the entry in it.'

Seale studied the slip of paper. 'It could be forged,' he said, and looked into eyes of chilled steel. 'I'm not saying it is——'

'The same fella baptised the child, an' there's people in Deepridge who remember she was called "Frankie" by her parents,' the puncher went on. 'Here is another document, which is genuine—I wrote it my own self.' His grin was not of the pleasant variety. 'It's the address o' the orphanage, where they'll show yu the record of Miss Darrell's stay there, an' give yu a pretty near description of her. Well, what d'yu think?'

All that the lawyer could think at the moment was that a substantial commission, together with the opportunity of vastly increasing it, were disappearing like a dream. He flogged his brain to discover some flaw in the evidence which would restore a glimmer of hope.

'Your facts about Miss Darrell may be correct, but you have not proved, as yet, that your claimant *is* that person,' Seale said.

The girl spoke for the first time: 'Did you ever see Mary Pavitt before she left home, Mister Seale?'

'Many times,' he replied absently.

She rose and moved forward into a better light. 'Would you say that I resemble her?'

He raised his head, and his mean little eyes opened to their fullest extent. 'God! You're her living image,' he cried, shocked into speaking the truth.

'I have been told so,' she said quietly. 'Are you satisfied?'

He was, but would not admit it; even now, there might be some way out. 'You certainly have a case,' he said. 'It will take time to examine it thoroughly.'

'Don't worry if yu lose that certificate,' Sudden said sardonically. 'The original an' the man who wrote it can be produced. Yu will inform the Governor, o' course?'

'No need—at present,' Seale said hurriedly. 'The matter is in my hands. As soon as I have come to a decision, I will take the necessary steps to put Miss Darrell in possession of the property.'

With which pompous statement he took his leave. The puncher accompanied him to the door. 'Speed is what we want, ol'-timer,' he said in a low voice. 'The lady has been without her inheritance long enough. Remember, yu can pay too high a price even for a thousand bucks.'

His face a pasty yellow, the man scuttled out of the house, scrambled into his conveyance, and grabbed the whip. Sudden's amused gaze followed him.

'Hell! I oughta mentioned the nearest way to the Big C,' he soliloquised.

Sudden's prediction as to the lawyer's destination was correct, and he proceeded there as quickly as the raw-boned beast he was driving could take him. Only when the buckboard was within sight of the Big C ranch-house did he slacken pace; he was not looking forward to the interview; the rancher's tongue was two-edged, and he never troubled to conceal his contempt for those he used.

'Well, what foul wind has blown you here?' was his greeting.

'I've news—bad news, Greg,' the lawyer replied.

'You shore look it. Bad for you, or for me?'

'For both of us—we've lost the S P.'

Cullin's frown deepened. 'Which means you've made a mess of things, I s'pose. How come?'

'The missing heir has turned up.'

'Well, with yore knowledge of how to evade the Law you oughta be able to upset the claim.'

Seale shook his head. 'It's as straight as a string—they have the proofs. I haven't said so—yet, but there isn't a doubt.'

'Who are *they*?'

'The claimant and the chap who found her—a cowpuncher from the Mexican Border.'

'Found *her*?' Cullin repeated. 'You told me the Pavitt woman had cashed, an' that it was her son you were lookin' for. You better spill the beans.'

The lawyer was ready enough; he knew that if there should be a means of evasion, the cattleman, with his acute, unscrupulous brain would find it. Cullin, poker-faced, listened without comment until he finished.

'You oughta done as I suggested—searched her out yoreself,' he said. 'Then we could've arranged that no claim would be made. What you gotta do now is make a friend o' the gal, put her in possession as soon as maybe, an'—not pointedly, slam the S P; it's been neglected, badly managed, the profit small, an' the outlook for the cattle trade generally—gloomy. Get her to let you sell an' invest the coin, leavin' her free to have a good time an' no anxiety. Play yore part right an' she'll fall for it, an' my offer to you still stands. By the way, where is that letter?'

'Burned—it was dangerous,' the lawyer lied. 'As for your plan, it's good—you still have the gift—but it will fail; the girl won't lack advisers; I forgot to mention that at present she's living in Shadow Valley.'

Cullin sprang from his seat. 'So it's that girl?' he cried. 'How'n hell did she get there, an' what's she doin'?'

'She skedaddled from her last job, and Drait found her adrift in the wilds,' Seale explained, adding with a sneer, 'As to what she's doing, it doesn't need two guesses.'

He got a black look. 'I wouldn't repeat that, Seale,' came the warning. 'I've seen her, an' she's not that sort.'

This left the man of law speechless; Cullin defending a woman's character was something he never dreamed of witnessing. He had expected an eruption, and here was the human volcano seated again, and wearing a slow smile of satisfaction. Indeed, the rancher had reason. The luck was breaking for him; the woman he wanted, the ranch for which he had schemed, and the man he hated, seemed to be almost within his grasp. He found himself wondering about the girl, for although he had closed Seale's evil mouth, it had been no tribute to her, but merely an automatic gesture—he would not permit a slur on one he intended to make his own. Presently he spoke again:

'Forget all I've said, Luke, except puttin' Miss Darrell in possession as quickly as possible. An' she's to have a straight deal. You can leave the rest to me; I'll see you don't lose by it.'

Fortified by a stiff dose of whisky, the lawyer set out for Midway, where he would stay the night and catch the coach in the morning. It had been a tiring day, both physically and mentally, and though cheered somewhat by the reflection that all was not yet lost, he was far from sanguine. Worry his wits as he might, utter failure resulted from his efforts to fathom Cullin's reaction to the news, but obviously the rancher had a plan, and the Weasel promised himself that he would discover and profit by it. The missing letter troubled him; he had only learned of the loss some days after it had been taken. The cowboy's farewell remark he put down as a shot in the dark, for he had completely forgotten the temporary absence of his keys.

Meanwhile, the man he had left was striding up and down his room, busily building a pleasing picture. Ownership of the Big C and the S P would make him the wealthiest cattleman for many miles round, and bring the corresponding power. Bardoe would have to be abolished, and Vasco eventually bought or squeezed out. Shadow Valley could be made use of.

'Might put up a fine house there, if she's keen on the spot,' he muttered. His thoughts went to this woman he had seen but once and desired so desperately. 'Beau said she don't care none for the fella, so she won't miss him.'

For Nicholas Drait was condemned; he was in the way.

*　　*　　*

Despite the fact that the day was young, Jack Gilman lay supine in the shade of the veranda, stretched out in a comfortable chair, feet on the railing, eyes closed and mouth open. He was awakened by a sharp command :

'Stick 'em up!'

He came alive instantly, started to obey, and then paused when he saw no weapon threatened him; the man who had given the order was merely regarding him with contemptuous amusement.

'You'd be easy, wouldn't you?' Cullin said, for he it was. 'One o' these days somebody'll take the ranch away from you.'

'Not while I got my health,' Gilman grinned. 'I had a hard day yestiddy.'

Cullin got down and stood surveying the range. It pleased him, but the neglected condition of the buildings had the opposite effect. He reached out a cigar, passed one to the foreman, and took a seat.

'Ol' Sam certainly had an eye for a location,' he remarked. 'Well, he was here first, an' it's on'y to be expected he'd get the best. You'll be sorry to leave it.'

'Leave it—me?' Gilman ejaculated. 'What's yore meanin'?'

Cullin shrugged. 'You don't appear to have heard the news. O' course, it ain't known but to a few yet.'

'Did you come to tell me?'

'No, just a neighbourly call—I allus had a fancy for this place,' the rancher replied. 'I certainly thought Seale would have sent you word.'

'Word of what?' the foreman snapped. 'If that dirty little runt is tryin' to put anythin' over on me. . . .'

The suspense was putting an edge on his temper as the visitor intended. He now struck—hard: 'There's no question o' that. The lawful owner o' the S P has turned up in the person o' Sam Pavitt's gran'daughter; "Frankie" wasn't a boy after all.'

He saw the man flinch as from a physical blow, and it gratified his delight in giving pain. But Gilman soon recovered.

'A girl, huh?' he said. 'That don't mean I gotta go. She'll need someone to manage things, I guess, knowin' nothin' about cattle.'

'I'm afraid you'll have to guess again,' Cullin said. 'You see, the heiress happens to be the girl I told you was residing with Drait. If she wants help. . . .'

This second blow shook the foreman to his very foundations. 'That damned nester,' he exploded, after a stunned silence.

'There's on'y one o' that name around here, thank God,' the other replied viciously. 'An' he's one too many. By the way, I hear the stock he has in the valley came from the S P. What about it?'

'If they did, he stole 'em,' Gilman retorted instantly.

'A hundred head, all without brands?' This incredulously. 'Ain't yore riders doin' anythin' for their pay?'

The foreman lifted his shoulders. 'Shouldn't wonder if there's more. I'm short-handed—to keep down expenses—an' with the future o' the ranch in the air, I reckon none of us feels like overworkin'—you wouldn't yoreself.'

'Possibly, but you'll have some explainin' to do; Drait's no tenderfoot.'

'Me too; mebbe he'll have some to do first.'

'O' course, if you could prove he helped hisself to those cows,' Cullin said softly.

The eyes of the two men met, and the foreman knew that his story was not accepted; he also read the meaning behind Cullin's last remark.

'Have to consider if somethin' can't be done 'bout that,' he said. 'If not, there's other ways.'

The rancher rose. 'It is, o' course, entirely yore affair, but we shall miss you, Gilman.'

The foreman's sullen gaze watched him cross the open and

disappear among the trees. 'Yeah, my affair,' he sneered. 'You want him got rid of, an' I'm to do it for you. Mebbe I will, because it suits my hand too, but if I have to start killin', look to yoreself, Cullin, you bastard.'

Though he failed to divine the malignity he had left behind, the Big C man knew he had not earned any gratitude. Nevertheless, he was satisfied with the morning's work. It was perfectly plain to him that Gilman had been robbing the S P, and pretty certain that Drait already knew, or would soon discover the fact. The removal of the nester therefore became imperative if the foreman was to retain his post, or even his ill-gotten gains. But Cullin was not the type to be content with only one chance in a lottery, and his mind was casting about for a second. It did not take long to decide; Bardoe's animosity towards Drait almost equalled his own.

From where he was, the route to the 8 B skirted Shadow Valley, and he was only a short distance from the entrance when he saw a rider ahead, a slight figure, dressed in grey, which he instantly recognised. Smothering a whoop of exultation, he loped after and soon overtook her. Hat in hand, he ranged alongside.

'This is certainly my lucky day,' he smiled. 'Didn't dream I'd have the pleasure o' seein' you again so soon. Do you often ride this way?'

She shook her head. 'I am venturing outside the valley for the first time.'

'I hope it won't be the last.'

For some moments they paced in silence. Thrilled by the nearness of her, the man was content to look, noting the easy grace with which she rode, the delicate colour under the faint tan of her cheeks, the curling tendrils of hair straying from beneath her hat-brim. Mary's eyes, though less searching, had not been entirely idle. Though he wore the garb of the country, she had seen that it was of superior quality, the shirt and neckerchief of silk, and his face newly-shaven. She would have described him as well-dressed, without the flashiness of Beau Lamond. Presently he laughed.

'Why, I have forgotten to congratulate you.' He saw she did not comprehend. 'Upon yore inheritance.'

'Oh, that,' she replied, with a tiny frown. 'Nothing is settled yet, and I'm sorry it is being talked about.'

'It isn't. Seale—who is also my lawyer—visited me last evening on business. He seemed very pleased about somethin' an' eventually admitted, in confidence, that it was because he is now in a position to clear up the Pavitt estate, havin' discovered the owner.'

'I would be much more grateful if he had found me three months ago,' the girl said, and there was an undercurrent in her tone which he could not guess at.

'I think you will have no more reason to complain on that score,' he assured her. 'Seale is under obligation to me, an' I've made it plain that any unnecessary delay in your case will be an unfriendly act to myself.'

'That was very kind of you, Mister Cullin,' she said warmly.

'Not a-tall, just fairness,' he replied, and then smiled. 'What does Drait think about yore good fortune?'

'We haven't discussed it yet,' she answered. 'I imagine that, like myself, he prefers to deal with facts.'

'You have known him long?'

'No,' she replied shortly, and he did not pursue the subject.

He offered no protest when she wished to return, but insisted on escorting her.

They parted at the spot where they had met, and the clasp of her hand made his blood burn. Holding it, he said : 'I want you to think of me as a friend, one who will always be ready to help you in case of need.'

Without waiting for any response, he turned abruptly and rode away. For a moment she sat gazing after him, astonished and rather impressed—as he had meant her to be. He did not look back.

Riding slowly back to Shadow Valley, she vainly endeavoured to arrange her ideas about her late companion. Though he had clearly shown that he admired her, it had not been done with the crude and offensive familiarity of Lamond. She liked him, and yet. . . .

The Big C man was in no doubt about his feelings—he wanted this woman and would have her, by fair means or foul. What she was to the nester he did not know, but should it prove an obstacle that was just too bad—for Drait. He rode on towards his destination, smiling grimly.

He was welcomed with some surprise and no great show of amiability, but was invited in and the customary bottle was produced.

'Well, Greg, you wouldn't come all this way 'less you wanted somethin',' Bardoe began. 'Let's have it.'

'My dear Bull,' the visitor protested mildly, and Bardoe stiffened; Cullin, in a polite mood, was to be suspected. 'The pleasure of seein' you . . .'

'Take a good long look an' then gimme the real reason,' the other said sourly.

'What a doubtin' Thomas you are, Bull,' Cullin smiled. 'But

there was an item of news I fancied might interest you; the S P is changin' hands.'

The other's eyes narrowed. Was it a guess, or had something leaked out? 'No,' he replied evenly. 'The missin' heir has been discovered—Pavitt's grand-daughter.'

'A gal, after all, huh. How should that interest me?'

'Jack Gilman'll have to go.'

'Can't see why—she'll need a foreman.'

'Will she? Nicholas Drait is at present takin' care of her,' Cullen said carelessly.

Bardoe's eyebrows climbed, his mouth opened ludicrously as this statement sank in. 'Are you mad, or am I?' he asked.

'Probably both of us, but what I've told you is a cold fact.'

Bull digested this in frowning silence. The girl he had lost was actually the possessor of the S P ranch, and the man who had stolen her—as he put it—was holding her. The shock was a staggering one. If only he—but that would not bear thinking of. Cullin was astonished at the effect of his news; Bull could not be so concerned about the foreman's future.

'It's tough luck on Gilman,' he remarked.

'To hell with Gilman,' Bardoe retorted. 'It's tough on me.'

'Afraid I don't get you.'

'Listen,' Bull growled. 'When Drait tried to bump me off that time up on Table Mesa, I had a gal ridin' behind me. I'd picked her up less'n an hour earlier, fair lost an' pretty well all in. Said she'd stampeded from the place she was workin' an' that she'd no folks an' nowhere to go. I offered her a job as housekeeper at the 8 B, an' she agreed. It warn't no hardship to look at her—young an' fresh, which is how I like 'em.' He leered at his listener. 'You know what happened, Drait did a pore job but knocked me out. He took the gal—they were together when my fellas catched him, an' if it hadn't bin for them two strangers—hell burn their bones—she'd 'a' bin fetched back to me. I want her, which is somethin' you wouldn't understand, an' I mean to have her, 'specially now; the S P would suit me fine.'

It was a tribute to Cullin's faculty of self-control that he was able to present a blank face during this brutal admission. But he had come to find a tool, and if it was keener and more dangerous than he had looked for, so much the better. When the work was done . . .

'You'll find Drait a hard nut,' he remarked. 'I expect he'll marry her—now.'

'All one to me,' Bardoe chuckled. 'I don't mind a widow if she's a good-looker.'

The Big C man emptied his glass. 'I wish you luck, Bull,' he said. 'Don't try anythin' too raw an' rely on gettin' away with it; Midway is more than a mite doubtful o' Camort, an' the Judge is jumpy. Losin' Gilman an' Vasco, we won't be too strong.'

'You needn't to worry,' Bardoe grinned. 'With that cursed nester attended to an' me in the saddle at the S P, we'll have 'em where's the hair's short.'

He accompanied his visitor to the door, and sent a satirical grimace after him. 'Eggs me on, an' then fobs me off,' he mused. 'Well, Mister Cullin, I dunno what yore game is but I'm playin' my own an' may the Devil take you.'

Cullin, riding with bent head, had plenty to occupy his mind. A bringer of news, he had also learned some. Presently he laughed.

'He downs Drait, an' we hang him for it,' he said, and this entirely satisfactory solution restored his temper to almost normal. At the Big C he found Lamond awaiting him.

'Want yore job back? So Drait fired you. Why?'

'Double-crossin' him, he said, but the real reason was he catched me sparkin' the gal an', believe me, she's worth a risk.'

'You were lucky; me, I'd a' beefed you,' the rancher said.

'So would he, but she begged him not to,' Lamond grinned. 'Said for me to leave the country, but I'm stayin'; I mean to git him—an' her.'

Again Cullin schooled his features to impassivity. Here was a third string to his bow, and he did not hesitate. 'Awright, when you've settled with the nester I'll put you on the pay-roll.'

'That's a bet,' the cowboy said jauntily, and went out.

The rancher smiled contentedly. 'The wise man gets others to run the risks, an' then, helps hisself to the stakes.'

CHAPTER X

NEARLY two weeks passed and nothing occurred to disturb the serenity of Shadow Valley. But the nester indulged in no false sense of security, and he was right—his enemies were not idle. The first evidence of this was provided by the arrival, in the early morning, of the sheriff, supported by a couple of deputies. Hammering on the gate, he demanded admittance 'in the name of the Law.'

Drait and his wife came out of the house just as the procession arrived; they were about to take their usual ride. The intruder surveyed them malevolently.

'Needin' me?' the nester enquired.

'You betcha,' Camort replied, and held up a paper. 'This is a warrant.'

'Another?' Drait grinned. 'Perseverin' fella, ain't you? What have you cooked up this time?'

'Just a little matter o' liftin' other folk's cattle, that's all,' the sheriff sneered, and turned to his assistants. 'Take his gun an' put the cuffs on him. If he resists, shoot.'

Wall-eye and his companion hesitated, and then began to dismount—slowly. Drait's harsh voice interrupted the operation.

'Stay in yore saddles—you'll be safer. I'm comin' with you, Stinker, free an' armed. In case you got other ideas, let me point out that Quilt is holdin' a rifle on you, an' if I nod, Midway will be able to elect a real sheriff. As for yore hirelin's, I could put 'em on the ground quicker'n they'd get there any other way. Next time you try to take me by force, you'd better bring the force.'

Camort's face was poisonous. 'There won't be no next time,' he snarled. 'We got the deadwood on you.'

It was at this point that Sudden and Yorky rode up. Drait grinned. 'Comin' to town, Jim? Stinker has issued an invite.' He turned to Mary. 'Yorky will take you along the valley.'

In a few moments they set out, the nester and Sudden in advance, with the sheriff and his deputies following. Quilt convoyed them to the gate.

'Say, Nick, let them polecats ride ahead, in case of an accident,' he advised loudly.

'You're forgettin' Stinker represents the Law, with a big L,' his boss smiled.

'Mis-represents it, you mean,' the foreman snorted. 'There's another big hell a-gapin' for him if he tries any tricks.'

'Threats from yore men won't help you, or scare me from doin' my dooty,' Camort growled.

'Quilt ain't threatenin' you, he's just makin' a promise,' Drait returned lightly. 'An' he's one o' those unusual people who keeps 'em.'

Comforting himself with the reflection that his turn was coming, the sheriff dropped into a sullen silence which his underlings forbore to break. A few yards in front of them Nick and his companion conversed in low tones.

The usually busy street of Midway seemed strangely empty. Outside the bank, Drait pulled up, slipped from his saddle, and went in. The sheriff uttered an exclamation and put a hand to his gun-butt, only to fetch it away with celerity when Sudden turned a chilly eye on him, the nester was back in a few moments. A little further along they were welcomed with a whoop by Pilch.

"Lo, Nick, you've won me ten bucks,' he greeted. 'I bet you'd face the music, come free, an' wearin' yore gun.'

'Good for you, ol'-timer,' Drait smiled. 'Hope it ain't one o' my friends yo're saltin'.'

'Not any; the victim is that happy-lookin' guy behind you, with a star on his manly buzzum.'

The nester stole a glance at the sheriff, whose face resembled a miniature thunder-cloud, and shook his head. 'Too bad to take advantage of a half-wit,' he said. 'Where's everybody?'

'Down to the court-room. Say, they got it all arranged—jury packed—Stinker would say "picked" but it's the same thing, witnesses primed up, and the Judge waitin' to walk in, sober, if possible. But you'll have a square deal, son, or the fur'll fly. I'll have that ten now, Camort; fat men like you is apt to die unexpected.'

The money was handed over; Pilch owned the principal store and had influence in the town, and the officer was well aware that his own popularity was on the wane. He was relying on this trial to re-establish it.

A group of idlers outside the court-house welcomed their arrival with a cheer and hurried in with the news. There was no demonstration when they entered beyond a murmur of excitement and a craning of necks to see how the accused was taking it. What they saw was an entirely unconcerned man, whose eyes twinkled when they encountered a friendly face, and froze for those which were hostile.

The room was spacious, with a raised platform at one end on which stood a desk for the Judge, and in front, a table for his clerk. At the right and left, were railed-in stands. The sheriff pointed to one of these.

'There's the dock,' he said.

'Try an' get me into it,' Drait retorted grimly, and approached two chairs in the first row for himself and his companion.

Camort decided not to insist. The place was full, those unable to find seats lounging against the walls. Sudden recognised some of them: Vasco and his foreman, with Cullin sitting next; Gilman, whispering with the sheriff, apparently not quite at ease; Bardoe and Lanty, whose eyes gleamed evilly when they rested on the accused; Merker, and to his surprise, the lawyer, Seale. He sought the jury and found it in an enclosure which afforded a good view of the witness-stand and the dock, and one glance told him that the members would be more at home in the latter place.

A door at the back of the platform opened, and the Judge entered, deposited his high hat on the desk, sat down, and surveyed the gathering through red-rimmed, watery eyes.

'He ain't feelin' so good,' someone remarked audibly. 'I'll bet breakfast meant just nothin' to him this mornin'.'

'Where's the prisoner?' the Judge snapped. 'Why isn't he in the dock?'

Drait stood up. 'Because I am not a prisoner,' he said. 'I came here o' my own free will.'

Towler apparently took no notice; he was listening to the sheriff's mumbled explanation.

'Most irregular,' he said irritably, and glared at the culprit. 'You are charged with stealing cattle from the S P ranch. Are you guilty or not guilty?'

'That's what you gotta find out,' Drait said drily.

The Judge made a gesture of impatience. 'Put Gilman in the box,' he told the sheriff, and when this had been done, added, 'State your case.'

'I'm accusin' Drait there o' rustlin' one hundred head, calves an' yearlin's, from the S P,' the foreman stated. 'Two o' my men saw him drivin' em off 'bout daybreak.'

'Yo're shore it was just a hundred?' the nester asked, and when Gilman nodded, 'Searchin' out that number o' unmarked beasts in the dark'd be a long an' pesky job.'

'You didn't have it to do; they was rounded up in the home pasture all ready for——'

'Me to take?' Nick finished blandly.

'No, for us to brand in the mornin'—that's how I know the tally,' Gilman grinned. He felt he had scored a point.

'Why didn't yore fellas do somethin'?'

'They was two to yore five. When I heard, I put it up to the sheriff. He suggested we lay a trap to make shore; we baited it with fifty more critters, an' you tumbled right into it.'

'Did you inform Mister Seale, yore boss, of these losses?'

'No, I ain't seen him, an' I expected to git the missin' cattle back.'

'I like yore second reason better,' Drait said, and turned to the Judge. 'Mebbe it'll shorten the proceedin's if I own to takin' the herds, but——'

'That's an admission of guilt, and I will not listen to excuses,' Towler cut in.

'You ain't goin' to hear any, an' a man in yore position shouldn't jump to conclusions, even if he is thirsty,' came the acid reply. 'I'm tellin' you facts, an' by God! yo're goin' to listen.'

Their eyes met and clashed, but the older man—his will

81

weakened by excess—was no match for his young, virile opponent. His head dropped, and he said wearily, 'I'll hear you.'

'The cattle were taken by arrangement with that dirty cur,' Drait resumed, pointing to the witness. 'That's why they were rounded up in readiness. He wanted 'em driven away early so it shouldn't be knowed he was sellin' stock—claimed the S P was short o' cash. Was that so, Mister Seale?'

'No,' the lawyer replied curtly.

'I paid for these beasts, seven bucks a head, all round,' Drait continued, amid a dead silence.

'Can you prove that?' the Judge asked, and Gilman laughed.

'I reckon,' the nester said. 'Mister Williams.'

The manager of the bank stood up; nearing fifty, with a keen, clever face, he took little part in the activities of the town outside his business, and was generally respected.

'Mister Drait is a customer,' he began quietly. 'Recently he drew out two sums of seven hundred and three hundred and fifty dollars exactly. At his request, I noted down the numbers of the bills.' He paused, and Sudden, watching Gilman, saw the swift dawn of apprehension in his eyes. 'Those identical bills, in amounts as issued, have returned to the bank,' Williams resumed. 'They were paid in by Mister Gilman to his private account.'

The simple statement hit the audience like a landslide. Cries of amazement and oaths of disgust came from all sides, and in the hubbub, Gilman—almost stunned by this crushing blow— lost his head.

'You made a mistake, Williams,' he shouted. 'I meant it for the ranch account.'

Instantly Drait cut in. 'Take notice, Judge; he admits I paid for the cattle.'

Williams spoke again. 'The bank does not make mistakes, Mister Gilman; I overheard your instruction to my clerk *on both occasions*. However, since you now say these sums belong to the S P, I will see that they are transferred.'

The foreman forgot to thank him. He realised that he had completely given himself away, and that personal peril had taken the place of the triumph for which he had plotted. He stood there, head down, shooting furtive glances in quest of a friendly face and failing to find it. But his ordeal was not yet over.

'Got rid of any other stock lately?' Drait asked, and when he got a sullen denial, 'What about the hundred three-year-olds sold to Bardoe? Lyin' won't help you, fella; I have it here in yore own fist.'

Gilman recognised the slip of paper, and despite the heat of the crowded room, was conscious of a chilliness. How much more did this devil of a nester know?

'I forgot,' he mumbled. 'They ain't bin settled for.'

'That coin was due to the S P?' The foreman nodded. 'Then you'll be glad to know it was placed to the credit o' the ranch some weeks back.'

Gilman turned a vindictive glare on Bardoe, which Drait easily interpreted. 'On'y partly right,' he said. 'Bull provided the gold, but I collected an' paid it in.'

Towler became aware that the 8 B man was regarding him with a heavy frown, and that he was expected to do something about it. He fired a question at Drait:

'Anything more to say?'

'On'y this,' Nick replied. 'I want you to get the layout. Gilman sold me the cattle an' put the proceeds in his pocket. Then he frames this charge, hopin' I'll hang. If it happens thataway, he gets the stock back, an' is one hundred an' fifty bucks to the good, with nobody the wiser. It's a safe bet he meant to play the same game when Bardoe paid up.'

As Drait sat down, Pilch shouted, 'Well done Shadow Valley,' and there was considerable applause. The Judge rapped sharply on the desk.

'Silence! or I'll clear the court,' he cried.

The storekeeper was not to be intimidated. 'Which I'd admire for you to try, Judge,' he said derisively, and raised a laugh.

The sheriff was whispering to the man on the Bench. 'He's got us cinched,' he said anxiously. 'Ain't there no way to ditch him?'

The Judge considered, and then his weak mouth twisted into a vicious smile, as he rapped again for attention. 'The case is not yet finished,' he said. 'It is clear that the cattle the accused claims to have bought were stolen by Gilman for his own profit. Now, if Drait knew this, he becomes liable to charges of conspiring and receiving.'

The foreman saw an opportunity to bite; he could hardly make his own situation worse. 'An' that's how it was, Judge,' he called out. 'We fixed it up atween us.'

'If the accused has any statement to make I am ready to listen,' Towler said blandly, as though conferring a favour.

Drait rose; this was an unexpected development, and he did not like it. 'Gilman, as foreman in charge, had the power to dispose o' stock,' he explained quietly. 'I bought, an' took steps to protect myself against a possible snare. What had I to gain by his crookedness?'

'You got yore cattle damned cheap,' Bardoe suggested.

'Not so damned cheap either—I would 'a' let him have some at the price,' Vasco chimed in. 'An' if seven a head is cheap for calves, what about the three-year-olds you got for ten?'

Bardoe subsided, inwardly cursing himself. In his eagerness to strike a blow at the nester, he had forgotten his own position.

Cullin had listened unmoved, but only to appearance. From the moment Gilman's dishonesty had been revealed, he knew the day was lost. Towler's persistency was only making matters worse—he was showing bias too plainly. With Gilman and Bardoe discredited, and Vasco in the other camp, the position was perilous. His agile brain evolved a master move to snatch a personal victory out of defeat; by defending Drait he would score with the townsfolk, and avert suspicion from himself if misfortune fell upon the nester in the future. He stood up, and the room became silent.

'In the interest of justice,' he began, 'I must point out that the on'y evidence against the accused is the word of a thief who has a'ready lied to the court.'

The Judge stared; he knew he was about to receive orders, but he had to present some sort of a front.

'What do you mean, sir?' he asked.

'Gilman said the stolen herds were gathered for brandin'! Now he claims that was done by arrangement with Drait. Which statement you goin' to accept?'

'I have not yet directed the jury, Mister Cullin,' Towler said loftily. 'Anything else?'

The rancher bit his lip. All right, if the old fool would have it. 'Yeah, I very much doubt if, havin' found a man innocent of the offence he was accused of, you have the right to bring in another charge. I know little o' the Law, but mebbe Mister Seale will give us an opinion.'

The lawyer was on his feet instantly, beady eyes agleam: at that moment he almost liked the rancher. Only a month or so previously he had sat in that same place, squirming under the castigating tongue of the man he now had an opportunity to repay. The Weasel was not one to forget.

'With due respect, I submit that the court is exceeding its powers, and there is nothing in the statutes to justify such procedure,' he said. 'In any case, a conviction on the testimony so far adduced would be a judicial crime.'

He sat down, and the room gasped. Towler's pale face had become purple, and he would have joyfully murdered the man who had brought this humiliation upon him. But he was impotent, and knew it. Ignoring the lawyer, he addressed Cullin:

'If you had been a little more patient, sir, you would have heard me instruct the jury to entirely exonerate the accused on both charges,' he explained ponderously. 'It was for his benefit I decided that the second—and possible—charge should be dealt with now.'

The verdict having been formally recorded, the Judge dismissed the jury, and remembered he still had a duty to perform.

'Sheriff, you will take the fellow, Gilman, into custody and hold him for trial,' he ordered.

Silent, chin on chest, the foreman slouched out, a deputy on either side. Camort followed, glad of an excuse to get away from friends and foes, neither of whom would spare him. The Judge too picked up his hat and departed, bitterly conscious that he had cut a sorry figure.

When Nick and the puncher tried to slip away they found themselves surrounded by a surging section of the crowd yelling crude congratulations, and struggling to get near enough to slap the nester on the back or grab a hand. He endured the ordeal with a sardonic grin, conscious that some of them, anyway, would have striven as strenuously to see him hanged.

'Awright, boys,' he called. 'The drinks are shore on me, but you'll have to go to Merker's for 'em.'

This started another stampede—in the direction of the saloon —and in a few moments, only a small group remained; they had remained aloof while the demonstration was on.

'I'm mighty obliged to you all,' Nick said quietly.

'Glad to see you clear of a nasty mess,' the banker said. 'If you hadn't thought of keeping those numbers. . . .'

'I didn't,' came the candid reply. 'That was Jim's idea.'

'A very good one,' Seale complimented. 'It wrecked the prosecution, and exposed a very shabby rogue.'

'Yeah, but what we didn't learn was the name o' the bigger rogue who put him up to it,' Pilch said meaningly.

'That may come out at the trial,' Cullin replied carelessly. 'He's the sort to squeal.'

'There'll be no trial,' Nick asserted. 'He'll get away.'

'They dasn't let him,' Pilch cried.

'They dasn't keep him,' Drait contradicted.

The Big C man laughed. 'You may be right. Anyway, he'll be no loss, an' we are to have a charmin' substitute. Any harm in sayin' that now, Seale?'

'No, everything is virtually settled,' the lawyer said. He looked at Drait. 'I shall be at the S P in the morning. Perhaps Miss Darrell would like to come over and inspect her property?'

The nester agreed that it was likely, and the matter having been explained to the other men, further congratulations were forthcoming, to be carried to the lady. Nick cut them short by suggesting an adjournment to the saloon:

'I wanta find out what I owe, an' add to it,' he said.

On the way, Cullin fell in beside him. 'If yo're gettin' rid o' Shadow Valley, gimme first offer, an' make yore own price,' he murmured.

'I'm not sellin'—at any figure, an' I'm not leavin' it,' Drait replied shortly.

Which was precisely the answer hoped for.

CHAPTER XI

THAT same evening the nester and his wife discussed, for the first time, the impending change. He had given her a brief account of the proceedings at Midway, but without revealing the gravity of the peril to which he had been exposed. Drait did not conceal that Cullin had taken his part.

'So you were wrong about him?' she said.

'Not any,' Nick replied. 'He was grand-standin'. Towler was givin' the game away, an' the boys were getting wise. It was a smart move, but it don't razzle-dazzle me. I'd bet a blue stack he's behind the whole dirty business.'

His apparent ingratitude appeared unnatural, but she said no more. The news that he would remain in the valley, leaving her free to go to the S P, came as a relief, and produced no protest. If her evident eagerness to get away from him hurt, he did not show it.

'You'll need a woman in the place,' he remarked. 'Better take Lindy.'

'Isn't there a cook at the ranch?'

'Yeah, one o' Sam's riders who got too old for the saddle, but he'll be no good alone.'

She gave in. Truth to tell, she did want the Negress, but would have died rather than ask for her; the prospect of going to the S P lacking a friendly face had been more than daunting.

'Then there's a foreman,' Nick went on. 'I can spare Quilt—for a time, anyway.'

'No,' she said sharply, and when his eyebrows went up, 'I prefer to give orders, not take them. I can find someone; if he knows his work, that's all I require.'

'Gilman knew that much,' he reminded. 'Trouble was, he didn't do it.'

'There was no-one in charge,' she argued. 'Men are all alike—they only need the opportunity to go off the rails.'

This bit of wisdom—a blow at himself—brought a smile.

'Shore, it's a wicked world,' he said. 'The men are devils an' the women saints—mebbe. I'll trail along with you to the S P.'

'There is no necessity,' she replied coldly. 'Mister Seale will be able to explain everything.'

'Seale knows little about the cattle business; don't trust him too much; yore appearance was a disappointment, remember.'

Instead, she recalled what Cullin had told her, and shrugged impatiently. 'Is there anyone you do not suspect?'

'Mighty few,' he agreed. 'We'll take Lindy with us—one o' the boys can drive her over; she'll see what is wanted to make the place comfortable.'

Mary knew she was being unreasonable, that the arrangements were sensible and for her welfare, but they chafed. Unconsciously, she thought aloud:

'Thank Heaven, I shall soon be able to do as I please.'

The stark exultation in her voice, coupled with an utter absence of gratitude, roused within him a fierce impatience. 'No matter where you are, you'll still be my wife,' he said sternly. 'If ever you forget that——'

'You will shoot me, of course,' she retorted hardily.

The spirit of anger had passed, leaving a cold grimness infinitely more sinister. 'You wouldn't be worth the cost of a cartridge,' he said deliberately. 'But I should shorely kill the man.'

He went out. For long she sat staring into the blazing logs, and, despite the heat, she was cold—inwardly. He would keep his word, for if she allowed him only one virtue, it was that. She was alone, save for Lindy, who almost worshipped her master, she had no friend. Her thoughts veered to Cullin, so different from her husband, kind, considerate, and more polished. No doubt he could be forceful, even ruthless—men had to be in that only semi-civilised land—but she did not believe he was responsible for the outrages in Shadow Valley. He had promised to help her. Comforted by the remembrance, she crept away to bed.

In the morning they set out for the S P, Yorky driving Lindy in the buckboard, escorted by the girl, Nick, and Sudden, on horseback. They found the lawyer awaiting them on the veranda, in conversation with a little, old, grey-bearded man. He greeted them cordially, and when they had dismounted, swept an arm around.

'Well, Miss Darrell, there's your domain,' he said.

She gazed at him, big-eyed. 'Do you mean that I possess all this land?' she cried.

Seale smiled, and shook his head. 'No, you actually own not much more than the buildings occupy, but you have priority grazing rights for many miles about, which is all you need.' He beckoned to the bearded man. 'This is Rod Milton, the cook, one of your grandfather's old servants.'

'Pleased to meetcha, ma'am,' Milton said, and then, as he saw her clearly, 'Gosh! I could a'most believe it was Miss Mary back agin.'

'You knew my mother?' the girl cried.

'I gentled her first pony,' he replied. 'But that was afore we come to these parts. Yo're as like her as one dollar is to another.'

'Rod was anxious about his job, but I told him you'd probably keep him on,' Seale said.

'But, of course. Lindy is coming as housekeeper, she'll need help in the kitchen.'

The little man grinned shyly as he regarded the Negress. 'I don' reckon my cookin' will grade up to your'n, by all accounts, but I'm ready to larn.'

Lindy's smile threatened to absorb her ears; praise for her cooking was a short cut to her good graces. Rod had made a friend.

At the lawyer's suggestion, they went into the house. It was of fair size, consisting of the usual parlour, three other rooms, kitchen, and an adjoining shack where the cook slept. It was substantially furnished but everything showed signs of neglect. Milton read the faces of the women.

'Gilman didn't care none, an' I had plenty to do,' was his excuse.

At one room he hesitated before he opened the door. 'This was Miss Mary's,' he said. 'Till he passed out, the Ol' Man had it tended, but nobody never used it.'

'I can see that later,' the girl said hurriedly. The cook nodded understandingly, turned the key, and gave it to her.

When they emerged into the open again, Lindy chuckled. 'We sho' got a passel o' work ahaid, honey,' she said. 'An' yoh gotta spen' consid'able.'

Mary's startled gaze went to the lawyer; she had not thought of the financial side of the matter. He smiled reassuringly.

'No need to worry. The exposure of that rascal foreman saved us over a thousand dollars, and there is another thousand owed by Bardoe which we could not have had if Mister Drait had not collected it for us. It results that the ranch has now a balance of three thousand, one hundred and fifty dollars at your disposal.'

If he wanted to impress her, he certainly succeeded; it was more money than she had ever dreamed of possessing. Another thought came; that was what happened to the gold taken from Bardoe, which she had accused the nester of stealing. She

88

glanced at him, glimpsed the shadow of a smile on his hard face, and looked quickly away. Seale was speaking again:

'Reminds me that you're a good prophet,' he said to the nester. 'Gilman broke gaol last night; overpowered, bound and gagged the deputy who brought his supper; helped himself to the keys, and walked out. They say Camort is furious.'

'He'd have to be,' Nick replied meaningly. 'Well, that's one more coyote we gotta watch out for.'

Five men who had been smoking and loafing near the corral now approached, removing their hats when they saw the lady. The lawyer addressed them:

'Boys, this is Miss Darrell, your new owner. You will take orders from her in future.'

Four of them were rugged, hard-bitten fellows, nearing or past forty. They muttered 'Howdy,' scuffed their feet, and appeared uncomfortable. The fifth was younger, and had the sallow complexion, black eyes, and lank hair which pointed plainly to mixed parentage.

'Ver' glad to meetcha, ma'am,' he said carefully, and to Seale, 'Meestair Geelman, he no come back.'

'He will not, Tomini,' the lawyer replied shortly. 'That's all.' When they made no move, he added, 'What are you waiting for?'

'Ordares,' the man replied, with a slinky look at the girl.

Drait stepped forward. 'If there ain't any work to do on this ranch, no outfit is needed,' he said sharply. 'If there is, get busy.'

The half-breed perceived that his malicious attempt to embarrass the new boss had failed signally: Nicholas Drait, whom he knew by repute, was clearly not a person to play jokes on. His companions were already moving away, and he followed.

'Any o' these fellas Pavitt's men?' Nick asked.

'No. Gilman got rid of all the old hands except Milton,' Seale informed.

'Guessed that. What do you think of 'em, Jim?'

'Pretty ornery bunch; that Greaser is a trouble-maker.'

'I'm agreein'; I didn't like his anxiety about the late foreman,' Nick said, and turned to Mary. 'You'd better fire him.'

This was a chance to assert herself. 'I'll think about it,' she replied.

'Worth while,' Drait returned carelessly.

After a meal which—to Milton's great satisfaction—earned a compliment from Lindy, the lawyer, Drait, and the puncher departed; Yorky remained to escort the women back to Shadow Valley in the evening. The Negress and Milton headed for the kitchen, Yorky went to unhitch the ponies and turn them into the corral, and Mary seized the opportunity to inspect her mother's room, which she had already decided should be her own.

It proved to be comfortably furnished, but the dust and decay had a depressing effect. The little chest of drawers had been cleared, but in a cupboard a few old dresses were hanging, mere moth-eaten rags. On a wall was the picture of a man approaching fifty, leaning against a fence, thumbs hooked in the cartridge-studded belt which supported a heavy revolver. From beneath the broad-brimmed Stetson keen eyes looked at her over a square, out-thrust jaw and close lips. Her grandfather. Violence, determination, self-will, she saw them all in the portrait, together with a dour, obstinate courage which would suffer to the utmost rather than give in.

Yet there must have been some underlying sense of justice in the old man, for though he would not forgive while he lived, his will showed a desire that what he had fought to create should not go to strangers. Impulsively, Mary made a mental promise to the picture, and fled from the room in a turmoil of doubt and despair.

Buried in one of the big chairs in the parlour, she strove to concentrate on possible changes there. Her mind fully occupied, she did not hear the long glass door to the veranda open.

'Well, if it ain't the Cattle Queen her own self,' said a jesting voice. 'Honey, I shore am glad to see you.'

She started to her feet. Beau Lamond, his hat pushed back, stood grinning at her. For a moment, surprise stilled her tongue, and then, as she realised the risk the man was taking, she cried:

'You must be mad to come here. If Mister Drait sees you...'

'I seen him first, an' his bodyguard, Green,' he replied.

'I scarcely think he needs protection,' something impelled her to say.

'No fella around here wants it as bad,' he asserted. 'I shouldn't tell you that, but I know you won't warn him.'

'You know so much, don't you?' she said ironically.

'I know you don't care two cents about him, an' that's why I'm here,' he said, with an impudent leer. 'I know too that this place is yourn, an' with Gilman on the run, you'll be needin' a foreman. How about it?'

Mary regarded him steadily, and had he been acquainted with Sam Pavitt, he would have remembered him at that moment. 'There is no place for you here, and never will be,' she said coldly. 'Please go.'

For an instant he did not comprehend; then the grin faded from his face and stark anger took possession. 'Puttin' on frills, huh?' he sneered. 'I ain't good enough for you—now. Well, I'll go when I damn please, but first, I'm takin' ...' He advanced into the room, arms outstretched, lawless desire in his savage eyes.

'I guess you'd better go, Beau,' a familiar voice chimed in.

The cowboy switched his gaze from the girl to a door leading into the house; Yorky was standing there. ''Lo, kid,' he said carelessly, and with sudden venom, 'Git, yoreself, or——' His hand streaked back to his gun but his fingers had no more found the butt when he saw that the boy's weapon was out and pointed at his midriff. Beau shook his head in bewilderment; he was reckoned fast, but ...

'You stopped just in time, *hombre*—another move an' you'd be travellin' up or down, 'cordin' to yore past life. Now march!'

Lamond marched, painfully conscious of a gun-barrel nudging his ribs. On the edge of the veranda he halted, and Yorky, placing his right heel in the small of Beau's back, suddenly straightened his leg. The resulting violent thrust sent the unsuspecting victim sprawling into a patch of sand and gravel, several feet of which he ploughed up with his face. When he rose, blood trickling from his abraded features, he was, as Yorky later put it to an amused audience in Shadow Valley, 'mad enough to bite hisself.' Instinctively, as he glared at the grinning youth on the veranda, his hand went towards his hip, only to halt when he recalled the swift draw which had brought about his defeat. With a volley of lurid imprecations, he flung himself on his horse and vanished in a cloud of dust.

Mary, pale and somewhat shaky, was sitting down. 'Thank you, Yorky,' she said. 'Did you hear why he came?'

'No, ma'am, I busted in right away.'

She believed him, which was not surprising, for Yorky was an artist. Early in his short but chequered career he had discovered that a lie, to be of use, must be accepted as truth, and he had studied the subject.

'Fetched his nerve along,' he said. 'D'you know why he's still hangin' around?'

Mary thought she could make a good guess, but shook her head.

'Waitin' for a break to bump off th' boss,' was the blunt reply. 'As foreman o' this ranch he'd shore get it.'

It was not the reason she had in mind, but remembering the cowboy's remark about 'a bonny widow,' and Drait's manhandling of him, it appeared likely enough. The peace she had hoped to find at the S P was becoming only a doubtful possibility. She made an abrupt decision.

'Mister Drait said I could have one of the Shadow Valley outfit. Would you ride for me, Yorky?'

91

'Why, ma'am, I'd be proud,' the boy said. 'But I gotta get back to the Circle Dot—I promised.'

'It would only be for a time, while I'm settling down,' she explained. 'You see, I know nothing about running a ranch, and you could keep me from appearing too ignorant. I would like to make you foreman, but . . .'

'That wouldn't do nohow—I'm too young to be givin' orders.' He saw her smile. 'Shore, I gave some to Beau, an' he took 'em, but you can't be pullin' a gun on yore men allatime. I don't claim to know everythin' about cattle, but Jim'll help me; he's the fella you oughta get.'

'He'd be too good—I'd have nothing to do or say,' she smiled. 'I'll arrange it this evening. Now, should I tell Mister Drait of—Lamond?' She read the reply in his blank stare of surprise. 'Of course I must.'

When he had gone she stepped out and walked clear of the building, so obtaining a wider view of the surrounding country. Plain, forest, desert, slashed with deep gorges, amidst which wound pathways of silver. And on the far horizon, amethystine purple mountains cutting off the rest of the world.

'Yeah, it shorely is worth lookin' at.'

Someone had spoken her own thought. She turned to find Cullin, hat in hand, standing a few yards away. Uneasily aware of her reddened cheeks, she murmured a welcome.

'Just rode over in the hope o' seein' you,' he said. 'Ain't settled in yet, o' course.'

'Not until the place has been made more habitable,' she explained. 'It is in a dreadful state; I would not care for anyone to see it.'

He laughed. 'Which means I don't get an invite. Well, I'm beginnin' to understand a woman's attitude thataway, an' I'm havin' a sort o' domestic revolution at the Big C. That Greaser o' mine thinks I've gone loco, an' maybe he's right.'

She gathered he was paying her a compliment—that the re-formation of his household was her doing. 'Cleanliness and comfort surely go together,' she said.

'Not to a Mexican. His motto is "manana"—never do today what you can put off till tomorrow, or later. But I didn't come to talk o' myself. Is Gilman's place filled yet?'

'No. Mister Drait offered me Quilt, but I told him I wanted to be boss of my own ranch.'

'Shorely,' he agreed. 'I've the very man for you; middle-aged, sober, level-headed, an' knows cattle. He also knows his place an' will keep it. His name is Sturm. I'll send him along in the mornin', but remember, you don't have to hire him because he comes from me; use yore judgment.'

He waved aside her thanks. 'Anythin' I can do for you is a pleasure.'

She had nothing to say to this, and he swung into his saddle and rode away. His receding figure was still in sight when Yorky came up.

'That was Mister Cullin,' she said. 'You don't like him, do you?'

The boy's face took on a whimsical expression. 'If I had to choose between him an' a rattler to cross th' plains with, I'd take th' rattler,' was how he put it.

Mary went indoors, trying to convince herself that he would naturally share the view of his employer. She failed; Yorky was eminently capable of forming his own opinion.

Dusk found them back at Shadow Valley. The presence of Sudden at the evening meal came as a relief to the girl, who had been awaiting it with some apprehension. She liked the puncher, and had confidence in him, though she knew that he too possessed dynamic possibilities for violence, and could be adamant when occasion demanded. The nester himself provided the opening she needed.

'I don't like you an' Lindy bein' up there alone,' he said. 'No doubt Milton's awright, but he's past his prime, an' the rest o' the outfit is just guess-work.'

'Perhaps you could spare Yorky?' Mary suggested.

'Shore could, but he's kind o' young,' Drait objected. 'What you think, Jim?'

'Yorky's head is a lot older than his body,' Sudden smiled. 'He'd be as pleased as a pup with two tails, an' he's useful in a tight corner.'

'As I've reason to know,' Mary said seriously. 'First, Bardoe, and today—Lamond.'

They listened gravely to her account, Drait's expression one of gloomy anger, Sudden's, of pride in his pupil.

'Well done, Yorky,' the former growled. 'Pity he couldn't finish the job.'

'If a fella won't draw, what can yu do?' the puncher queried. 'So he booted him off the veranda, huh? Wonder who learned him that trick?'

'I believe I could guess,' Mary said demurely.

'Yu'd likely be wrong, ma'am,' Sudden returned. 'I started his education, but I ain't takin' the blame for all of it; them rapscallions at Rainbow took over when I left.'

'I had another visitor too—Mister Cullin; he came to offer me one of his riders as foreman.'

It astonished her to find that Nick received the news quite calmly; she had expected an outburst, which would only have

93

made her further inclined to engage the man. Drait divined this.

'What's his name?' he asked, and when she told him, shook his head. 'Maybe a newcomer, an' honest, which might account for Cullin wantin' to get rid of him,' was his caustic comment.

By the time Sudden had returned to the bunkhouse Mary was facing her husband; she never found it easy to speak to him.

'Yorky thinks that Lamond is staying in the country to kill you,' she said.

'Do you also believe that?' he asked.

'I don't know,' she replied dully. 'Any savage act of revenge seems possible in this land without law.'

'Revenge, yeah, naturally he'd hate me for beatin' him up,' Nick mused. 'An' success would convert you into a most attractive widow. Have you thought o' that?'

The blood burned in her cheeks. 'Obviously,' she cried sarcastically. 'Why else should I be warning you?'

'I've had no encouragement to think you'd be sorry.'

'Have I any reason to be?'

'Mebbe not,' he said slowly, 'but mistress o' the S P, even at the cost o' bearin' my name, in secret, is better than bein' Bardoe's—toy. I'm obliged for yore warnin'.'

He went, leaving her angry, perplexed, but silenced. His last words, brutally blunt, were nevertheless true; looked at in that way, she ought to be grateful. Passionately she told herself she was not.

In the morning, Yorky convoyed his new boss and Lindy to the S P. Again they found a visitor waiting, but this time it was a sturdily-built, blue-jowled cowboy, with a craggy face in which the only distinguishing feature was a pronounced cast in one eye. This was Cullin's man, Sturm. Leaving Mary to speak with him, Yorky made for the bunkhouse, eager to inspect his new quarters. He was about to push the door back when a sneering voice came from within:

'I tell you, *hombres*, eet weel be easy. Lamond say dees gal know no t'ing of de ranch beesness. She weel give us de feefty bucks a mont'. She young, pretty, an' weel be lonely; een a leetle time, I sleep at ze ranch-house.'

The listener slammed the door back and stepped in. The five men sitting at the table rose to their feet, staring at him.

'Tomini, you are a filthy, foul-mouthed liar,' Yorky said, with deliberate stress upon the epithets. 'Pull yore gun.'

The half-breed's eyes grew ugly. He knew he had been overheard, and that this would ruin his plans, unless . . . He folded his arms, keeping his hands well away from his belt.

'I do not war wit' cheeldren,' he said loftily.

'No, women are yore mark,' the boy retorted. 'Do I have to slap yore face, you spawn of an Injun?'

The bitter taut had the desired effect, but not quite in the expected way. The man's right hand flashed up from his shoulder and down again. Only just in time Yorky caught the gleam of steel, snatched out his gun and fired. The heavy throwing-knife fanned his cheek as it passed to bury several inches of its blade in the jamb of the door. Tomini, reeling under the shook of a bullet in his shoulder, and mouthing curses in his own tongue, was fumbling for his pistol.

'Freeze!' Yorky barked. 'Th' next slug goes through yore gizzard.'

It was at this moment that Sturm, followed by the breathless girl, appeared; they had heard the shot.

'What is happening?' she cried.

'Nothin'—now, ma'am,' Yorky told her, as he shoved a cartridge into the empty chamber of his weapon. He was seething with anger. 'This yeller-bellied son of a bitch called'—he hesitated—'me names, an' I don't take that from nobody. Then he threw a knife an' I winged him.'

He pointed to the weapon and Mary shivered. Violence seemed to pursue her.

'But why should he abuse you?'

'Heard 'em plannin' to sting you for a ten bucks a month raise all round. Lamond put 'em up to it.'

A tiny crease showed between her level brows at the mention of the cowboy. She looked at the sullen faces of her outfit, decided that the situation was beyond her, and turned to Sturm; 'Are you prepared to start at once?'

'Shore. I fetched my warbags along—hopin',' he replied. 'Want I should handle this?'

'Yes,' she said, and to the men, 'This is my and your, foreman.'

The newcomer wasted no time. 'Yo're fired,' he said to the half-breed, who, nursing his damaged arm had slumped down on a form. 'Git yore hurt fixed, an' travel.' To the other four, 'The pay is forty per; any o' you honin' to go with this fella?'

All were silent; it was months yet to the Fall roundups and work would not be easy to find.

'Right, now listen to me,' Sturm went on. 'Do yore job an' you'll find me not difficult to git on with, but I won't stand for quarrellin' an' gun-plays.' He swung on Yorky. 'If yo're in this outfit, make a note o' that.'

Yorky looked him straight in the face, his eyes hot. 'You can go plumb to hell,' he said, and walked out of the bunkhouse. He had gone but a few yards when Mary caught him up. Her distress was evident.

'I'm sorry, Yorky, he shouldn't have spoken like that,' she began.

'Yo're shoutin',' he replied roughly. 'I ain't goin' to be bawled out afore the outfit by any cock-eyed cow-wrastler that ever wore shoe-leather. I'll get back to the Valley; I on'y make trouble. I reckon yo're no good at choosin'.'

'What do you mean?'

'Sturm ain't straight.'

'You say that because he comes from the Big C.'

'No, ma'am. I've met plenty crooks, an' I say th' same if he stepped right outa Paradise; there's mean blood in him. He's comin' now—to soap me over.'

Another moment and the man was with them, a smile on his lips. 'I guess I gotta 'pologise,' he began. 'I've bin diggin' the facts outa them dumb-heads an' it 'pears the Greaser was lettin' his tongue wag purty scand'lous 'bout you, ma'am, an' our friend here told him what he was—made it plain too. Tomini buzzed a knife, an' if this young fella hadn't bin almighty slick with a gun he'd be lyin' back there with his face split open; as it was, he come close to losin' an ear. Seein' he was just bein' loyal to his boss, I'm eatin' crow. No hard feelin's, son.'

Yorky shook the extended hand, but without enthusiasm, and the foreman beamed. 'Good. I'll git back an' giv them loafers somethin' else to think about.'

'So that was it?' Mary said softly. 'You risked your life for my good name. Do you still think I'm a bad chooser?'

'Yeah, Sturm knowed he'd got off on the wrong foot,' the boy persisted.

Mary smiled. 'Stubborn as Sam Pavitt, they used to say of my grandfather I've been told. Yorky, if Sturm is not honest, I'll need you all the more.'

CHAPTER XII

BOTH Sudden and Yorky ate at the ranch-house that evening. Despite a harassing day, the girl seemed in better spirits, and her husband too appeared less constrained than usual in her presence.

'So you got yore foreman,' he remarked.

'Yes,' she replied. 'He seems—capable.'

'An' Jim was right about the Greaser?' He read her reproachful look at Yorky. 'Oh, he didn't blab; I heard from Lindy, an' she got it from Milton. I guess. Ain't it true?'

'Yes, Mister Green——'

'That shore makes me feel like a stranger,' Sudden said.

'Well, Jim then,' she smiled, 'sized the creature up correctly. Yorky was—fine.'

Drait's harsh features softened. 'You two fellas are pilin' a debt I can never pay,' he said gruffly.

'Shucks!' Sudden protested, and the pair of them had the air of criminals caught in the act.

Nick, who knew exactly how they felt, switched to another subject. 'Have yore range combed an' cattle gathered,' he advised. 'Then brand the unmarked beasts an' count 'em. I guess Gilman was more than careless thataway.'

The talk drifted. Mary told them she was taking Lindy to town in the morning to buy things for the house, and her sparkling eyes showed that she was looking forward to the essentially feminine delight of shopping. Her companions, all of whom had seen big cities, knew that she was due for a disappointment.

'Don't expect too much,' the nester warned. 'Midway is a one-hoss, an' mighty near a one-store town, 'cept for liquor.'

'Which is not on my list,' she laughed, and then, 'Which is the best store?'

'There ain't any best, but Pilch will give you a square deal,' Nick replied. 'He's one o' my few friends in that dump.'

She thanked him with a smile, and after that he was content to leave the conversation to the others, though his gaze was never far from her. In truth, he was trying to convince himself that this really was the girl he had wed. The slimness was still there, but the curves of her figure were fuller, more alluring; the delicately-tanned cheeks had a bloom, and her voice was low, lacking the bitter note he had come to expect. She had a disturbing beauty, new to him.

As the visitors strolled back to the bunkhouse, Sudden heard the full story of the happenings at the S P. 'Yu got off better'n yu'd a right to,' was his comment. 'Didn't yu know a Greaser allus carries a sticker back of his neck or under an armpit?'

'I was watchin' his gun—shore oughta knowed when he folded his wings,' the boy said ruefully.

'Yo're a quarrelsome young devil,' Sudden admonished. 'Keep a hold o' yourself tomorrow; the third time can be unlucky.'

Back in the ranch-house the nester was talking to himself as he undressed; 'Pore kid. She's never had money to spend on the things women prize. Mebbe, someday—But hell, she hates me anyway.' Nevertheless, as he flung himself on the bed, his last

97

waking thought was that one word, 'Someday,' and then, being a healthy animal, he dropped into a slumber which was dreamless.

* * *

Yorky swung his team with a flourish as he pulled up in front of the ranch-house, where Mary and the Negress waited.

'You Yorky, drive'm kearful now,' Lindy urged. 'Dere's no hurry—we sho' got time a-plenty. If I gotta meet ma Maker, I aim to be in one piece.'

'That goes for me too,' Mary smiled, as he helped her into the vehicle.

'Never had a complaint from a passenger yet,' Yorky said boastfully.

The black woman's face split into a wide grin. 'Must allus 'a' druv a hearse,' she said.

A low laugh came from the veranda. 'Best not argue with her, boy,' Drait said. 'She's a woman, bound to have the last word.' He waved his hat as the buckboard shot away.

With Yorky exercising unusual restraint, the journey proved uneventful.

As they drew up outside the bank, Mary became aware of a horseman reigning in, and a voice said, 'Well, if I'm lucky.' She looked up into the smiling face of the Big C rancher. 'I was over to the S P, on'y to learn they weren't expectin' you. So yo're givin' Sturm a try-out?'

'Yes, and thank you for sending him,' she replied. 'He seems capable.' It was the description she had given Drait, she recalled.

'If he's not, send him packin'—don't hesitate,' Cullin said heartily. 'I've found the job, but it's up to him to keep it.' He made no reference to the affair with the half-breed, but she saw him studying Yorky interestedly. Then his glance went to the bank, and he laughed. 'Easy to guess yore errand is to get rid of money.'

'Quite correct,' she told him. 'I'm going to find out how much I can afford, and spend it; the list of things I must have is simply terrifying.'

'Don't hope for much beyond the barest necessities,' he told her. 'Midway is far from civilisation, an' freightin' an expensive business. When do I see this paradise you'll make at the S P?'

She turned startled eyes on him. 'Oh, it won't be ready for ever so long.'

'Then I gotta be patient, which isn't my habit,' he said, in a low, meaning tone. 'Well, mustn't delay you. Good huntin'.'

He rode on down the street, nodding to passers-by, and the

girl watched uneasily. For no definite reason she wished they had not met.

* * *

When Cullin arrived opposite the sheriff's quarters he became aware of that officer beckoning to him. He rode over, got down, and entered. 'Well?' he asked.

'A chance to hit at that cursed nester,' Camort said.

The rancher's lips curled disdainfully. 'I'd 'a' thought you were tired o' swallowin' the dirt he feeds you.'

'I'll never git tired till he's under the turf,' came the vicious answer. 'It's like this, Greg——'

'When did I give you leave to use my front name?'

The sheriff swallowed hard. 'Fancied we was friends.'

'Fancy is misleadin'. I employ you, that's all. Go on.'

'There was a ruckus at the S P yestiddy,' Camort continued sulkily. 'One o' Drait's men shot up Tomini, who hadn't reached for his shootin'-iron. He swears this fella was fetched over to get him. We could charge the gal an' the gunslinger with attempted murder.'

Cullin clenched his fists to keep his temper under control. 'Listen to me, you idiot,' he rasped. 'The Greaser was befoulin' the reputation of a lady, his boss. Taxed with it, he threw a knife an' got shot. The on'y mistake the lad who downed him made was not killin'. Now, go ahead with yore fool case an' I'll bring five witnesses to prove the truth.'

The sheriff's eyeballs bulged; active opposition was the last thing he had expected. Disappointment and anger nerved him. 'Well, if you want I should lay off Drait, I ain't carin',' he said.

The rancher leaned forward, tight-lipped. 'You can do what you please with the nester an' I'll thank you, but raise one finger against Miss Darrell or the S P an' I'll take the hide off you with a bull-whip; that's a promise.'

He stalked from the office, leaving a well-nigh paralysed man floundering in a mental mire. It was some time before he arrived at a satisfactory solution : Cullin not only coveted the ranch but the woman who possessed it. With a long-drawn whistle, the sheriff got out his makings and tried to roll a cigarette. His shaking fingers tore the paper and spilled the weed. Flinging them aside, he stood up.

'Better warn the Judge,' he concluded.

Towler was draped over a chair, snoring raucously; as usual, he had gone to bed early that day instead of the night before, and was not too pleased to have his slumbers disturbed.

'Oh, it's you?' he growled. 'What's the bad news?'

'Cullin is mad,' the visitor said.

99

'What about?'

'I don't mean thataway—just plain loco.'

'That isn't news,' the jurist said disgustedly. 'We all are—must be to stay in this God-forgotten hole. I take it he turned down your stupid plan and forgot to thank you.'

The ironic reminder stirred the sheriff's bile. 'I'm gittin' mighty tired o' bein' bullied by that fella,' was his answer.

'Did you say as much?' Mildly.

'No, but I've half a mind——'

'Don't boast, Camort. Well, well, only my joke, but have you considered your chance of retaining your position—you were not elected for life—at least, we'll hope not.'

This could be taken in two ways, one sinister and the other unflattering, and neither added to the sheriff's ease of mind. But it made him think. Perhaps the 'old soak' wasn't quite the fool he had imagined.

'You have lost the support of the S P, Vasco made his attitude very plain, and Bardoe is not pleased with the publicity you provided,' the Judge went on. 'Quarrel with Cullin and where are you to look for honey? Is your popularity with the townsfolk growing?'

''Bout keepin' step with yore own, I guess,' the officer replied, with a flash of insolence. It was a sore point that of late he had to pay for more of his liquor.

'Then it is on the down grade,' Towler returned equably. 'But my post is different, in that it does not depend on the favour of the populace.'

'If the Governor knowed what——' He stopped abruptly.

'If,' the Judge smiled. 'A remarkable word, Camort; it suggests so many things. If, for example, this town knew how much Cullin and Bardoe paid you to help Gilman escape . . .'

The sheriff started. 'That's a——'

'Secret, of course,' the other finished, and then, sharply, 'Enough of this. What I am trying to get into your thick skull is that if you fall out with the Big C you're finished. On the other hand, with Drait out of the way, and Cullin in the saddle at the S P, he'll call the tune and Midway will dance. If you've helped him, Camort . . .' He rose and picked up his hat. 'Talking is dry work. The drinks are on you—for awaking me.'

*   *   *

That evening the sheriff left Midway to the care of itself and his deputies without informing it or them of his intention. In fact, he waited until dusk enabled him to leave unobserved, and then set off in the direction of Rideout. After covering something less than a couple of miles, he turned into a narrow pathway—no more than a bridle-track, and presently arrived at a dilapidated wooden shack from the broken window of which a light gleamed. Trees and brush surrounded it on all sides, and it seemed a queer spot for a habitation. Yet it had been built, lived, and died in, by a mystery man, was known as 'Stranger's,' and reputed to be haunted. The sheriff was not superstitious; he tied his mount, knocked, and entered. Three men, playing cards on an up-ended packing-case, unobtrusively sheathed the guns they had drawn.

"Lo, Stinker, we didn't know it was you,' Gilman explained. Beau Lamond and Tomini, his companions, nodded agreement.

'Expectin' anyone else?' Camort asked suspiciously.

'Shorely not, but we ain't takin' chances neither.'

'That's a pity; I've come on a fool's errand then.'

'Stop stallin' an' tell us what's on yore mind.'

'Thought mebbe you'd like to pick up some loose change an' wipe out a few scores into the bargain, but if you ain't interested . . .'

Beau swore, and began to shuffle the pack.

'I figure none o' you is over fond o' Nick Drait,' the sheriff went on, and then waited until the volley of curses had died out. 'I seem to 'a' guessed right. Well, there's others, an' among 'em, Greg Cullin. Any idea what he's after?'

They had not, and he told them, in practically the Judge's words. They listened eagerly enough now, but without remark; only from Beau's narrowed lids, fire flashed when the Big C man's ultimate object was revealed.

'What's in it for us?' Gilman wanted to know.

'Plenty,' was the confident reply. 'Greg's no piker, an' the fella who helps him is helpin' hisself. The nester is the first job.'

'Cullin spoke for him at the trial,' Gilman reminded.

'Shore, he's deep; if I'd bin Drait that would 'a' made me nervous,' Camort explained. 'I'm tellin' you, a fatal accident in that quarter would be good news at the Big C.'

'We on'y got yore word for that,' Lamond grumbled. 'We pull it off, an' find ourselves in the air, with a rope round our throttles to keep us from fallin' too far.'

'My word's all you get,' Stinker said irritably. 'Did you s'pose I'd have a signed promise to pay in my pocket? You can count on two hundred apiece.'

'What about my case, Meestair?' the half-breed enquired.

'No good, Tomini. I saw that when I looked into it. There are witnesses to prove you were insultin' the woman an' started the ruckus by throwin' a knife. You can't git away with that in a white man's court; they'd likely have lynched you.'

'I weel revenge myself,' the man said darkly.

'Well, here's yore chance; the chap who drilled you was sent by Drait, probably on purpose. How's yore wing gettin' on?'

'Ver' good,' Tomini replied. 'Ze slug bre'k no bone. Een a week, I shoot.'

'Who's this jasper, Sturm?' Gilman asked.

'Dunno. Greg provided him, part of his plan. I s'pose.'

'Huh!' the late S P foreman grunted. 'Other folk can make plans.'

'That's so, but his come off an' theirs don't,' Camort replied pointedly. 'Think it over, boys, an' please yoreselves.'

CHAPTER XIII

ONE afternoon a week later, Sudden suggested a visit to Vasco, whom they had not seen since the trial. Nick agreed, and they set out, unaware that keen, vengeful eyes were on the watch. The owner of the Double V welcomed them cordially, and his Texas foreman also nodded a welcome.

'Anythin' I can do?' Vasco asked.

'Mebbe there is,' Drait replied. 'I'd like you to tell me, man to man, how you feel about Shadow Valley bein' occupied?'

'This is thirsty weather,' the rancher said. 'Let's irrigate.'

In the cool of the front room, they sampled their drinks, and rolled smokes. Then Vasco resumed the conversation:

'Yores is a fair question. Rawlin was just a nester, knowin' little about cattle, an' ownin' none to speak of. It seemed likely he'd help hisself to some of ourn, so I throwed in with the other ranchers. I suggested he be bought out, we puttin' up the coin an' holdin' the valley as our joint property. That warn't popular, and anyway, he wouldn't sell, so they tried somethin' else, as they did on you. I'm askin' you to believe that I knew nothin' o' the killin's until after; it's God's truth.'

'I'm takin' yore word,' Nick said quietly.

Vasco looked relieved. 'You ain't a Rawlin,' he went on. 'If you aim to raise cattle in the valley an' outside, well, it's free range, with plenty room. Yore beasts'll get mixed with Big C an' mine, but that's no reason for not bein' good neighbours.'

'I'll shake with you on that,' Drait said, and did so. When he spoke again, his voice was harder. 'That don't go for Bardoe an' Cullin, you understand.'

'Bardoe is a rustler,' Vasco replied sternly. 'Yeah, we found the Double X critters you spoke of'—this to Sudden—'But I wanta catch him in the act o' blottin' the brands.'

'It'll save argument,' Sudden agreed.

'Shore thing,' Vasco replied. 'As for Greg, he's got some big ideas but I don't like his methods, an' I've told him so.'

'He's bein' friendly just now,' Nick smiled. 'Offered to buy the Valley, at my figure.'

Vasco whistled. 'The devil he did. Then keep yore eyes peeled, an' remember you got friends at the Double V.'

'Which is worth ridin' a long way to hear,' the nester said heartily. 'An' it goes both ways, you savvy.'

Drait's too-frequently saturnine features wore a smile of satisfaction as he and his companion headed for home. 'It was a lucky day when you found them rustled steers an' put Vasco wise,' he remarked. 'The odds against me were five to one, an' now they're three to two, leavin' out the S P.'

'Gilman got away, an' Lamond hasn't skipped.'

'That's so, but they dasn't show theirselves, an' can't do much alone.'

Just as the nester spoke, a flash of fire darted from the brush about a hundred yards ahead and something tugged at his hat. Then the crack of the exploding cartridge came to them.

'C'mon,' Sudden cried, and swinging his horse, dashed for the nearest bank, forced the animal up the incline and vanished amid the foliage. Drait followed, but not before another slug whined past his ear.

'That came from fifty feet further along,' the puncher informed. ''Pears there's a pair of 'em. Gotta hide the hosses first.'

A jutting outcrop of rock provided the necessary shelter, and having securely tied the animals, they grabbed their rifles and crawled to a spot which afforded a clear view of the depression. A wisp of smoke hanging in the still air, showed whence the second shot had been despatched. The nester was examining his headgear ruefully.

'She was a perfectly good lid,' he said.

'Still is—what's a coupla ventilation holes, anyway,' his friend consoled. 'Good thing you ducked though.'

Drait stared, saw the grin and joined in. 'Ducked? Shore, I allus do when I see lead comin'.'

Prone on the ground, cheeks cuddling rifle-stocks, they watched; nothing happened.

'Think they've dusted?' Nick asked.

'Waitin' for us to move,' the puncher said. 'We'll give 'em a mark to aim at. If they bite, shoot twice, right and left o' the smoke; s'pos'n the fella dodges yu may nail him thataway.'

He found a rock and lobbed it into a bush some six yards to their right. Instantly, from across the hollow, guns blazed, three of them, the bullets shredding the shrub to which the missile had given movement. The ambushed pair returned the fire, and lay close. More shots followed, this time whistling a foot or so above their heads, and bringing down twigs and leaves. Sudden noted, with a grim smile, that only two of the unknown were now shooting.

'Third *hombre* seems to have got into the game a bit late,' he remarked.

'Yeah, an' by the look of it one of 'em has got out early,' Drait replied.

They lay there, lynx-eyed, but the peace of the place remained unbroken. Then came the hoot of an owl, followed by another.

Sudden laughed. 'A signal, an' the jasper who gave it is goin' to be worried at on'y gettin' one answer.'

'Yo're right, Jim. There he goes to investigate.'

At the spot whence the furthest marksman had been shooting, a branch shook, and a little to the left tall grasses swayed; since there was not a breath of wind this meant someone or something was on the move. The keen eyes of the plainsmen tracked the tell-tale signs along the face of the slope to where a second gunman had been hidden. Then Drait's rifle barked viciously, twice, and the movement became more violent, taking an upward direction towards the rim where there was thicker cover. The cattlemen caught fleeting glimpses of darting forms and pumped lead persistently. A savage curse floated back, and stillness came again.

'Any luck, d'you think?' the nester asked.

'No sayin',' Sudden replied. 'Better stay put for a space, it may be a dodge to draw us out.'

They smoked and waited. Presently, at the far end of the bowl, two riders burst from the brush and spurred their mounts madly in the direction of Midway. One of them had his head swathed in a bandage and was rocking in his saddle. Nick swore.

'Hell's bells, that's Beau—I'd know his hoss anywhere. An' the other is Gilman. Where's the third?'

'We'll go find him, guess we needn't to hurry though,' the puncher said sardonically.

They got their horses, crossed the hollow, and soon found what they sought. Sudden had guessed correctly; there was no need for haste. Behind a bullet-riddled bush lay the figure of Tomini, face downwards, his rifle beside him. Apparently he was dead, but when Sudden turned the body over, to reveal a spreading crimson stain above the heart, the eyes opened, and the pallid lips framed two whispered words, 'Steenker—Cullin.' Then the head rolled sideways.

'So now we know,' Drait said.

'Yeah, but what we say he said don't prove a thing.'

'That's so. Well, I was goin' to leave him here, but I got a better idea. We'll tote him in for the sheriff.'

They found the dead man's mount nearby, slung the limp form across the saddle, and secured it with his own rope. A search of the pockets produced nothing but a few coins and the 'makings.' They started out, the half-breed's horse tugging back on its lead.

It was a long, tiresome journey, and night was spreading its blanket over the town when they arrived. Naturally, their gruesome burden aroused interest, and a crowd followed them to the sheriff's office, the lighted window of which only served to deepen the darkness. Drait rapped with the butt of a gun and reined back, leaving the led horse well to the fore. Camort opened the door, and gave one look, and with evident satisfaction, cried:

'So you got him, huh?' Noticing the two riders, he added, 'Where Tomini?'

'Right under yore nose,' Drait replied sternly. 'Whose corpse were you hopin' for?'

The officer's eyes having adjusted themselves to the gloom, he now became aware of the onlookers. He had to think fast, and that was not one of the things he did best. However, inspiration came.

'I figured my boys had fetched in Gilman—they bin out lookin' for him half the day.'

A sneering laugh from one of the crowd greeted this explanation. 'Yore boys come into Merker's this arternoon, too tight to talk, an' are there yet, sleepin' it off.'

Camort had the hide of a horse; a mere insinuation that he was lying could not penetrate. Flattering himself that he had redeemed his bad break, he remembered he had a duty to do.

'I wanta know how this come about,' he said, pointing to the corpse.

'Yo're goin' to,' Drait assured him. 'Tomini an' two others waylaid me an' Jim in Little Basin. They missed—there's a coupla holes in my hat to prove it warn't by much—an' we had an argument. The Greaser got the worst of it, an' his friends 'peared to lose their enthusiasm. One of 'em was Beau Lamond.'

'I ain't seen him for a week or more,' Camort said.

'Then you musta bin blind drunk night afore last, for you were drinkin' with him in Pinto Pete's,' an onlooker contradicted.

'That is a——'

'What?' The speaker stepped into the light, a huge fellow,

105

well over six feet, with the thews of a giant; he was the Midway blacksmith. He could, indeed had, slain a man with a blow of his fist. The sheriff wilted.

'I'd forgotten, Jules,' he hastened to say. 'Fact is, I'm still a bit hazy 'bout that evenin'.'

'The other fella was Gilman,' the nester went on.

The sheriff blundered again. 'Who's left the country,' he jeered.

'Yet you sent yore deputies to search for him?'

'I was told he'd gone, but I wanted to make shore. That's why I was s'prised when I thought they'd got him.'

'Not surprised—delighted, because you figured it was me bein' brought in,' Drait corrected. 'Don't lie any more, but listen: any further attempts o' this kind an' I start gunnin' for you right away; yore star won't save you. Tomini hadn't cashed when we reached him, *an' he talked.*'

Camort trembled. 'I had nothin' to do with it,' he protested. 'All three o' these *hombres* had somethin' agin you.'

'Tomini talked, Stinker,' Drait repeated grimly. 'You've tripped up again an' yore boss won't be pleased. Tell Gilman an' Beau—who will have his head tied up—that I'm shootin' on sight. C'mon, Jim, let's go.'

They swung their horses round and disappeared into the darkness, leaving a most uncomfortable peace-officer with an unwelcome corpse, a few sceptical spectators, and a gnawing fear in his mind. How much had Tomini 'talked'?

CHAPTER XIV

AT the S P the routine of ranch life was being resumed. The excitement of arranging her new home over, Mary began to take an active interest in the outside work. Here she found Yorky invaluable, for though he was far from being the complete cattleman, Sudden and the Circle Dot outfit had taught him a great deal, and his sharp wits enabled him to apply his knowledge. So the girl was in a position to tackle her task not entirely as a novice.

'That lawyer chap at Rideout must be either dumb or crooked to let these figures get by,' Yorky remarked.

They were examining Gilman's record of expenditure; the book was an amazing specimen of inefficiency or carelessness, to put it mildly. There were no receipts, dates often omitted, and payments made without any reason being given. All the riders appeared to have drawn 'advances' but there was nothing to show these had been repaid. A constantly recurring item was 'Stores,' always purchased—as Mary had already learned from Milton—by the foreman.

'An' if he spent forty bucks an' charged fifty, nobody's any th' wiser,' Yorky pointed out.

The girl was studying the book with knitted brows. 'It seems to me that none of the outfit is entitled to wages for at least a month,' she said.

'I wouldn't gamble on that, ma'am,' he replied. 'They all say Gilman was easy to deal with, allus ready to make an advance, but he never forgot to deduct it on pay-day. I'll bet he pocketed those repayments, an' with full wages entered agin his name, how's th' hand goin' to prove he made 'em? Either Seale never saw this book, or he was gettin' a rake-off.'

'But he's a lawyer.'

'Th' more a fella knows 'bout the laws th' easier for him to break 'em.'

'I'll destroy the wretched thing, start another, and keep it myself.'

'Don't you,' Yorky urged. 'Take care o' that book; there's evidence to send Gilman to th' pen for a long spell.'

'But I've no wish for that. It's clear he robbed the ranch, but he did not know I existed.'

'He did his durndest to get an innocent man strung up for rustlin',' the boy reminded. 'An' failin', tried to bump him off.'

'What do you mean?' she cried.

Yorky had ridden into Midway that morning, where he heard various versions of the bushwhacking episode, and from them had gleaned a fairly accurate statement of the facts. White of face, she listened to his bald recital, and in a voice which had a strain of harshness, gave her decision:

'I will put the book in a safe place.'

'There's another reason for keepin' it. You ain't had yore bill from Seale yet, have you?'

'Why, no, but——'

'Mebbe if you ask him to explain it, he'll take a more modest view of his services,' Yorky grinned. 'Life's a game, an' you can't afford to throw away good cards.'

She laughed too, and shook a finger at him. 'You are older than your age.'

'I growed fast—fella had to where I was raised. Don't you trust th' law-sharp, ma'am. Jim reckons he's a twister.'

'And Jim is always right.' In a tone of gentle raillery.

'Shore thing,' Yorky said stoutly. 'If he said I was a waster, I'd believe it.'

107

'I'm not saying a word against your Jim—I owe him too much. I only hope he approves of poor me.'

'I'll say he does, or you wouldn't be here—Jim don't help th' wrong 'uns,' Yorky asserted, and then frowned in perplexity. 'But he helped me, an' I was pretty ornery.' His face cleared as he arrived at a solution. 'Reckon there's a spot o' good in me I don't savvy.'

He went out, unmindful of the fact that her eyes were moist. The thought of the bushwhacking chilled her blood. Two inches lower and Shadow Valley would have lost its master, and she. . . . No, that was unthinkable—horrible.

Sturm, when she informed him of her decision about the ranch accounts, looked somewhat glum. 'Meanin' you don't trust me?' he asked bluntly.

'Certainly not,' she replied. 'You have enough to do, and I need something to occupy my own time. One thing more: I want to know how much stock I have. Please have the cattle collected, counted, and properly marked.'

Yorky had told her, 'rounded up, tallied, and branded,' but nervousness in giving the first real order to her foreman brought forgetfulness. Sturm received the suggestion without enthusiasm.

'That's a big job, ma'am, an' we ain't got the men to handle it,' he objected. 'Likewise, with the Fall round-up due in a few months—when it'll have to be done again—it shore looks a waste o' time. You ain't crowded here, the grass is good, an' stock not liable to stray. I'm advisin' you to wait; in the meantime, the boys can carry strait irons, an' watch out for un-branded beasts.'

'I'll think it over, Sturm,' she said, and went to where her pony was waiting.

The morning ride was something she would not willingly miss.

She did not ride far, however, confining her excursions to an area within easy reach of the ranch-house. Frequently, after traversing a shaded aisle, or emerging from a brake, she would come upon groups of long-horned, fierce-eyed cattle which scattered at the sight of her, but putting into practice Yorky's advice to 'edge up on 'em like you wasn't interested,' she was able to make out the brand. On this morning the discovery of several on which it was missing brought Sturm's suggestion to her mind again. She must have another opinion.

Returning to the ranch-house, she saw the foreman conversing with a visitor; it was Cullin. Sturm led her pony away as she greeted the rancher.

'Just had to come,' he said. 'Seems a long time since I saw you.'

'But it isn't,' she protested.

'I said "seems,"' he reminded. 'My, but the air up here certainly suits you.' The warmth in eyes and voice told her it was no empty compliment, and the flush it caused added to her charm.

'A hard-working cattle-woman has no leisure for pretty speeches,' she said lightly. 'A little advice would be more acceptable.'

'About countin' yore stock? Yeah, Sturm mentioned it— 'peared uneasy at havin' to oppose you. But he was right, you know.'

'If I haven't the hands now, I shan't have them in the Fall,' she argued.

'Let me explain,' he said. 'For the Spring an' Fall round-ups the cattlemen work together, arranging the time for each ranch. When yore turn comes, you will have two riders from the Big C, Double V, an' 8 B. In return, you will help them out the same way. This saves all of us the trouble an' excuse o' takin' on extra hands for short periods. Of course, if yo're set on it, I could spare——'

'No, I see it is unnecessary,' she interrupted. 'I should have had more faith in my foreman.'

'Well, he might have made it clearer,' Cullin excused. 'He's mighty anxious to please you an' I envy him the opportunity.' She ignored that, and he went on, 'House open for inspection yet?'

There was no escape. 'The sitting-room is presentable,' she admitted.

They went in, and, as at Shadow Valley, he was struck by the neatness, taste, and comfort. The furniture he had seen before, in the former owner's time, but now it was polished until it shone; a large square of carpet hid the board floor, dainty curtains draped the long glass door leading on to the veranda, and a sheaf of flowers—the waxen blooms of the Spanish bayonet— decorated the table. Cullin sank into one of the roomy chairs.

'Wonderful!' he said, and it was evident that he meant it.

'You mustn't give me all the credit,' she said earnestly. 'Aunt Lindy helped enormously.'

'I'm not interested in Aunt Lindy,' he replied.

Mary repressed a smile; the Negress felt that way too. His eyes followed her covetously as, remembering her duty as hostess, she produced whisky, a tumbler, and water.

'This was the easiest bit of our shopping,' she laughed. 'I was cautioned that no ranch-house would be complete without it.'

'Must 'a' been a cattleman or a saloon-keeper who said that.' He helped himself and lifted the glass. 'Here's—my love to you.' Her swift gravity warned him, and he hurried an excuse. 'That's a common toast to the ladies where I was raised; don't you like it?'

'No,' she said.

Curiously enough, her prudishness pleased him; here was a woman worth winning. 'I haven't had much to do with yore sex,' he told her. 'You must forgive me if I blunder sometimes.'

He looked so crestfallen that her smile came back. He went on to speak of the great cities he had seen, the crowds, hustle and bustle, the big stores, and places of amusement.

Having created the desired impression, he took his departure. From his saddle he smiled down upon her. 'You must show me yore range. I'm a lonely man, an' it does me good to talk to you.' Without waiting for an answer, he rode away.

Recalling the conversation, Gregory Cullin chuckled several times. He was, in fact, entirely pleased with Gregory Cullin, and also with Mary Darrell. Why he, who had always despised women, should now so passionately desire this one, he could not explain. But he knew it was so, and that there was no length to which he would not go.

'Blast those clumsy fools,' he muttered. 'Two inches lower. . . .'

Shortly after Cullin left, the S P had another visitor. Mary, day-dreaming in a chair on the veranda, awoke to find her husband regarding her quizzically.

'Runnin' a ranch shorely keeps one on the jump,' he said.

'I've been riding, and I suppose I dozed,' she excused. 'Won't you step in?'

He followed her, and gazed round with both amazement and appreciation. 'Fine,' was his verdict. 'You certainly have the gift.'

'Of what?' she asked.

'Home-makin',' he replied, and the look in his grave eyes brought the warm blood into her face.

'Lindy did a lot,' was all she found to say.

'Skittles!' Nick smiled. 'Nobody thinks more o' Lindy than I do, but I'm wise to her limitations.' The bottle attracted his notice. 'Must 'a' been expectin' me.'

'Mister Cullin called,' she explained. 'He wanted to see the place.'

Drait's expression was wooden. 'Yeah, he allus fancied this range,' he returned, and began to roll a cigarette.

She found herself studying him anew. He was not so carefully attired as the Big C man, nor so obviously anxious to impress, yet she was conscious that he had something the other lacked, that mysterious 'quality' the Negress had spoken of perhaps; she did not know. She invited him to stay and eat. Cullin would have seized the opportunity for a compliment; Nick did the opposite.

'Shore is a temptation to sample Lindy's grub again. Not that the boys ain't doin' pretty well—considerin'.'

'I feel mean about taking her away.'

'Don't you, it's doin' us all good; we didn't know how well off we were.'

When Lindy brought in the meal she scrutinised the nester closely. 'Massa Nick, yoh ain't lookin' too peart,' she announced. 'I sho' hab a fohbodin' dem hellions ain't feedin' yoh right.'

'Yo're all wrong, woman,' Nick teased. 'It's just grief over the absence o' my housekeeper.' He shot a mischievous smile at Mary as he spoke, and, without thinking, she returned it.

There was little conversation until the meal was over, and then he asked, 'Started counting yore cattle yet?'

'I'm going to wait for the Fall round-up,' she replied, and gave her reasons. 'It was Sturm's suggestion, and Mister Cullin agreed.'

'Sturm was his man,' Nick said. 'Well, yo're the doc.'

'Isn't it possible you are mistaken about Cullin? He helped you, and now me.'

'Must be a change of heart; his reputation is for on'y helpin' hisself.'

He had picked up his hat, and she saw the sinister holes in the front and back of the crown. The reminder brought a look of concern which he read.

'Now what fool had to tell you?' he asked. 'Cullin?'

'No, I already knew. He seemed very upset about it.'

' "Disappointed" would be a better word,' Nick said harshly. 'An' how did you feel?'

Her steady eyes met his squarely. 'I was very glad you escaped injury.'

His grin was back. 'That makes it a'most worth while. Now, remember, any time yo're in a difficulty, send Yorky, an' we'll come a-runnin'.'

He strode from the room, stepped into his saddle, and with a wave of the perforated hat, spurred across the plain.

CHAPTER XV

I⊤ was a week later that Gregory Cullin halted his horse outside the hotel at Rideout, and having made an enquiry, mounted to an upstairs room. He entered without knocking, and the occupant took his hand away from a gun-butt only when he recognised the visitor. He was a middle-aged man, of medium build, with a thin, sour face and restless eyes. He wore two guns, the holsters tied down. A bottle and two glasses before him.

'Well, Lukor, how's the world treatin' you?' the rancher said.

'Too damn seldom,' was the growled reply. He pointed to a chair and the whisky. 'Help yoreself.'

'I will, but I'm really here to help you.'

This attempt at humour produced only a contortion of the close-shut, almost bloodless lips which was more like a sneer than a smile. 'Can that kind o' chatter,' their owner said. 'I never could figure you as a charitable institootion.'

'But I pay well,' the rancher retorted. He poured out some spirit, and as the other grabbed the bottle and half-filled his own glass, added, 'I'd go light on that stuff.'

'Bah! It never does nothin' to me, I was weaned on it. They carried me to bed las' night, an' look.' He held the tumbler high; the liquid in it might have been solid. He gulped the greater part. 'Well, what's to do?'

'There's a man in my way,' Cullin told him.

'On'y one?' the gunman jeered. 'You used to be fairly handy with a six-shooter yoreself.'

'There's also a reason why I mustn't appear in this.'

'Shore.' The tone turned the word into an insult.

The cattleman's patience was at an end; he did not relish being called a coward. He stood up. 'I gather you don't want five hundred bucks,' he said coldly.

The ruffian knew his man, and was not to be bluffed.

'Yo're damn right, I don't; a thousand's the lowest—take it or leave it.'

Cullin hesitated, but only as a matter of form; he was prepared to pay double the amount, for success.

'I'm takin' it, Lukor,' he said. 'You come to Midway an' hang about, givin' any excuse you like, waitin' yore chance. Don't use yore own name—it might be known.'

The other revealed his tobacco-stained teeth in a wolfish grin. 'I reckon. Figure I'm a greenhorn, huh?'

'The cleverest can make mistakes,' Cullin replied. 'Fella's name is Nicholas Drait, an' he's about my size, mebbe a shade bigger; a nester an' a cattle-thief. You don't like nesters, do you?'

'They ain't fit to live,' Lukor said, and spat in disgust. 'Leave it to me. I'll want fifty for expenses, an' it ain't an advance, mind.'

The rancher peeled off some bills from his roll. 'Needn't to rush things. It's gotta look natural, an' don't let him get his hands on you—he'd smear you on the wall.'

'If he got past a dozen slugs, mebbe,' the gunmen said scornfully. 'Hell, it's good as done; you can wipe him off'n yore worry list right now.'

Cullin left Rideout immediately, unaware of a pair of youthful but sharp eyes watching from the angle of a building across the street. Yorky, having by chance seen Cullin pass through Midway heading east, conceived a desire to discover his destination. When he vanished into the hotel, Yorky followed, got into conversation with the clerk, a youth of his own age, and learned that business was bad—they had only one guest.

'Calls hisself "Fish," drinks like one, an' has all the earmarks of a gunslinger,' the clerk said.

Yorky returned to his hiding-place, saw Cullin come out, but still waited. Presently his patience was rewarded; Lukor emerged and slouched towards the nearest saloon. The watcher noted the pair of revolvers, the deeply-bronzed right hand, the ever-alert glances.

Satisfied he could glean no more he started for home, arriving there as dusk was falling. Outside the house, he met Mary.

'Why, Yorky, we were becoming anxious,' she cried. 'Where on earth have you been?'

Naturally he did not want to tell, and the only plausible pretext he could think of would put the laugh on himself, but it had to be.

'All over it—the earth, I mean, ma'am,' he replied dolefully. 'Guessed I could find a shorter way back an' got proper lost. Wandered about for hours—got mighty near Noo York, I reckon—an' there I was in Midway again. So I come th' old road.'

At the bunkhouse Sturm gave him a sour look. 'Where the blazes you bin all day?' he enquired. 'The Boss'll want an explanation.'

'She's had one,' Yorky said, and closed up like a clam.

His problem now was to get his news to Sudden; he could not ask for time to ride to the Valley. His luck was in—the puncher arrived during the next afternoon.

'Nick's so full o' the change yu've made that I just had to

113

come,' was his excuse to the lady of the house, whereupon she smiled delightedly and invited him in.

His eyes travelled about the room. 'Shore is great,' was his verdict. 'Thought Nick might be romancin' but that ain't so, an' with some flower-beds in front o' the veranda. . . .'

'But what a splendid idea,' she cried. 'Thank you.'

He shook his head. 'It was Nick's notion; I'm on'y passin' it on.'

'Then you must pass on my gratitude,' she replied warmly.

He enquired about Yorky, and listened to the tale of his mis-adventure with a gravity he was far from feeling.

'He's new to these parts; might happen to anybody,' he said.

As he rode away in search of the boy he spoke to the black: 'Nig, a fella who can't lie for a friend, ain't much; I must remember to wise up Nick 'bout them flower-beds. Wonder what that li'l devil was doin'?'

He found the 'li'l devil' forcing steers from a thorny thicket, and exuding moisture and expletives with equal frequency. He was nearing the end of his vocabulary when a low, amused voice remarked: 'Mind yu don't get lost in there.'

Yorky smote an obstreperous steer on the flank with the end of his rope, and came piling out of the bush.

'Yo're th' very fella I wanted to see,' he cried, and then, as the significance of his friend's words dawned, 'You didn't think I lost myself, did you, Jim?'

'Well, no, I figured mebbe there was a reason,' Sudden admitted.

'Shore is,' the boy said, and told his discovery.

'Yu done fine,' Sudden complimented. 'I'm glad I fetched yu along.'

Praise from this quarter was priceless to Yorky, and having watched the black race out of sight, he murmured, 'You ol' pirut,' and returned to his labours quite happily.

On reaching the Valley, Sudden sought out the nester and warned him about the flower-beds. Drait regarded him curiously.

'I'm obliged, Jim; oughta thought o' that myself.'

It was not until several days later that Nick announced his intention of going to Midway; stores had to be purchased.

'I was aimin' to visit town my own self,' Sudden said.

'Mebbe I can do yore errand?'

'I guess not; some things a fella's gotta do for hisself an' gettin' a hair-cut is one. But gimme a list an' I'll order yore goods.'

'Why o' course. Where's my head?'

So Sudden solved a problem which had been worrying him.

For the trip he selected a mount from the corral, leaving Nigger behind. Exactly why, he could not have explained; the thought came and he acted upon it. Pilch, the storekeeper, welcomed him joyfully, and business being soon concluded, Sudden perched himself on the counter, swiped a handful of raisins from a nearby tub, and prepared to chat.

'Nick all right?' Pilch began, and when the customer nodded, "Bout time he got his rope on that gal at the S P an' won hisself a fine ranch.'

Sudden took some more fruit. 'Good, these. Add a dozen pounds to our list, ol'-timer, Nick must 'a' forgot 'em; the boys like plum duff.'

'You seem partial to the plum part yoreself,' Pilch retorted, with a meaning glance at the puncher's not too small paws. 'Now stop side-steppin'—you heard what I said.'

'I don't know a thing 'cept Nick ain't lost his appetite, which I'm told is a sign. Anythin' new in town?'

'A hard-lookin' stranger, mean-mouthed, carries a couple o' sixes, an' claims to be waitin' for someone.'

'An' he doesn't deal with yu.'

'How d'you——? Well, yo're right. I don't sell liquor, an' that's all he buys. Been around 'bout three-four days, an' the quicker he leaves the sooner we shan't miss him.'

Sudden laughed, purchased some tobacco, and went in search of a barber and a meal. These matters attended to, he proceeded to Merker's, failing to notice that a pedestrian had stopped as he passed, turned, and followed him. Lukor had seen the N D brand, and the somewhat sketchy description he had received seemed to fit the rider. But he had to be sure. He entered, and saw his quarry at the bar, talking to the proprietor. Strolling to an adjacent table he sat down. Merker was speaking.

'I'm tellin' you, Nick'—he dropped his voice to little more than a whisper—'is in danger; somebody's out to get him.'

'Sound reasonin', but where's the proof?'

'We'll get it, but in the meantime, don't run risks.'

'Shore, they cool the blood an' hamper digestion,' Sudden smiled. 'Know the genial-lookin' gent at the table?' He had noted the man's entrance in the mirror behind the bar, and recognised him from Yorky's description.

'A newcomer—been hangin' about recent.'

Lukor who had heard—as he believed—the saloon-keeper address the puncher as 'Nick,' was satisfied that he had found his man. An evil grin twisted his lips as he reflected that soon he would shake the dust of this 'prairie-dog settlement' from his feet, easy in mind and rich in pocket. The victim was a big fellow, but he expected that; Cullin had warned him. The two guns brought a sneer, they were the sort of bluff a nester might put up. The low-drawn hat-brim concealed most of the face. He stepped to the bar and spun a dollar. Picking up his change plainly revealed that the little finger of his left hand was missing. Sudden's eyes narrowed. Lukor sampled his drink—a moderate one—and facing round on the company, said:

'Nesters is rank pizen.'

His raucous voice rang through the room, the buzz of conversation ceased, and every eye was turned upon him.

The speaker went on:

'They digs their selves in among the ranges, which gives 'em plenty chances to steal cattle.'

This produced no result, the least interested man in the place being the one who should have resented it. Leaning against the bar, with one heel hooked over the foot-rail, he was rolling a smoke, and taking unusual care.

The gunman went on with greater confidence; it was going to be easy money.

'Sneakin' coward an' coyote—that's yore nester,' he rasped. 'Any self-respectin' c'munity'd string 'em up on sight.' The savage gibe evoked no response, and he stabbed a finger at Sudden. 'You agreein' with me?'

The puncher was lighting his cigarette. His mind recalled 'Whitey,' a killer of the same type whom he had been forced to slay during those hectic weeks at Windy.* A cold rage possessed him. This man had come to butcher, in cold blood, someone he had never seen, and for mere gain. Well, he would not act, unless he must.

'Did yu say somethin'?' he asked indifferently.

'On'y that nesters is cowardly thieves an' oughta be wiped out,' Lukor snapped.

'Mebbe yu know best,' came the mild answer. 'I ain't lost any nesters.'

A tinge of red in the bully's cheeks showed that he was becoming really angry; this stupid fool was making it difficult. He must depart from his usual routine, and force the issue.

'No, an' you ain't got no guts neither, you——'

With the words, he had fallen into a crouch, his right hand hovering, claw-like, over the butt of his gun. Sudden, watching the other hand, saw it drop, with the speed of a striking hawk, to the holster on that side; the weapon was clear of its container when fire jetted from the puncher's left hip and Lukor staggered. For an instant he kept his feet, and then, with a choking grunt, lurched forward, and as his knees gave, collapsed on the sanded floor, his drawn gun thudding beside him.

* Related in *Sudden*.

116

Sudden knelt and raised his shoulders, disclosing a gaping wound at the base of the throat. As he did so, the eyes opened, and a spark of recognition shone in them.

'Yo're—not—Drait,' the man muttered thickly. 'Yo're——' The head fell to one side, and another gunman had died—as did most of his kind—'with his boots on.' Sudden straightened out the body, placed the hat over the face, and stood up.

At that moment the sheriff came bustling in, elbowed a way through the crowd which had swarmed round as soon as the shooting was over, and demanded:

'What's happenin' here?'

'Nothin'—now,' the puncher told him drily. 'Yo're in time to take charge o' the corpse—as usual.'

'I'm in time to take charge o' the killer, too,' Camort retorted. 'You know this fella?'

'On'y by hearsay,' Sudden replied. 'Name of Lukor—knowed too as "Finger-shy." His guns were for hire, an' there's a sheaf o' sheriffs further East honin' to hang him. His dodge was to make a show o' goin' for the right-hand gun an' usin' the left, in spite o' the missin' finger. By all accounts, it fooled a lot o' fellas.'

'An' you knew about it, o' course?' Camort sneered.

'No, he told me,' Sudden said. 'You see, he picked up some change so clumsily that it was plain he wanted me to notice the crippled paw, an' I wondered why.'

'Which o' you started the trouble?' A dozen voices told him. 'Awright, I ain't deaf,' he said testily.

'Why shouldn't you be?' Pilch asked. 'Gawd knows yo're dumb.'

When the laughter had subsided, Merker explained that the puncher had done everything to avoid a clash.

'So Green was—cautious, huh?' the sheriff sneered. 'Tried to duck out, in fact?'

Sudden looked at him, and before those frosty eyes Camort's assumed merriment died swiftly.

'Listen, yu makeshift,' the puncher said. 'I didn't wanta fight that fella because I knew he wasn't after me, an' his last words proved it. When you came in just now it was Drait's body you expected to see. One thing more: yu are a liar, twister, an' a yaller dawg. Got any ideas?'

The challenged man had one—to save his skin. 'I am also the sheriff,' he reminded.

'Yu'll be the late sheriff unless you get out, *pronto*,' was the scornful retort.

Camort looked at the stony, threatening face, then at the grinning spectators, and slunk out like a punished puppy. An ironical cheer followed him through the swing-door.

CHAPTER XVI

TIDINGS of the tragedy arrived at Shadow Valley before the chief actor returned. One of Vasco's riders had been in Merker's, and running into Shorty on his way home, told the story in detail. 'An' say,' he finished, 'Don't git fresh with that Green person—who shore has a most misleadin' monicker—an' handles a six-shooter like he'd cut his teeth on one.'

'Fast, huh?' Shorty queried.

'Lightnin's that, but you can see it,' the newsbringer replied. 'There's nothin' wrong with my eyes, but Green's draw beat 'em. An' he had to hump hisself, that trick o' goin' for one gun an' usin' t'other was mighty bafflin'. An' that's Gawspel truth. Well, gotta be pushin' along—I'd just hate for anyone to beat me in with *this* news.'

'I'm aimin' to be early my own self,' Shorty grinned.

He got his wish, and by the time Sudden arrived, the story was common property in the Valley. Quilt opened the gate for him.

'Anythin' fresh in town, Jim?' he asked casually.

'Nothin' to speak of,' was the equivocal reply.

He rode on, and Quilt scratched his head. 'Cool?' he asked himself. 'I guess ice on him'd on'y git harder. An' he shore is closely related to a clam.'

Having unsaddled and turned his mount into the corral, Sudden was making for the bunkhouse when Drait hailed him. The nester did not beat about the bush.

'So you've been takin' my place in Midway?' he began.

'Shucks!' was the disgusted reply. 'This is the most chatter-some country I ever was in. Did they tell yu I bought seegars in Merker's too? Have one.'

Nick lit up. 'Then it's true?' he said.

'I dunno what yu've heard,' Sudden replied, and when he had been told, went on. 'That's about the size of it.'

'How come he took you for me?'

'We're both biggish, an' I had my hat pulled down. Likewise, I was ridin' one o' yore hosses.'

Drait looked at him sharply. 'Anythin' wrong with Nigger?'

'I've been workin' him middlin' hard; he was due for a rest.'

'You steered me off town. Were you lookin' for trouble?'

'Never had to yet,' Sudden laughed.

Drait digested this evasion in silence; he was no fool, and he knew that he again owed, perhaps his life, to this chance-met comrade.

'Jim, yo're on'y a passable liar an' Yorky ain't much better,' he said. 'Don't think I ain't grateful, but this has gotta stop; I'm too old for dry-nursin'.'

'Nick, I wasn't expectin' a showdown, but I did hope to get a line on what was afoot,' Sudden said soberly. 'He rushed me.'

'Did you know this Finger-shy gent?'

'On'y by repute; he was just a professional killer an' crooked at that, but he was over-confident an' *showed his hand* too plain,' Sudden said with a sinister smile. 'What about grub? I'm as empty as the sheriff's head.'

There was no demonstration when they entered the bunkhouse, nor any reference to the day's happening; with innate delicacy, the cowboys knew that taking life, even justifiably, was not a thing a man would want to talk about. Smoky just grinned and said:

'Glad yo're back for supper, Jim. Long has threatened somethin' special tonight.'

'An' "threatened" is the right word,' Shorty supplemented. 'When Long passes in his checks, someone else will be the worst cook in the world.'

Which specimen of brotherly love restored the normal atmosphere and put everyone at ease.

* * *

Cullin called the S P the following morning, and finding that Mary knew nothing of the gun-fight, gave her the details, dwelling especially on Lukor's error.

'He intended to kill Mister Drait?' she cried. 'But why, if they were strangers?'

'If,' the rancher shrugged. 'I'm told that the fella talked o' bein' in Midway to avenge a sister's honour, but mebbe it was on'y an excuse; his kind has to have one.'

He saw her face darken; however little a wife may care for her husband, the advent of another woman is rarely welcome. But she did not speak.

'That cowboy, Green, is a mighty good watch-dog,' Cullin continued. 'He's done a lot for Nick.'

'I, also, am in his debt,' she reminded quietly.

'Same here,' he smiled. 'For what he has done for you; I wish it had been my luck.'

'But you have helped, and I am grateful.'

'On'y that? Well, I mustn't be impatient, but I want you to like me very much—Mary.'

She flushed—it was the first time he had used her front name —but she affected not to notice. He left soon after, to her relief. Staring, almost with unseeing eyes, at the great panorama before

119

her, she tried to analyse her feeling for Cullin. Did she really like him, or was it the fascination a forceful man who knew the world must have for a young, inexperienced girl? She could not decide. Admiring him, enjoying his company, at the back of her mind was an instinctive warning, vague but insistent. She shook her head and was glad to see Yorky rocketing towards her. The boy was bursting with excitement; Smoky had brought him a note from Jim, and of course, spilled the whole story.

'You heard 'bout th' ruckus in town, ma'am?' he blurted out, as he flung himself from the saddle.

'Yes,' she said. 'Mister Cullin told me.'

'Cullin? Why he—was here then?' She did not notice the hesitation, due to the warning Smoky had delivered.

'Naturally,' she said, and very gravely. 'It is a terrible affair; I am glad Mister Green escaped injury.'

'It'll take a damned good man to git Jim, by fair means,' Yorky replied pridefully. 'If he'd done it, I'd 'a' got him—somehow.'

The hardening of the youthful face, firmed lips, and slitted vengeful eyes told that this was no vain brag. Then, ashamed of the emotion he had displayed, came the excuse, 'Jim's been awful good to me, ma'am.'

'I understand,' she replied gently. 'He's been awful good to me also. Someday, I hope he'll let me tell him so.'

'He'd ruther you didn't,' the boy said bluntly. 'Sooner be cussed than thanked, durn him.'

'I'm afraid that's true,' she smiled. 'Yorky, why did that wretched man want to kill Mister Drait? Was it because of some old score?'

'Guess not. If Lukor had knowed the Boss, he'd never 'a' mistaken Jim for him.'

'Why, of course,' she cried, and wondered at the sudden warm glow in her breast.

'He was hired for the job,' the boy went on. 'An' got just what he deserved. As for the white-livered houn' who employed him....'

'It is hard to believe such monsters exist,' she said. 'Do you think it might be Bardoe? They fought before.'

'Mebbe, but Smoky sez Bull would 'a' done the deed hisself an' saved his dollars.'

'I'm afraid of that man,' she confessed.

'You don't have to be, ma'am,' he told her. 'We're all a-lookin' after you.'

'I know it,' she smiled. 'I mustn't be foolish.'

When she had gone, Yorky relieved his feelings with a mild oath. Something was troubling her.

'Why didn't Nick come along here with th' outfit an' take hold for her?' he asked the world. 'Stuck on showin' Midway he could hang on to Shadow Valley, I s'pose.'

Which was only part of the truth, and by no means the most important.

CHAPTER XVII

THE extinction of a gunman as a topic of interest lasted less than two weeks, and the town resumed the uneven tenor of its way.

By this time, Cullin's impatience reached its limit. He had paid several visits to the S P, only to realise that he was making no progress. The girl was friendly, but that was all, and he began to suspect more interest in Drait than she would admit; the thought made him furious. The removal of the nester was not enough; he must be discredited in her eyes. His plans were taking shape, and they carried him to the 8 B. As he rode up, two men came out, Gilman and Lamond.

'I heard you'd skipped,' he said. 'Ridin' for Bull?'

'Gotta do somethin' for our chuck,' was how Beau described it. His head was still bandaged.

'A change for you,' Cullin replied. His humour generally contained a sting. 'You come near not needin' any, I understand.'

At that moment Bardoe came out; he had heard the voices. 'What's the trouble?' he asked.

The Big C man saw that he had overplayed his hand. 'Aw, forget it. Mebbe I ribbed 'em too hard; I was on'y joshin'.'

It was an apology, of a kind, but two pairs of baleful eyes followed him as he disappeared into the house. His host pointed to a chair, and said, 'Ain't you got more sense than to quarrel with men who might yet be useful?'

'They've bungled everythin' so far.'

'You ain't bin such a howlin' success. Drait's still in the Valley, firmer rooted than ever, an' with the town lookin' sideways at Camort. . . .'

'Yo're tellin' me news,' Cullin said sarcastically.

'You act like you didn't know it,' Bull returned, in the same vein. 'What do you want now, anyway?'

Cullin hesitated, purposely, and then, 'I did have a proposition, but if yo're buryin' the hatchet with Drait, I'll be off.'

'Please yoreself,' Bull shrugged. 'But any hatchet I bury'll be in the beggar's skull.'

'He's had the devil's own luck.'

'An' friends he can trust. That's where you fall down, you've on'y got people you pay, an' don't trust. What was Lukor's price?'

'How should I know?'

'Like I said,' Bardoe sniggered. 'Shall we mention a thousand bucks?' The rancher's slight start of surprise told the guess was a near one. 'It would 'a' bin worth it, if—but there's allus an "if," Greg, ain't there?'

The visitor lit a cigar and rolled another across the table. Inwardly boiling, he forced himself to speak calmly. 'S'pose you stop yappin' about what doesn't concern you an' listen to some-thin' that may.'

'Shoot.' Bull leaned back in his chair and expelled a screen of smoke, behind which he grinned in real enjoyment.

'I want some cattle lifted, an' it's goin' to be worth more than a thousand to you,' Cullin began. 'It's the S P. Rustle a few, at short intervals, an' don't monkey with the brand. Keep 'em hidden some place, an' I'll pay ten a head when I take over.'

Bardoe pondered. 'I don't savvy the game.'

'It ain't necessary you should.'

'That's what you think,' the other said curtly. 'Find a bigger fool.'

Cullin swallowed the word 'Impossible' and managed to say quietly, 'I'm aimin' to bleed the S P white, give the owner a lesson, an' compel her to sell.'

'You bin after that range a good while. Too bad that cowboy routin' out the gal. Why don't you marry her?'

'That's another reason for carryin' out my plan; poverty is a fine reducer o' pride. Get on with it, Bull, an' when we're good an' ready, we'll take another whirl at that cussed nester.'

'It's a bet,' Bardoe said. 'Sturm was one o' yore men, huh?'

'Yeah, you'll find the beasts bunched up—preparations for a round-up, likely. The outfit is bone-lazy 'cept one—Green's side-kick, Yorky; he's awake.'

'That damned young cub?' Bull exploded. 'I've a score to settle with him. Awright, Greg; you've hired a man.'

When the visitor had departed, Bardoe indulged in a burst of laughter. 'Bleedin' is a game two can play at, Mister Clever Cullin, but I'm with you part o' the way. Then mebbe it'll be you to git the lesson.'

The rustler's face was never pleasing; now it was hideous—a jeering mask of hatred.

* * *

The sun, slowly climbing into the blue vault above, was warming the keen, sage-scented air, which was yet cool enough

122

to make movement pleasurable. Away on the horizon the mountains were beginning to unwind their swathed wrappings of mist. It was a grand sight, but Drait's eyes were more often—unknown to her—on the girl by his side, noting the upright poise of her lissome body, the curve of her cheek, or the errant curl with which the light breeze was playing.

Mary too, was less attentive to the view. She was thinking of a ride with Cullin two days earlier. The contrast was marked. But she had to admit that he was more restful than the impetuous admirer from the Big C.

'Feed looks fine,' he remarked presently. 'Not many cattle showin'.'

It was not long before they came across a score or more, and got near enough to look them over. 'In good shape,' Drait conceded. 'But there's some need brandin'.'

Mary looked annoyed. 'That should have been attended to. I told Sturm he would find several about here.'

'How's he shapin'?'

She said the man was satisfactory, so far. They reached another small herd, containing more which had 'missed the iron.' 'I guess Gilman's fellas had an easy time,' Drait commented.

'They're still having it, apparently,' Mary said bitterly. It hurt her pride that this man, especially, should find subject for criticism when she had hoped for praise; Sturm must be made to understand he was there to obey orders.

'Know anythin' about yore fellas?'

'They close right up when I'm near. All I get out of them is "Yes, ma'am," or "No, ma'am." They're different from the Valley men.'

Drait grinned. 'You bet they are. I'm boss, but those rascals are my friends, an' they know that, come what may, I'll stand by any or all of 'em to the finish. Such wouldn't serve under a Gilman. Now, what's yore trouble?'

She was about to deny, but he interrupted: 'Don't say it; yore lips weren't made for lyin'—Mary.' The word slipped out —he had not meant to use it. He saw the red tide rise in her cheeks, but he could not know that her veins were tingling as they had not done when Cullin took the same liberty. 'You see,' he went on hurriedly: 'This is a stiff job you've taken on, an' it can't be mastered in a few weeks, though you've done amazin' well. O' course, you don't have to tell me, but. . . .'

'I'm losing cattle,' she confessed helplessly. 'Just a score perhaps at a time.'

'What's yore foreman doin' about it?'

'The men are night-riding, but while they watch one part of the range, the thieves visit another.'

'Someone's gettin' information. Don't worry; these things happen, an' you must expect a loss now an' again, but it's gotta be looked into.'

Presently they encountered Yorky. 'Able to find yore way around better?' Drait wanted to know.

'I'm learnin' how th' land lies,' the boy replied.

'Mind the land don't learn how you lie,' the nester grinned. 'These missin' steers now; got anythin' to tell us?'

'Yestiddy there was fifty right here, an' today I can't round up thirty; also, hoss-tracks in circles don't come o' theirselves.'

'Have you reported to Sturm?' Mary asked.

'No, ma'am, I was aimin' to try an' track 'em down m'self.'

'You any good at trailin'?' Nick asked.

'Not very,' was the modest reply. 'Jim can read sign like an Injun.'

'We'll try him out. He'll be over in the mornin', an' we won't tell even the foreman. Sabe?'

'I'll be as dumb as a dead nigger,' Yorky promised.

When they reached the house, the sight of newly-turned soil jogged her memory. 'I haven't thanked you for that suggestion,' she said.

Nick looked unhappy. 'It warn't mine,' he blurted out. 'It was Jim's, an' he fathered it on me, I dunno why. Don't let on I told you—I expect he had a reason.'

Her woman's instinct enabled her to make a near guess, and neither of the men suffered in her estimation by the disclosure.

'We'll round up some roots for you—there's plenty in the Valley,' Drait went on.

'I'd rather have those than any,' she replied eagerly, and saw his grave face light up.

'Which is fine to hear,' he said.

The firm clasp of his fingers remained after he had left. Her eyes softened at the puncher's attempt to do his friend a good turn, and that friend's refusal to accept credit not due to him. She went into the kitchen.

'Lindy, what do you think of Mister Green?'

'Reckon he's all man, honey, an' dey's sca'ce. Massa Nick's one, foh sho', but dat Cullin——'

'Is kind to me,' Mary reminded sharply.

The black woman shook her head; she was not to be convinced.

CHAPTER XVIII

EARLY morning found Sudden at the S P, and having collected Yorky, heading for the scene of the latest raid. Sturm saw them, but having been told that the boy was showing the visitor over the range, was not interested; if the time of a hand was wasted, it was the owner's affair.

The evidence on the spot was plain enough. Sudden studied the tracks closely.

'About twenty-five cows, convoyed by five riders,' he decided. 'One of 'em forkin' a shod hoss, with a cross in the off hind shoe, for luck, mebbe.'

The depth of the imprints told that the beasts had been hard-driven, but after a mile had been covered, the pace fell off as the undulating plain gave place to broken, wild country.

'I ain't envying' 'em,' Sudden remarked. 'Must 'a' been a moon that night.'

'There was,' Yorky said. 'An' they wasn't usin' th' trail for the first time neither.'

They had arrived at the edge of a miniature desert, roughly circular in shape, and about a mile across. Into this the trail plunged and ceased abruptly; a wind had swept the light, powdery sand into tiny ridges, obliterating every trace.

'Gotta ride around her an' find out where they came off,' the puncher said. 'Take the left an' keep agoin' till we meet.'

It was Yorky who found the spot, the rustlers having borne well to his side in crossing the arid expanse. This was their first real attempt to blind their tracks, but it was followed by another necessitating a search of the banks of a stream along which the stolen cattle had been driven. A stretch of gravel next gave trouble, but after that the raiders apparently regarded themselves as safe. Finally, a stone-littered, winding pathway brought the trailers to what appeared to be a pile of rock. Closer inspection revealed an opening, masked by foliage, and secured by a barrier of newly-cut poles. Within was a cuplike depression, grass-carpeted, on which a herd was grazing. There was no sign of any herders, so they entered and walked their mounts forward until the brands were discernible.

'S P—over a hundred of 'em,' the puncher said. 'An' as this place can't be far from Bardoe's range, it's an easy guess who fetched 'em here. Well, gotta get back an' report to Nick; I ain't trustin' Sturm.'

They took their time on the return journey, and evening was approaching when Shadow Valley was reached. Drait was awaiting them.

'Bardoe, no doubt,' he agreed. 'That place is the Devil's Pocket; we'll have 'em out o' there tomorrow.'

'An' take 'em back to the S P?' Sudden asked.

'To be lifted again? No, they'll be safer here. We'll say nothin'; it'll be a pleasant surprise for—Miss Darrell. You two'll have to let her think you've failed, just for the time.'

'That's no matter,' Sudden smiled. 'But ain't it rather risky to have stolen cows in the Valley?'

'Won't be for long, an' who's to know?' Nick argued. 'Folks has to get permission to come in here now.'

He seemed set on the plan, and the puncher said no more but he did not like it; some intuition told him it would spell trouble.

When the first streak of grey on the horizon proclaimed the coming of the dawn, Drait and his four men set out. Yorky had returned to the S P the night before; Sudden remained in charge of the Valley. It was late in the day when the outfit appeared again, driving a bawling bunch of steers; the Pocket had been emptied.

'Everythin' went slick as a greased rope,' the nester said. 'We took it easy, fogged the trail some, an' went on a wide sweep to miss Bardoe's range. Never saw hide nor hair o' anyone.'

But the operation had not been quite so unobserved as he believed. When they were but a mile or so from home, one of Cullin's men had seen the herd from a distance and promptly investigated. Having dogged it to its destination, he carried the news to his employer, who frowned in perplexity when he heard it.

'Which direction were they comin' from when you first saw 'em?' he asked.

'West,' the rider said, adding, 'Must 'a' taken a helleva road round if they were from the S P.'

Cullin dismissed him, and then tried to puzzle it out. The only conclusion he came to was that it required attention. Accordingly, in the morning, he journeyed—not unwillingly— to the S P, but instead of going to the ranch-house he swung off into the brush, and waited until he saw the man he wanted. A whistle brought Sturm to him—they had met there before.

'Mornin',' Cullin greeted. 'Cattle still *strayin'*?' with an emphasis on the last word.

'Over a hundred head—it's that simple you can skin the range if you want.'

'I don't. Any more news?'

'That Yorky kid was showin' Green around day afore yes-tiddy,' Sturm replied. 'I saw 'em start an' that's all any of us did see; the boy showed up agin at night—alone.'

As the rancher rode back to approach the house in the usual

way, his brain was busy with this piece of information. Green was an experienced cowboy, and would know about trailing cattle. He had spent a whole day looking over a range the like of which he must have seen on scores of occasions. In the circumstances, Bardoe's men would hardly trouble about leaving tracks. It was all plain: Drait had the stolen steers in Shadow Valley. A Satanic smile distorted his lips; the nester had handed him the winning card.

The girl's welcome seemed less cordial than usual, and though the possibility angered him, there was no sign of it. After a compliment on her appearance, he asked casually, 'Have you been partin' with cows lately?'

The question rubbed a sore spot. Sudden's failure to run down the raiders had been a sharp disappointment, and Mary had a vision of continued losses, and an end to her hopes of making the S P a success.

'Yes,' she replied ruefully. 'Parting with them, but not willingly; they've been spirited away—in the night.'

'My, that's tough,' he said, in a shocked tone. 'Lost many?'

'More than five score, Sturm estimates.'

'I'm terribly sorry. The rustler is the bane o' the cattle business; there's on'y one cure—the rope. I'd hang every one caught with the goods.'

He spoke with vehemence, and the girl, smarting under her sense of loss, was disposed to agree. 'I hate violence, but crime must be checked, and certainly these wretches deserve no mercy,' she said.

'Come for a ride,' he suggested, and when she was about to refuse, added, 'I've somethin' to show you.'

He took her in a westerly direction, away from his own range. After nearly an hour, they reached a line of high bushes, pierced here and there with grotesqucly-shaped spires and pinnacles of stone which appeared oddly familiar.

'We have a few yards to walk now,' Cullin told her.

He went ahead, making a path for her, paused, and pointed to a sapling. 'Put an arm round that and look down,' he said, drawing aside a branch.

'Why, this is Shadow Valley!' she cried.

'True. What do you see down there?'

'Only cattle grazing.'

He passed her a pair of binoculars. 'Try these.'

She did so, and the powerful lenses seemed to fling the nearest cow in her face. On its rump were the letters S P—her own brand. Wonderingly she directed the glasses to others of the herd; all bore the same mark. She turned to her companion.

'What does it mean?'

'I can't say. By chance I learned that over a hundred head, wearing yore iron, had been driven into the Valley yesterday evenin', an' when you told me you hadn't sold any, I guessed you oughta know about it.'

'Thank you,' she said, her face like pale marble, and returned the binoculars.

'Look again, an' make sure,' he urged. 'Mebbe there's just a few strays.'

'I saw several dozen of my three-year-olds, picked animals,' she replied harshly. 'I wouldn't have believed a man could stoop so low.'

'It looks bad, but seems incredible,' Cullin mused. 'I wish I could help you.'

The ride to the S P was made in silence, and Cullin was content it should be so. He had sown the seed; solitude, and the outraged pride of a woman would bring fruition. When they reached the ranch, she did not invite him to remain. He played the hypocrite once more.

'Don't think too hardly of Nick,' he begged. 'This is a lawless land, an' he is hot-blooded, impulsive——'

'It was a mean, cruel act,' she interrupted icily, and then her voice broke a little. 'He could have had them for the asking.'

With these words ringing in his ears, he went away. Somehow, he did not quite like the sound of them, but he had done a good morning's work, and things were going well.

The girl he had left was far from sharing his satisfaction. Puzzled, angry, and utterly miserable, she sought her bedroom, to be alone her one desire. Her husband had behaved vilely, Green and Yorky had helped him. In all the world she had no one to whom she could turn for aid or counsel. Cullin had been kind—even to the point of pleading for the offender; he seemed to be her only friend. To confide in Lindy would be useless; the black woman would not hear a word against 'Massa Nick.'

Why had he done it? she asked, over and over again, and always it was the same answer: because of a ruthless, masterful nature which took what it wanted, regardless of who might suffer.

Another explanation suggested itself. Drait resented her taking charge of the S P, and this was his revenge—the planning of a humiliating failure which would drag her pride in the dust, and bring her to him, disillusioned, begging for aid. Instinctively she looked at the portrait on the wall, and in the hard eyes and grim lips read a message: 'Fight.' As though she had actually heard the word, she replied: 'Yes, you had troubles too, and fought them. I am of your blood. If Drait has done this despicable deed, he shall answer for it.'

*   *   *

On leaving the S P Cullin had ridden at a sharp pace to the 8 B, the owner of which welcomed him with a grin.

"Lo, Greg, I shore hope you've fetched yore roll along; I got a li'l bill for you.'

'You don't have to worry,' the visitor returned. 'What's the tally so far, an' where are they?'

'Six score, an' they're in the Devil's Pocket.'

'I'll stake the amount I owe you they ain't.'

Bull's glance was one of suspicion. 'If you've fetched 'em away——' he began.

'Don't talk foolish,' Cullin said. 'In the first place I didn't want 'em—yet; in the second, I'd no notion where yore cache was; in the third, I shouldn't 'a' taken 'em to Shadow Valley.'

Bardoe's eyes bulged. 'Shadow Valley? What'n hell they doin' there?'

'Grazin', I shouldn't wonder,' Cullin replied. He liked to irritate, and the other's volley of oaths merely amused him. 'Drait an' his men drove 'em in yesterday.'

'How'd they know where to look?'

'Green an' his young friend trailed you, is my guess.'

Bull damned the pair at length—he could see his li'l bill becoming waste paper; Greg Cullin was not the man to pay for nothing. For once he was mistaken. The rancher must have divined his thought, for producing a big wad of currency, he pushed a portion of it across the table.

'I'm payin' just the same,' he said. 'It so happens that Drait has stepped right into the loop that's goin' to hang him.'

The rustler pouched the money. 'How come?'

'You wouldn't care to be found with stolen stock in yore possession, I expect,' Cullin replied ironically.

'By God, yo're right, an' o' course, he stole 'em straight from the S P.'

'He an' his men'll tell a different tale, but who's goin' to swallow it? Besides, he could 'a' hidden 'em in the Pocket; found there, he'd never be suspected, but you would.'

Bardoe scowled. 'That's so. Allasame, I owe Green somethin'.'

'Better let the debt run—Finger-shy was no slouch,' Cullin reminded drily. 'Listen: the sheriff will pull Drait in tomorrow mornin' an' shove him in the calaboose to await trial. Now, in case the girl turns soft, I want her out o' the way till the whole affair is over, an' that's where you come in. Get the idea?'

'I'm to carry her off an' keep her hid,' Bardoe said.

'It's a pleasure to work with you,' Cullin complimented. 'Where can you take her?'

'My cabin on Black Ridge, the other side o' the Big Quake. She'll be safe enough—ain't many know of it.'

The Big C man nodded. He had seen the place, an extensive and wide strip of morass which had proved a death-trap to many hundreds of cattle. An expanse of brilliant green, dotted with tussocks of coarse grass and reeds, it appeared innocent enough. But the pressure of a foot brought the moisture squelching up, and to stand still even on the brink for a few moments was to court disaster.

'It must be done tonight,' Cullin went on. 'In a little while, when Drait has been dealt with, I shall discover where she is and rescue her, payin' you a ransom of three thousand dollars.'

Bardoe was too cunning to jump at the proposition. 'I shall have to split with my fellas,' he objected.

'You won't need many—Sturm an' his crew will be out on the range watchin' for rustlers, so you'll have a clear field. There must be no violence; if the girl is hurt in any way, payment will be in—lead.'

'Ain't threatenin' me, are you, Greg?' Bull fleered. 'Be easy, I'll take care o' yore ladylove, an' mebbe shake a leg at yore weddin'.'

But when the Big C owner was receding in the distance, he shook a fist instead, and growled, 'Damned mongrel. Lead, huh? You'll settle in gold, my friend, an' I'll fix the figure; the S P, with the dame thrown in, is worth a lot more'n three thousand.'

CHAPTER XIX

At the Big C, Cullin bolted a meal, saddled a fresh mount, and hastened to Midway. Camort, lolling drowsily in his office, woke with a start when the great man entered.

"Lo, Greg, anythin' new?' he enquired.

'Yeah, we've got him.'

'Meanin'?'

Cullin swore impatiently. 'That infernal nester, o' course. Where are yore wits?'

The sheriff smothered a sigh; he was rather weary of battling against the 'infernal nester.' With a dubious expression, he remarked, 'That jasper's as hard to hold as a greased rattler, an' as dangerous.'

'Don't talk like a weak-kneed quitter,' Cullin snapped, and proceeded to explain the situation. Camort brightened visibly.

'It shore does seem we got him where the hair's short,' he admitted. 'But if the gal lets us down. . . .'

'She won't appear a-tall—I'm arrangin' that. Yo're actin' on a complaint about the rustlin' an' request for the punishment o' the culprits, received from her.'

'I ain't——' the sheriff commenced, but got no farther.

'Don't be dumb,' Cullin said angrily. 'Her protest was made to me, an' I'm handin' it on; she won't be there to deny it. In any case, you have yore duty to do.'

'Shore,' the officer smirked. 'What she wants don't really matter—the welfare o' the public comes first.'

'Quite, but keep that admirable sentiment for the court. You will arrest Drait in the mornin', lock him up, an' see he stays that way. If _he_ gets out, you'd better climb a tree, tallest you can find.'

'S'pose he resists?'

'Six o' my outfit'll be in town; you can use 'em. I don't fancy he'll fight, but if he does, it's yore duty to get him—dead or alive. Understand?'

'You bet. I'd rather hang him, but I ain't one to think o' my own pleasure.'

Cullin's next call was on the Judge, and again the position was set forth. Towler's fear of the rancher exceeded his dislike, but he had no affection for the nester either, so he readily promised to do his part.

'Within the Law, Mister Cullin,' he said. 'Strictly inside the bounds of my office.'

'Of course, Judge,' Cullin smiled. 'Have I ever asked you to do otherwise?'

'No, sir, you knew that such a request would be futile. This trouble-maker appears to have so acted that the Law can now deal with him—effectively.'

'Well, it's up to you an' the sheriff. I don't think he can wriggle out as he did last time.'

The reminder was unnecessary, the Judge had not yet forgotten the fiasco of the former trial. He frowned and said:

'We will endeavour to see he does not, sir,' which was the assurance the visitor wanted.

*　　　*　　　*

Midnight was near when a rider with a led horse paced noiselessly up to the S P ranch-house, dismounted, and dropped the reins, leaving the animals a few yards from the building. He had already ascertained that only one light was showing—from the parlour. Cat-footed, he stepped on the veranda and peered through the glass door. The girl he had come to find had fallen asleep over the fire, an account book lay on the floor beside her. He noted, with satisfaction, that her hat and coat were on another chair; this simplified matters. Pulling his own hat well over his eyes, and covering the lower portion of his face with his neckerchief, he stepped inside.

'Keep yore tongue still an' you won't be hurt,' he said, in a low tone.

Mary awoke with a jerk, made to rise, and sank back again as she saw the muzzle of a six-shooter within a few inches of her face.

'What do you want?' she managed to whisper.

'Obedience, just that,' was the reply. 'Put yore things on. We're goin' for a ride, an' remember, one scream'll be yore last.'

She knew it was useless to resist. Lindy would be snoring, Milton, in his little shack next the kitchen, would hear nothing, and Sturm had told her that the men would be out on the range till dawn.

When she was ready, he motioned her to the door, turned out the lamp, and followed; she felt the barrel of the weapon against her spine. They reached the horses, mounted, and set off, the man still holding the lead-rope. Almost at once, four riders emerged from the shadows and fell in behind them.

It was very dark, the few stars, pin-points of light in the sky, seeming only to increase the gloom. Mary could form no idea as to the direction in which they were travelling, but from the fact that progress was slow, and frequent turns necessary to avoid black masses of foliage, she guessed they were breaking a new trail through the brush.

The captive, tired and despondent, rode like one in a dream, holding the reins slackly, and making no attempt to guide the beast she bestrode. Fortunately the animal was docile, sure-footed, and the shapeless dark bulk beside her was watchful. She was almost sure this was Bardoe, and the possibility filled her with dismay; she had heard much about him since their first meeting, none of it to his credit. She became aware that he was speaking:

'Too damned dark to risk the Quake tonight, boys. Have to ride around her. Better be safe than sorry.'

'Yo're whistlin', Boss,' one of the men agreed.

'Shore is one hell of a place,' the leader remarked. 'I hate crossin' it; one wrong step an' it's—curtains.'

The dreary miles dropped behind, and then Mary became aware that they were climbing, and that the stars were no longer visible. Also, the riders had strung out in single file. She surmised, correctly, that they were mounting a narrow pathway through a forest. The air grew colder, and there was a breeze which increased as they mounted higher. Then she saw a light, and one of the men said fervently:

'Home, sweet home, boys, an' I hope to Gawd grub's ready.'

'Well, here we are,' the leader remarked, as he drew rein opposite the light, which proved to be an open door.

Mary got down, so stiff and fatigued that she would have fallen had he not placed an arm about her. Instantly, she straightened and recoiled.

'I'm all right,' she said.

'You done noble,' he replied gruffly. 'There's warmth an' food waitin'.'

'I need sleep—that only. Where is my—prison?'

He conducted her to a small room, with a floor of bare boards, and an unglazed window only a cat could get through. The candle he lighted brought to view a pile of blankets on a pallet bed, a chair, pail of water, and a torn but clean towel. On one of the log walls a cracked mirror was hanging.

'Rough quarters, ma'am, but we'd little time,' the man said. 'I ain't tyin' you up, but remember that the Quake lies between here an' the S P. The key o' the door will be in my pocket, so you can sleep easy.'

'Why have I been brought here?' she demanded.

'I dunno,' he lied. 'All I can say is that if you make no trouble, you'll meet no trouble.'

The key grated in the lock. She bathed her face, removed hat and coat, spread her blankets, and lay down. Despite her determination to remain awake, she slept.

Bardoe returned to the big room, where, at a long table, the men who had accompanied him were eating, and washing the food down with generous doses of spirit. Four others were smoking round the log fire. One was Gilman, who looked up with a leer.

'So you got her?' he said. 'I hear she was dressed ready, too. Yo're allus lucky.'

'Lucky?' chimed in Lamond from the table. 'An' Bull all fixed to play the part o' lady's maid.'

Some of them laughed, but their leader's face was mirthless. 'Beau, I hate to tell a man he's a damn fool twice in one night,' he said, and looked at Gilman. 'The girl's got grit; that ride would 'a' taxed a man some, but she never let out a squeak.'

'Hell, Bull, whatsa use gittin' sore over the dame? Drait's no saint, an' it wouldn't surprise me if she's feelin' lonely.'

Bardoe whirled on him, ferocity in every feature. 'Listen to me,' he barked. 'If I catch anyone near the gal's door I'm shootin' first an' enquirin' after. Get me?' His threatening gaze swept the room. 'A complaint from her an' Cullin'll go back on his bargain, an' we'll have a battle with the Big C on our hands.'

'Bull's right, boys, as usual,' Lanty put in. 'It ain't worth the risk; me for the dollars, every time.'

The muttered agreement appeared to guarantee that the prisoner would be undisturbed, but the leader was taking no chances, and when retired to his own room, he did not sleep. His followers piled fuel on the fire, got their blankets, and made themselves comfortable.

Bardoe, in the darkness, sat listening to the snores which mingled with the crackling of the logs. Presently he caught another sound—stealthy footsteps in the passage. They paused, waited, and then went on. He slipped off his boots, drew his gun, and noiselessly followed. He could hear someone fumbling at the girl's door, seemingly searching for the keyhole. The rustler raised his gun. The report, deafening in the confined space, brought the sleepers from the big room, one of them carrying a blazing brand from the fire.

'Hell, what's broke loose?' Lanty cried.

'Somebody after the girl,' Bardoe replied.

By the unsteady light of the improvised torch they surveyed the crumpled, supine form of Lamond; a key was gripped in his right hand.

'Well, I warned him,' the killer said dispassionately.

'Where'd he git that key?' Lanty asked.

'One o' the other doors, I guess; thought it'd fit, which it might've,' Bull said. 'Take him away—she's stirrin'.' He called out: 'It's awright, ma'am; a gun went off accidental-like.'

Two of the men carried the limp body into an empty room. 'He allus was a fool 'bout females,' one of them said, as they dumped it on the floor.

CHAPTER XX

Breakfast was over in Shadow Valley, and the nester, with Sudden, had ridden down to the gate, where Quilt was on duty. The foreman seemed worried.

'Hope you ain't keepin' them S P steers long, Nick,' he said. 'Our feed is limited, an' they make me uneasy, anyway.'

'They'll be gone soon,' was the reply. 'Who in blazes is this a-comin'?'

Sudden studied the approaching bunch of riders, ten in all. 'It's the sheriff, an' seein' he's fetched along plenty assistance, it spells trouble,' he remarked.

'Get the other boys, Quilt,' Drait said. 'It may come to a scrap, but we'll hear what he has to say first.'

Emboldened by his superior force, Camort rode right up to the barrier. Drait, standing in his stirrups, asked, 'What might you want?'

'You,' was the blunt answer. 'I got a warrant.'

'Again?' Nick said, with a shrug. 'Don't you ever get tired o' doin' the same things?'

'This'll be the last time. Open up, we're comin' in.'

'You don't say?' The rest of the outfit had arrived. 'There's on'y six of us, but we're good, an' this wall ain't easy to climb. Let's have a look at yore authority.'

The sheriff handed up the document, and Drait read it. 'The old charge—stealin' cows from the S P. Dug up some fresh evidence, Stinker?'

'Yeah, an' we're here to see it don't run away.'

Nick was studying the visitors. 'Half o' you from the Big C. So Cullin's in this, huh?'

'Quit foolin' an' let us in,' the officer said. 'I want them cows.'

'To put in as witnesses?' Drait asked. 'Now, I'll give you a choice; the herd stays where it is until the Judge makes an order, an' I give myself up, or—you can let yore wolf loose.'

Camort considered the proposition. His main purpose was to secure the person named in his warrant. He had talked boldly to Cullin, but faced with danger, he had no stomach for it. His followers showed no enthusiasm for the task of scaling that wall in the face of six skilled gun-wielders. In a battle his office would not protect him. Sudden's sardonic eye settled the matter; he seemed to be deciding where to plant his bullet.

'Well, that's fair enough,' the sheriff said.

Drait turned to his companions. 'Take notice I'm goin' willin'ly. If I'm shot in the back. . . .'

'I'm comin' with yu, Nick,' Sudden put in. 'Any dirty work an' Midway will be shy a sheriff.'

Camort scowled; he did not like the arrangement, but was powerless to prevent it. Drait unbuckled his belt and tossed it to his foreman.

'Take care o' that, an' hold the Valley against all comers,' he said.

'Shore will,' Quilt said dourly. 'Yo're playin' the hand, Nick; me, I'd sooner argued with 'em.'

With a gloomy face, he saw them depart, Drait and the puncher riding together, the posse—split into two groups—in front and behind, a disposition which evoked the nester's contempt.

135

'Cautious man, Stinker,' he commented. 'Well, Jim, once more yo're right—I was a bonehead to cache the cattle in the Valley. Wonder how that worm got on to it?'

'Somebody saw you fetch 'em in,' Sudden surmised. 'It's serious this time.'

'I'm believin' you. Rustlin' is bad, but robbin' a woman, my—friend, is damned bad. An' the truth ain't worth tellin'.'

Their arrival in town was witnessed by many. Looking at the faces, Drait soon realised that public feeling was not in his favour; men he knew well avoided his eye. Pilch was not of these; the size of the posse gave him an opening.

'On'y ten to bring in a desp'rit character like Nick?' he said loudly. 'Yo're takin' chances, Stinker. Think what a loss you'd be; we'd have nobody to laugh at.'

Having seen his friend safely installed in the calaboose and made a mental plan of the place, Sudden returned to the Valley in the late afternoon and found another problem awaiting him. Yorky had come racing in with the news that the mistress of the S P had vanished. At first it was assumed that she had gone for an early morning ride, as her saddle and pony were missing, but when, after some hours she did not appear, it was discovered that her bed had not been used. Then the saddled pony drifted in, and the outfit spread out to scour the range. Yorky came for help. No, the foreman didn't send him.

Sudden nodded. 'How does he figure this out?'

'Well, her hat an' coat is gone, an' the door to the veranda unbolted. Sturm suggests she went to sleep over th' fire an' wakin' in daylight, took a tide to freshen up an' met with an accident. Brownie was a pet an' would come at her call.'

'Mighty ingenious, but it don't add up,' the puncher said. 'She's been carried off, an' the hoss turned loose as a blind, mebbe by Sturm. Where was he last night?'

'With th' rest of us, watchin' for cattle-thieves what never showed up.'

'They were after other game. Yorky, we got a job to do. No, Quilt, two will be enough. The rest get some sleep; we'll be on the move early.'

It was late that night when the sheriff, dozing in his office and feeling the effects of a lavish celebration of his capture—mostly at the expense of others—heard a light tap at his window. He was rather unsteady, but he managed to open the door, and nearly lost a tooth on the muzzle of a revolver.

'One chirp, an' they'll be fittin' yu with wings—mebbe,' the masked man holding the weapon growled.

The sheriff allowed himself to be pushed into the room, and turned round obediently when ordered. The gun-barrel boring into the small of his back, he submitted to his wrists being handcuffed behind, a gag jammed into his jaws and secured by a handkerchief—his own—which also deprived him of sight. A final operation roped him in his chair so that movement became impossible. In picking up a bunch of keys on the desk, the visitor observed a paper. It read: 'I have the girl. Rush the trial and carry out verdict *pronto*.'

It was signed with a sprawling 'C,' and went into the finder's pocket. On a shelf, a dusty, little-used volume attracted him; it was a copy of the State laws. He took it down, read a certain section, and replaced it thoughtfully. Then he turned to a door on the left, which he knew must lead into the prison. Opening it softly, he saw a wide, dimly-lighted passage. At one end was the main entrance, heavily-barred, and at the other, the cell where the nester was confined. A thin line of light, almost opposite where he stood, indicated a room from which came the murmur of voices—deputies on guard, no doubt.

Silent as a shadow he stole to the cell, took out the bunch of keys, and at the third attempt found the right one. The prisoner was deep in dreamland; he must be awakened without noise. Sudden tried the old hunter device—pressure below the left ear, and in a few moments the sleeper quietly came back to consciousness.

'It's Jim,' Sudden whispered. 'Follow me, and not a sound.'

Drait obeyed, without argument. Stealthily they crept back to the sheriff's office, and the nester smiled widely when he saw the helpless, muffled figure. The puncher extinguished the light and they slid outside. Yorky was waiting for them; his task had been to procure the prisoner's horse and saddle from the sheriff's corral. In five minutes, keeping behind the buildings, they were clear of the town. Then the released man put a question.

'Tell yu all about it at the Valley,' Sudden promised. 'For now, we gotta ride.'

It was not until they entered the bunkhouse, and the cheers which greeted their appearance had subsided, that Nick got his answer.

'An' you figured I'd like to help find her?' he said. 'I'm thankin' you.'

'Solitude has dulled yore wits some,' the puncher smiled. 'Ain't it plain they want the girl out o' the way till yu've been disposed of, an' to leave yu in the calaboose would be handin' 'em the pot?'

'You think that's why she's been taken?'

'Yeah, they're scared she'd plead for yu. There'll be mostly men in the court, an' Miss Darrell is a mighty attractive person—though mebbe yu ain't noticed it.'

137

The mild irony reddened the nester's cheeks. 'That's one time yo're wrong, Jim,' he said quietly. 'What else?'

'This,' Sudden replied, and showed the message he had found on the sheriff's desk.

'Cullin?' Drait exclaimed. 'If he's harmed her I'll cut his heart out.'

'If yu can find it,' Sudden said. 'That can wait; we gotta get Miss Darrell.'

'She wouldn't be at the Big C?'

'No, that'd be too raw; someone is workin' for him. We can be at the S P by daylight an' mebbe pick up a trail.'

'Line yore bellies, boys, it looks like bein' a long day,' Drait warned. 'I shall want all o' you, an' fetch yore rifles. The Valley must take care of itself.'

The eastern sky was lightening when they arrived at the S P. No one was about. Sudden sent the others into hiding, and proceeded on foot to the ranch-house. At the end of the building he found a spot where two horses had stood. Tracks of two people came to the place from the veranda, and the narrow sole and high heel of one set pointed to a woman. They had mounted there and moved away in a westerly direction. Occasional indentations led him to an opening in the brush where hoof-pitted ground and cigarette butts proclaimed that a party of riders had waited; one print showed a cross in the off hind shoe.

'Pretty much as I guessed,' Sudden reported, when he re-joined the others. 'If we can keep on their trail . . .'

Keeping on the trail proved to be a trying and slow affair, for much of it passed over coarse grass; often they completely lost it, and all of them had to dismount, circle, and search on foot. Time after time, however, patience and perseverance prevailed, and in due course they reached the Big Quake. No one of them had seen the place before, but the tracks, showing plainly in the softer ground, led straight to the morass. Drait, who was getting impatient, quickened pace, but Sudden caught his arm.

'I don't like the look of it,' he cried. 'Why's the grass green there an' burned up here?'

'But they went,' Nick argued.

'Yeah, a couple of 'em rode past here an' backed their hosses mighty brisk. Look at Nig; he knows.'

In fact, the black, with a snort of fear, had commenced to sift its feet uneasily. Nick looked down and found his own animal had sunk to the fetlocks. Hurriedly they retreated. Sudden, swinging down in his saddle, picked up a chunk of wood and slung it on the line they would have taken. For a moment, they saw it, and then it was gone.

'Nice place—on a dark night,' he said.

Retracing their steps, they found where the quarry had jumped aside on to firm footing. Circling the morass involved another wearisome ride, but at length they got to the pine-clothed slope, and saw, about halfway up, a tiny ribbon of smoke spiralling out of the tops of the trees. As they paced up the narrow pathway, rifles were examined in readiness. Soon they heard someone whistling, and could see the cabin through the trees.

'We'll leave the hosses in that bunch o' bush off the trail,' Sudden suggested. 'Quilt, Shorty, an' Smoky can sneak round back o' the buildin', case they try to vamoose. We'll give yu fifteen minutes to get into position. The firin' will tell yu when the dance is on; then use yore judgment.'

The three men melted away into the undergrowth, and the others waited, silently. The quarter of an hour seemed endless, but presently Drait gave the word, and they moved forward, spread out, and using the tree-trunks as cover. When the cleared space in front of the cabin was reached, the nester shouted, 'Hello, the house.'

At once the door opened and Bardoe appeared, rifle in hand. 'Who's there?' he called. 'Come ahead, with yore paws up.'

Nick stepped out. 'You know me, Bardoe,' he said.

'So you got away?' he said, amazement evident in his tone, and damned himself for the slip. 'What you want?'

'Miss Darrell, an' you needn't lie; I know she's here—Cullin has given the game away.'

'Then I play my own hand,' Bull replied, and with a sneering laugh, 'Go to hell.'

With the last word he fired, sprang back, and slammed the door. His bullet whined past the other's ear. An instant later came darts of flame from the two windows and several loopholes; no damage was done.

'Me an' Yorky'll deal with the windows, Nick,' Sudden called out. 'Yu an' Long take the loopholes.'

For some moments the stream of lead continued, but beyond trimming the trees and bringing down showers of twigs and leaves, it accomplished nothing. In both directions, lead threaded the air, chipping bark from the trunks sheltering the assailants, and zooming through the now glassless windows beneath which the defenders crouched. The latter had not been lucky; two would never fight again, and several were hurt. Bardoe strode up and down the room; things were going ill. Frayle, his left arm useless, had an idea.

'Why not git away, an' take the gal with us? If they foller, we can wait for 'em—under cover. Shall I see if the back's clear?'

139

Bull nodded; it seemed the only chance. He was wondering if indeed Cullin had weakened? 'He would, curse him, to save his hide,' he muttered. 'Where in hell is Frayle?'

That individual was having troubles of his own. Incautiously poking his head out of the rear door, he received a rap with a revolver butt which dropped him senseless.

'Tally one,' Smoky chuckled. 'Next please.' No more victims offered. 'What do we do now?'

The spiteful crack of the rifles had ceased again when Quilt answered: 'If they won't come out, we just naturally gotta go in. I'll give Nick the signal.'

He sent three rapid shots skyward, and they dashed into the building, guns out and spitting lead. The foreman's first objective was the big door, which he unbolted and flung wide. He caught a glimpse of his friends racing for it, and twisted only just in time to dodge a rifle-butt which would have split his skull.

For the next few minutes the invaders had a hectic time, for they were outnumbered and fighting desperate men. Even the advent of their comrades did not at once settle the issue. Choking in the acrid reek of burnt powder and dust raised by stamping feet, the battle continued. At such close quarters reloading was impossible, and the combat soon resolved itself into single-handed tussles in which rifle or pistol-butts, fists, or feet were the weapons.

In this wild melee, Yorky was pounced upon by Bardoe, who had not forgiven the Shadow Valley incident. The boy fought like a wildcat, striking, kicking, biting, but he was outsized and out-weighted, and a crashing blow sent him reeling to the floor. Sudden, who had just accounted for one opponent, turned on the rustler.

'Try one yore own size,' he gritted, and drove a granite fist to the body, following it up with another to the jaw which jolted the big man back on his heels.

Bull grunted and cast a swift glance around; it told him that the day was lost. With a headlong rush, and a rain of furious punches, he forced his man to give ground, and then, twisting, leapt through a nearby window to vanish in the undergrowth a few yards distant. Sudden swore; he had set his mind on getting Bardoe.

So he too used the window, but instead of following the runaway, he made for his own horse. He conjectured that the man would head for the 8 B, and he knew Nigger could overtake anything in the shape of horseflesh Bull might possess. Passing down the winding trail, he re-charged his weapons, and halted in the fringe of the pines. His reasoning proved correct;

after a short wait, the fugitive emerged well to the left, and he was mounted.

Sudden rose into view, hoping the fellow would turn and face him, but apparently Bardoe had but one idea—to get away, for he at once began to spur and thrash his horse furiously. A word, and the big black shot forward as though on springs, the mighty muscles moving to and fro beneath the satin skin like the well-oiled parts of a machine. Swiftly the gap between the two animals was closing up, and Sudden saw the man in front making frantic efforts to get more speed.

'If he thinks he can tire Nig out, he's due for a surprise,' the pursuer reflected.

Then comprehension came; Bardoe was galloping straight for the Big Quake; the inviting green patches were already plain.

'There's a road across an' he knows it. Quit dawdlin', yu imp o' darkness.'

A lengthened stride resulted, and when the black, scenting danger, stopped abruptly on the brink of the morass, the fugitive was less than a dozen yards distant. Sudden slid his drawn gun slowly back into the holster; there was no need for it. One of two things had happened; either Bardoe, in his haste, had mistaken the crossing-place, or the treacherous sub-structure of the bog had shifted. Apparently he had soon learned his peril and swung his horse round to return, but too late. The violent struggles of the terrified beast only hastened the end; already, its head alone protruded. Standing in the stirrups, with distended, horrified eyes, the rustler voiced an agonised appeal:

'Shoot, damn you, an' finish it.'

'Had yu a hand in killin' Olsen?'

'That was Cullin's work. I was there, an' spoke agin it; he wouldn't listen.'

'Will yu bear witness to that, if I save yu?'

'I'll spill everythin'—I swear it,' Bardoe said earnestly. 'For Gawd's sake, hurry.'

The last words were almost screamed. The trapped man's mount had disappeared, and only by holding his arms high could they be kept clear of the churned-up, vicious mess which, like a live thing, seemed to be reaching for them. He strove to move his legs, close-clamped by the clinging mud, but fiends below were tugging at them. A vile smell of rotting vegetation almost choked him. In a spasm of frenzied fear, he repeated his promise and his oath to keep it.

With what must have been maddening deliberation, Sudden lifted his rope from where it hung and made his cast. The loop fell truly over the up-stretched arms to be grabbed and pulled tight below the arm-pits by feverish hands. The puncher twisted the other end round the horn of his saddle, and spoke to the horse:

'Back, boy, but slow, mighty slow, at first; we don't wanta tear him in two.'

Inch by inch, the man was drawn from the clammy clasp, and at length lay spent and gasping, but safe. When Sudden removed the rope, Bardoe sat up, gazed at the hell from which he had escaped, and shook as with an ague.

'I couldn't bear it,' he muttered brokenly. 'To see it comin'— that filthy muck fillin' my mouth, nose, an' eyes, suffocatin', stranglin', an' me—helpless as a babe. I've allus figured I could face death with the next fella, but not thataway. S'pose I'm a coward?'

Sudden shook his head. 'It's an ugly end.' He rolled a smoke, passed it over, and proffered a light. 'I guess yore makin's are wet.'

Bardoe took it eagerly, regarding the giver with a puzzled expression. The tobacco soothed his frayed nerves. 'Yo're a curious cuss,' he said. 'Half an hour back you'd 'a' blowed me to hellangone, an' now....'

'I've a use for yu,' Sudden reminded. 'I've done my part o' the bargain.'

'You shore have,' Bull agreed, and drew a deep breath. 'It's fine to be alive. What you want me to do?'

Sudden told him, in detail, and the rustler replied. 'I get you, an' I won't fail, whatever comes to me,' he said quietly.

'I'll do what I can about that,' the puncher promised, and stepped into his saddle. 'Reckon my friends have cleaned house by now.'

Bardoe saw him vanish into the wood, and only then became aware of a tobacco sack, papers, and matches lying where the rescued man must see them. His eyes gleamed.

'There goes a fella who could beat me every time,' he told the world.

CHAPTER XXI

BARDOE'S flight finished the battle, such of his men as were able following his example, and disappearing into the surrounding forest. Drait at once went in search of the prisoner. He found a locked door, rapped, and got no response. Lifting a heel, he drove it at the fastening. With a splintering crash it gave way, swinging drunkenly back on its hinges. Mary was standing at the far side of the room; the fear in her eyes died out when she saw him.

'You?' she cried.

'Were you expectin' someone else?' he asked drily.

In truth she was, having jumped to the conclusion that Cullin had come to her rescue. 'You might have been one of the brutes who brought me here,' she explained.

Lack of warmth in her reception angered him. 'No, I'm one o' the brutes who has come to take you away,' he retorted. 'Better stay here till we've straightened up.'

He went out, leaving her with the knowledge that she had behaved badly; but the picture of her cattle feeding in Shadow Valley would not be blotted out. Yet he had fought for her freedom, risking his life—she recalled the trickle of blood down one cheek. She must apologise. She nerved herself to again seek the nester, and found him with Quilt in the big room, bending over a prostrate form.

'This is no place for you,' he said.

'Who is it?' she asked, and when they told her it was Gilman, she knelt beside the man who had robbed her. Even to inexperienced eyes, the haggard, pain-wracked face and loose jaw showed that the end was near.

'I wanna drink,' he mumbled weakly, but when she called for water, a ghastly grin trembled on his lips as he added, 'I said—a drink—ma'am.'

A half-empty bottle of whisky was on the table. Drait poured a stiff dose and Quilt tipped it down the eager throat. The fiery spirit gave a temporary strength. The weeping girl looked appealingly at the nester, and the dying man understood.

'Ain't nothin' to be done,' he murmured. 'Sorry—'bout yore cattle, ma'am. If I could make amends. . . .'

'You can, Jack,' Drait said. 'Tell me who murdered Eddie.'

'Cullin—strangled him—hisself.' His voice grew feebler. 'Off'n thought o' Eddie, an' now—it's—my turn.'

Quilt laid the limp form gently on the floor, and placed his hat over the staring, lifeless eyes. Drait led the girl away.

'Was that true—about Cullin?' she whispered.

'Yeah, a man don't lie at such a moment,' he replied. 'Get some rest; it's a long ride back.'

She was glad to be alone. Seated in her late prison, she strove to reconstruct her disrupted world. Cullin, her one friend—as she had believed—was a heartless, brutal murderer. She could not doubt it. And if she had been wrong there, had she erred in other judgments? What did it all mean? She could find no answer. Voices broke in.

'Glad yo're back, Jim,' she heard her husband say. 'What about Bull?'

'He got away.'

'So did some o' his men, Lanty among 'em,' Drait grumbled. 'We've three to plant, an' Frayle has a busted arm. No, we've been lucky—a few grazes.'

At the end of an hour, preparations for departure were complete, graves dug and filled, mounts found for the lady and prisoner. The nester decided to strike south-east for Shadow Valley, which would cut down the distance considerably. He and Sudden led the way, with Mary and Yorky following, and the others, shepherding Frayle, behind. All were too tired to talk, and even Yorky lost his loquacity.

It was dark when at length they reached the Valley to find Lindy awaiting them. The S P without her mistress had proved too much, and she had prevailed on Milton to drive her over, to a greater loneliness. She received them with voluble expressions of delight, but her chief concern seemed to be the state of the kitchen.

'Yoh'd sca'cely b'lieve, honey, a passel o' men——'

'We're tuckered out an' hungry, woman; get some grub,' Drait said brusquely. He looked at Mary. 'You'll stay here to-night.'

He was gone before she could reply, and she smiled a little; that was his way. But she wanted to thank him, and since the moment he smashed the door of her prison, he had given her no opportunity. Was he purposely avoiding her? The thought was curiously disturbing. Sitting in the parlour, she waited for his return. She heard Sudden speaking to Lindy and called him in.

'Where is—Mister Drait?' she asked.

'Well on the road to Midway, by this. Didn't he tell yu?' Sudden replied. He saw she did not understand, and went on to tell of the arrest and subsequent escape, passing lightly over his own part in the latter. She listened with mounting colour, and then cried indignantly:

'You let him go?'

He smothered a smile. 'Nick is full-growed, an' when he decides on somethin' he's mighty liable to do it. About yore cattle——'

'Oh, damn the cattle,' she burst out, and then, 'I'm sorry. You were saying?'

'He didn't steal 'em, on'y got 'em back from the fella who did, an' fetched the herd here for safety, an' meanin' to surprise yu.'

'Then you and Yorky did find them?'

Sudden's grin was entirely unrepentant. 'Yeah, but it would 'a' spoiled Nick's plan to let on.'

'I still don't see any reason for returning to prison.'

144

'He has to face the music. To run would admit guilt.'

'I see that now,' she said. 'Who is bringing the charge?'

'The sheriff, backed by Cullin.'

'But surely, what you have discovered about the wretch. . . .' She paused as the puncher shook his head.

'Rustlin' is a capital crime in a cattle country,' he told her. 'What Cullin is, or has done, won't explain away yore steers in Shadow Valley.'

'But there is an explanation,' she persisted. 'His men——'

'Are accomplices,' he reminded. 'Besides, they'd be expected to swear black was white to get their boss outa trouble, an' they would.'

'What had kidnapping me to do with it?'

'They feared yu *might* 'a' stood up for him.'

'Might?' she repeated. 'Of course I would—and will. When does this infamous trial take place?'

'In the mornin', I'd say; they won't lose time. We'll all be there.' Then, inconsequently, 'Nick's a real fella, but terrible unseein'—times.'

His kind but probing gaze confused her. 'Thank you, Jim,' she murmured. 'We must save him.'

'Shore we will,' he replied. 'Mebbe we got a card they don't know about.'

*   *   *

The silver light of the moon which softened the crudities of Midway, only revealed the identity of the late visitor as he rode nonchalantly along the one street. Citizens stood still, stared, and rubbed their eyes in disbelief. The prisoner who had effected a sensational escape from the calaboose was the last person they dreamed of seeing. To a man they followed dumbly, and when—indifferent to the excitement he was causing—he got down at Merker's and stopped in, they crowded after him. Within, the paralysing amazement was repeated, and the saloon-keeper, who was serving a customer, nearly dropped the bottle.

'Goda'mighty, Nick, are you mad?' he asked, as the nester ranged himself at the bar.

'No, on'y thirsty.' He helped himself. 'Where's Stinker?'

'Just comin' in,' was the disgusted reply.

The sheriff was pushing his way importantly through the throng, gun out, and an unholy expression of joy on his face. 'So it's true,' he muttered, for he had doubted the news. 'Stick 'em up, Drait.'

The nester laughed. 'Cut out the play-actin', Stinker. I'm not heeled an' came to find you. I want five hundred bucks.'

The sheriff's bloodshot eyes bulged. 'Whaffor?' he asked.

'Bringin' myself in—alive, which is a disappointment, I know, but it had to be that way. Who put up that reward—the town or—Cullin?'

'None o' yore business,' Camort growled uneasily.

Pilch pounced on him. 'Mebbe, but it's our business if yo're spendin' money to git back prisoners you've let go, an' we wanta know.'

The sheriff was cornered, and knew it. 'It warn't town money,' he admitted sullenly. 'A private citizen, who don't want to be named——'

'Cullin's modesty is well known,' the nester broke in.

The sheriff flared up. 'You oughta talk, robbin' a young gal under cover o' purtendin' to help her.'

This time he scored, and Nick was aware of hard looks. He clenched his fists in an effort to fight down the fury surging within him. Then he spoke:

'Stinker, if I didn't know yo're just achin' for an excuse to pour lead into me, I'd shake yore teeth out an' cram yore lyin' tongue down yore throat,' he said. 'Now, I've had a busy day, an' need sleep.'

The officer reluctantly emptied his glass and signed to his deputies. 'If he flaps a wing, drill him, good an' plenty,' he ordered.

'I'll come an' tuck you up, Nick,' Pilch grinned, and to the sheriff. 'If there's any funny business, you'll be tried in the mornin'—by yore Maker.'

Having seen the prisoner duly incarcerated, and posted guards at door and window, Camort called on the Judge, who was—surprisingly at that hour—sober. He listened to the news with a dubious air.

'Surrendered after getting clear away. He must have an answer to the charge.'

'It's yore affair to see he don't have any such thing,' the sheriff said. 'Cullin——'

The Judge held up a hand. 'Listen: my affair is to administer the Law. Cullin, to me, is just another man, and I'm weary of his name; don't mention it again.'

The visitor gaped; decidedly the Judge was sober, dangerously so. 'I thought——' he began.

'Don't over-tax my credulity,' Towler said cuttingly. 'I will hear the case in the morning, and hope the accused will not be missing.' Camort told of his precautions. 'Better have someone to watch over your own slumbers,' came the acid comment. 'The girl will be absent.'

'That's so.'

'Unavoidably detained, one might say.'

146

The other agreed, and came away somewhat perturbed. He comforted himself with the reflection that Cullin would soon bring him to heel.

CHAPTER XXII

THE court-room was filling rapidly when the Shadow Valley party arrived. The hum of conversation increased as they marched up the middle gangway, and many glances of admiration were directed to the girl. Pale, but with head high, she appeared indifferent to the interest their entry occasioned. When they reached the front row of seats, which was empty, Wall-eye came bustling up.

'Them's for the witnesses,' he warned.

'I guessed as much,' the puncher said curtly, and sat down. The deputy decided not to argue.

Vasco, his foreman, and three riders were a couple of rows behind, and Sudden went to speak with them.

'What'n hell was Nick thinkin' of to come back?' the rancher queried.

'On'y the guilty run away, ol'-timer,' Sudden smiled. 'He'll make the grade.'

'Shore hope so, but if anythin' goes awry, there's five here you can depend on—to the limit.'

'That's good listenin'. I'm not forgettin' it.'

'Pickles! You did me a service. We ain't catched Bull yet, but he's keepin' his han's off.'

'Been busy other ways, but I've a notion he won't trouble yu no more.'

'Which'll suit me fine. So that's the S P heiress? She certainly rests the eyes.'

'I'll tell her yu said so,' Sudden grinned.

'Don't you, or I'll light out,' Vasco threatened. 'Hello, there's Greg, an' he's lookin' kind o' surprised.'

He was right, but 'surprised' was a pallid description of the Big C man's state. He had seated himself at the end of the front row, near the jury-box, before he saw the girl; he started to rise, only to sink down again under the freezing glance she gave him. How did she come to be here? A qualm of uneasiness shot through him.

The appearance of the accused, escorted by the sheriff, was the next incident. He nodded to his friends as he passed, stepped unconcernedly into the dock, and surveyed the jury critically.

147

The Judge slouched in, the jury was sworn, and Towler turned to the dock.

'Nicholas Drait, you are charged with stealing stock from the S P ranch,' he said. 'Do you plead guilty or not guilty?'

'Which would you advise, Judge?' Seriously.

'I'm not here to give you advice,' Towler snapped.

'I keep forgettin' yo're on the other side,' Nick said ruefully, a naive expression which brought titters from the audience, and made the Judge angry.

'I am not on either side, sir,' he thundered. 'And let me warn you that facetiousness will not help your case. Answer my question.'

'When in doubt, toss for it.' Nick spun a coin and studied the result anxiously. 'Not guilty. Well, what's fairer'n that? D'you mind tellin' me who's bringin' the charge?'

The Judge did not see the sheriff's negative headshake. 'Naturally the person who was robbed,' he replied drily.

Mary stood up. 'I am that person, and I know nothing of it.'

Towler frowned; he had been misled again. He referred to a paper. 'My information is that you lodged a complaint with the sheriff and asked for action to be taken.'

'I have neither spoken nor written to him at any time.'

The Judge's silence told Camort he must get out of the difficulty himself. 'The message came by another party, an' warn't written,' he explained.

'The name, please,' Mary insisted.

The sheriff hesitated, but there was no alternative; for once in his tortuous career he must tell the truth. 'Gregory Cullin.'

Her contemptuous gaze travelled to where the rancher sat. 'Mister Cullin had no authority whatever to bring a message from me.'

The rancher rose. 'Miss Darrell told me of her loss an' expressed the view that no punishment was too severe for a rustler. I believed I was carryin' out her wishes in gettin' the sheriff to move in the matter,' he said heavily.

Mary ignored him. 'It is admitted I did not authorise this—this——'

'Prosecution?' Towler suggested, with a smile which acted like a goad on the girl.

' "Persecution" was the word I was seeking,' she retorted. 'I have no wish for it to go on, and ask you to dismiss the accused forthwith.'

Flushed and breathless, she sank into her seat amidst general applause. Coarse-fibred as most of the audience were, they could appreciate beauty, and above that, courage. She found her real reward in the warm eyes of the man in the dock.

Silence fell on the court; everyone was waiting for the decision. Towler, listening to Camort, noticed that Cullin was talking to one of the jury.

'You must not do that, Mister Cullin,' he said sharply. 'If it happens again, I shall have you removed.'

The rancher drew back, his face rigid. 'Sorry,' he drawled and with a palpable sneer, 'I thought the case was ended.'

The Judge bent his gaze on the girl. 'The matter is less simple than you imagine, ma'am,' he began. 'You may condone a crime, but I cannot; it is my duty to protect the public.'

'No crime has been committed,' she replied hotly. 'Mister Drait did not steal the cattle.'

'That is what we are here to determine; the trial must go on.'

She sat down, her eyes flaming. Sudden patted her shoulder, rose, and smiled apologetically at the Judge. 'She's just naturally disappointed, seh,' he said. 'Ain't wishin' to delay proceedin's none, but I'm wonderin' if yu'd settle a triflin' argument for me? A fella claimed that when a woman marries, any property she has becomes the property o' the husband. I didn't agree, an' we had a li'l bet.'

'Which you have lost,' Towler said. 'That is the law.'

'Never was lucky,' Sudden said sadly. 'I'm obliged.'

But his expression as he sat down belied his voice, and the meaning look he gave the girl beside him electrified her. Red-faced, eyes shining, she cried : 'I again demand the release of the accused.'

The Judge gestured wearily. 'On what grounds now?'

'You have just stated them. Nicholas Drait is my husband, and owner of the S P. Even this court cannot convict a man of stealing what already belongs to him. Here is the proof.' She produced the paper the minister had given her on that fateful morning.

Again the paralysed silence as the Judge bent over it. When he looked up it was to ask sternly : 'Why wasn't I told of this earlier?'

'The marriage was kept secret, at my request—the whim of a foolish woman.' Mary said steadily. 'I did not know about the law until you answered Mister Green.' She smiled, enjoying her triumph. 'They say a little knowledge is dangerous, but it seems to me that a little ignorance is more destructive.'

The Judge did not reply; he was tasting the bitterness of defeat and not liking it. But there was no escape. In his best judicial manner, he said : 'The evidence now before the Court completely destroys the case for the prosecution, and exonerates the accused.'

The effort was received in silence. The cheering broke out

only when Nick walked from the dock, gripped his wife's hand hard enough to account for the wetness in her eyes, and turned to thank his friend.

'Forget it,' Sudden said hastily. 'The Judge is goin' to dismiss the jury; he mustn't do that.'

He stepped on the platform, to be greeted with a sour look of surprise, and a sharp, 'Well, sir?'

'This business ain't finished,' the puncher said bluntly. 'Mebbe this'll interest you.' He laid a letter on the desk.

Fear gripped the jurist as he read. Briefly, the document informed all whom it might concern, that the bearer, James Green, was deputed to enquire into the Pavitt succession, and other irregularities in and around Midway, and to deal with them as he thought fit. All officials were required to give him every assistance. It was signed, 'Bleke, Governor.'

The Judge drew a difficult breath. He could vision himself losing everything, even his liberty, for the Governor's attitude to ill-doers justified his name. 'I wish you had made yourself known to me earlier.' Sudden smiled. 'What do you wish me to do?'

'Tell 'em the show ain't over.'

The Judge rapped for silence, and made the announcement, rather more grandiloquently than the puncher had put it, and the audience, eager for the excitement, quietened down.

'What next?'

Sudden pointed to Cullin, who, slumped in his seat, chin on chest, seemed oblivious to what was happening. Indeed, the revelation that the woman he coveted was married to the man he hated, following by the latter's triumph, had mentally stunned him. 'Put that man in the dock.'

Towler gasped, doubting his own ears. 'Cullin's the most powerful man in these parts,' he expostulated.

'Not just now,' Sudden reminded.

The old man shivered, called the sheriff, and gave the order. Camort convinced that his chief had gone mad, stammered, 'Ain't feelin' sick, are you?'

The Judge was—very sick. 'Do as I tell you,' he snapped.

Like one awaking from an evil dream, Cullin sprang to his feet. 'What the hell's the meanin' o' this, Towler? Are you crazy?' he cried.

'Charges have been made against you, Mister Cullin, and must be investigated—in your own interest.'

The mild answer brought reason. Cullin felt no apprehension; he had covered his trail too cleverly, but it would be foolish to antagonise those present. So he dropped his bluster, and laughed.

'Never thought of it thataway, but yo're right.' He stepped jauntily into the dock, and as he passed, the sheriff deftly lifted the gun from his holster. At any other time he would have been struck down, but the rancher merely shrugged; he had a part to play.

He did it well. As he faced the whispering, excited crowd, few suspected the furnace of fury raging in his breast. One thing puzzled him—what had the cowboy to do with it?

'Well, Towler, trot out yore charges,' he challenged.

It was the cowboy who answered. 'What amount did yu promise Seale if he succeeded in *not* findin' the heir, an' got permission to sell the ranch?'

'I made no promise an' knew nothin' of his plans. I was willin' to buy the range if it came on the market.'

Sudden produced the letter found in the lawyer's office, and the Judge read it aloud.

'I never wrote that,' Cullin denied. 'It's a forgery.'

'A small matter, anyway,' Sudden remarked carelessly. 'But that don't go for yore plot to get Drait plugged in Little Basin.'

'With which I had no connection.'

'On'y to put up the money, two hundred apiece; Tomini talked, Cullin,' the puncher said sternly. 'Well, they bungled it, so yu had to try again. This time yu raised the ante, an' offered a thousand to Lukor, a notorious professional killer.'

'Whose name I never heard till after the shootin',' the rancher sneered.

'Two witnesses can testify yu called on him at the Rideout hotel the day afore he came to Midway.'

'Liars are easy found.'

'Yu oughta know. Lukor fell down on the job, an' stayed down,' Sudden went on grimly. 'He picked the wrong man; yore description must 'a' been lackin' some. For yore own safety, yu decided to let Drait live a little longer, an' turned yore attention to grabbin' the S P. As usual, yu hired others to do the dirty work. They were to steal an' hide cattle so that yu could collect 'em when the owner had been scared into sellin' yu the ranch. Yore rustlers were careless, the cows traced an' fetched back to Shadow Valley.'

'You oughta be writin' dime novels,' Cullin said, but his eyes were uneasy.

'That gave you yore chance; it shore looked like an open an' shut case o' rustlin',' Sudden continued. 'The sheriff was instructed to arrest Drait, an' yu had the S P owner kidnapped so that she could not interfere.'

'That's an infernal lie,' Cullin cried, with a fine air of indignation.

151

The puncher's reply was to hand the Judge the letter he had found on the sheriff's desk. The reading caused a sensation.

Cullin dismissed it in two words: 'Another forgery.'

'No,' the Judge said firmly. 'Comparing these with others in my possession, I find the writing identical.'

'On the strength of two letters I never wrote, and a lot o' guess-work, I've been accused of attempts to break the law, but Drait is still alive, the lady is back in our midst, an' I still do not own the S P. My career of crime seems to be a failure.'

'Not quite,' Sudden corrected. 'Once yu succeeded, an' that once will hang yu, Cullin. I mean the murder of Eddie Olsen.'

The blow went home. Confidence left him, fear taking its place.

'Easy to accuse,' he said. 'Where's yore proof?'

'With his last breath, Gilman named yu.'

'He allus hated me. A dead man's word; is that all?' Cullin jeered.

Sudden beckoned towards the door, and two men sitting by it rose and walked to the platform. Exclamations of wonder followed their recognition. 'Bull an' Frayle. What's comin' now?' men asked.

'Bardoe, yu saw Olsen die. What happened?'

'Nine of us went to throw a scare into Drait. Olsen said he warn't to home. Cullin called him a liar, clutched his throat, an' swore to choke the truth out'n him; he choked the life out instead. Me an' Frayle protested, but he was past listenin', just murder-mad. When it was done, he told two o' his men to hang the body from a limb, and said it would show Drait we meant business.'

Sudden looked at Frayle. 'Anythin' to add?'

'No, that's just how it was.'

The pitiful story brought a low, threatening growl, mixed with forcible expressions of disgust. Cullin shot a furtive glance at the spectators; contempt, cold condemnation, ironical curiosity, satisfaction, all these things he read in the hard faces, but no pity. He made a last effort:

'What are they payin' you for these lies, Bardoe?' he asked.

'A lot less'n you offered me for robbin' the S P an' carryin' off its mistress,' was the reply. The rustler's fierce eyes swept the gathering. 'Every word I've said is God's own truth, an' if I have to follow you into the dock, I won't squeal—if they clean it out first. I ain't proud o' my record but it don't include guzzlin' an unarmed cripple.'

Cries of 'Good for you, Bull,' followed the rustler's denunciation, and the prisoner's last shred of hope vanished. In the moment of deadly peril, he was without a friend. Even the quaking tool he had used and abused was solely concerned with his own danger. In every grim face he read the fate awaiting him. The twisted, tortured features of Eddie dangled before his eyes, mocking him. An icy hand seemed to clutch his heart as he looked at Drait and the girl who had cheated him. Frenziedly he strove to think, and then, in a flash, hope was reborn, mad, fantastic, but possible. Towler was turning to the jury; he must act now.

'Judge, I would like a private word with Drait an' his wife,' he said, all arrogance gone from his voice. 'It's vital—to them.'

The Judge nodded, and head bowed in an attitude of dejection, Cullin watched the approach of the woman he hungered for and the man he hated. Not until they were quite close did he look up.

'Well, Cullin, what is it?' Nick asked.

'This,' the rancher hissed. His right hand flashed to his shoulder, the gun cracked, and even as Drait was falling, the assassin's left hand swung the girl round, and the still-smoking muzzle of his weapon was pressed against her head.

'Freeze, all o' you,' he shouted. 'A hurt to me, kills her.'

It was true; the hammer of his gun was held back only by a thumb, and her life depended on it remaining so. Many present could have shot him down, but it meant two lives. So they sat in their seats, petrified, helpless, while he strode from the dock, thrusting his captive before him.

Dazed by the swiftness of the tragedy, and kept conscious only by the biting grip of steel talons which seemed to penetrate to the bone, the girl moved forward. Cullin did not hurry—he knew he was safe, and a fiendish snarl of triumph distorted his lips. Savage, impotent men watched his progress to the door, which he forced the girl to open, and heard the gibing 'Adios' as it slammed behind him, and the key turn.

For a moment they stared at one another, and then Sudden acted. Picking up a heavy chair, he hurled it at the nearest window; glass and framework vanished together. He leapt through, dashed to his horse, and flung himself into the saddle. Which way?

'He'll make for the Big C to get cash an' fresh hosses,' he told himself.

He found the trail, a mere wagon-way, which after crossing a brush-dotted mile or so of plain, zigzagged through a procession of shallow wooded ravines and low ridges. It was from one of the latter that he got a glimpse of the killer. He had not waited to take a second horse, and the girl—who appeared to be unconscious—was slung across the saddlebow. Only for a moment

153

they were visible before entering a timbered tract, but the puncher's knowledge of horseflesh told him something.

'He's got a good start, Nig, but that hoss is weakenin'.'

He stroked the curving silken neck, and the black quickened its pace, eager to show this master who never ill-treated, what it could do. When next they sighted the fugitive he was appreciably nearer, and commencing a long, gradual incline. Sudden smiled mirthlessly.

'We've got him, ol' fella,' he said. 'That rise'll bust his bronc wide open.'

He was right. The double burden and killing speed had already taken toll, and only incessant spurring kept the exhausted beast going. The climb proved the last straw, and the black began to gain rapidly. Cullin glanced back, and his right arm rose and fell furiously as the brute above flogged the nobler brute beneath. Somehow the gallant animal, dying on its feet, reached the crest and was lost to sight. Sudden was a scant fifty yards behind.

This distance covered, the ground dropped a little and then rose sharply, and here the trail swung off along a rather narrow shelf, with vertical cliff on one side, and a precipice on the other. An outflung natural buttress engaged Sudden's attention. His dismounted.

'He's got a gun,' he said. 'Better "look afore we leap"—into sight.'

There was no trap. Cullin's horse had foundered, and lay on its side, breathing, but useless. The rancher was standing near the brink of the abyss, holding the drooping girl to his side. Sudden walked towards them stopping a dozen paces away.

'Well, Green, I still hold the high card,' he taunted. 'Listen: I wanted this woman, so bad I was willin' to kill to get her. That dream's gone. I'm just usin' her. An' see, my gun's empty.' He pulled out the weapon, snapped the hammer six times, and thrust it behind his waist-belt, not without some difficulty.

'What's yore proposition?'

'I'll trade her life for mine. Give yore word to let me go unhurt an' I'll place her in safety.'

Sudden reflected a moment. He suspected a ruse, but could not divine it. In any case, if he got the girl away from that horrible chasm, he could take care of himself.

'It's a deal,' he said.

With every sense alert, he watched the rancher convoy his prisoner to the cliff wall, where she subsided listlessly. Then Cullin turned and walked away, his right arm swinging by his side. Sudden's eyes narrowed; the swing was lengthening, the hand going nearly waist-high, where the empty weapon had

154

been stowed. Tensed and ready, he stood, watching and waiting. Then it happened. Cullin had gone but a few steps when he whirled and fired, doubtless counting on a surprise. But Sudden had caught the beginning of the movement and his own gun was spouting flame at the same instant. He felt the scorch of the lead on his cheek, and saw the traitor stagger back under the impact of the heavy slug. His face drawn with pain and fraught with fear, the murderer tottered, fighting to regain his balance, only to lurch sideways, step on nothing, and with a strangling cry, vanish into the void.

The puncher pushed his hat back and wiped the clammy moisture from his brow. Not till then did he become aware of voices. Yorky, Pilch, and half a dozen others were beside him.

'You ain't hurt, Jim?' the boy asked fearfully. 'Gawd, you were quick.'

'Shore had to be,' Sudden replied. 'It was a close call.' He explained the desperate trick Cullin had tried.

'Well, saves soilin' a rope,' Pilch said callously. 'Though I wouldn't 'a' grudged it.'

The girl, ashen-faced and moving shakily, joined them, anxious for news of her husband. Only Yorky, who had started behind the others and caught them up, could tell her anything:

'He's hard hit, an' they're takin' him to Merker's, an' sendin' to Rideout for a doctor; Midway don't have none.'

With this she had to be content.

CHAPTER XXIII

DOCTOR BOLUS—so he called himself—was middle-aged, and slight of frame, with a kindly face in which the eyes smiled. Why he chose to reside in this wild region nobody knew or cared; he was skilled, liked, and respected. The citizens gathered in Merker's bar to await his first report fell silent when they noted the gravity of his expression.

'It's a bad business, but he has a chance—a very slim one,' he announced. 'Cannot be moved, so you can say farewell to your bedroom for some weeks, Merker.'

After a moment's thought, Merker said, 'Not reflectin' nohow on yore ability, doc, I'm layin' you twenty dollars to one you don't save Nick.'

His eyes twinkling, Bolus accepted the wager, and the others on the same terms which followed. Merker, busy making out a list, said:

'How far you prepared to go, doc? More o' the boys'll want in on this.'

'The sky's the limit,' the little man smiled. 'And I'm staying in Midway to win the money.'

'That's good to hear, sir,' the Judge said. 'You'll be the town's guest, and anything your patient needs will be got.'

So it came to pass that Midway went about both business and pleasure on tiptoe, as it were. Every day men stepped softly into the saloon to read the latest bulletin, and for the first two weeks went away with disconsolate faces. To their queries the doctor had but one reply:

'I am doing all that is possible, and he has the most devoted nurse I ever met; she's just killing herself, and I'll have to speak to her.'

He did so, to be met with a stubborn refusal to leave the sickroom. He had his argument ready: 'What's going to happen if your health breaks down?'

The possibility appalled her, and she capitulated on the condition that the doctor took her place, to which he readily agreed. Her first excursion brought astonishment. Every few yards men she had never seen stopped and shyly asked for news of the nester. This universal anxiety delighted her until an enquirer provided an apparent explanation.

'You just gotta pull him through, ma'am,' he said. 'There's a lot o' dollars dependin' on it.'

She returned to the saloon seething with anger. Her crimson face told the doctor something had gone wrong.

'The callous brutes!' she cried. 'They are actually gambling on my husband's life.'

'You misjudge them,' Bolus returned quietly, and gave the facts. 'So you see,' he concluded, 'it is their way of offering me a fantastic fee to insure I will do my best. Do you know what happened this morning when I gave Merker a favourable report? Most of the wagers were doubled. You see, they *want* to lose.'

'I shall never understand the Westerner,' she said ruefully.

A day or so later Mary met Sudden, whom she had not seen since the tragedy, and asked a question: 'Jim, how did you know we were married?'

'I didn't; it was just a hunch,' he replied.

'Was that the card they might not know of?'

'Yeah, but I wanted yu to play it,' he grinned.

She did not quite believe his ignorance—he had most discerning eyes, this Mister Green, and the twinkle in them wrought confusion in her cheeks. Perhaps this was why he changed the subject.

156

'When am I goin' to see Nick?'

'Soon,' she promised.

But a week passed before the meeting came about, and Sudden received a shock. The nester, propped up by pillows, was a mere shadow of his former self. However, there was a smile on the gaunt, pale face.

'My, Jim, it's good to see you,' he said. 'Me? I'm doin' fine. Tell me the news.'

'Ain't much. Quilt an' the rest of us are lookin' after the S P an' the Valley, Sturm an' his riders bein' plenty absent. Seale took a notion to travel. The Judge gave Camort ten years in the pen, but we had to sneak him out after dark to save his neck. Cullin? Oh, he fell over the cliff.'

'Yeah, that's what Mary told me, but she used more words,' Drait said drily. 'Jim, I've been tryin' to figure out my debt to you.' Sudden started to rise. 'Awright, cuss you, I'll be dumb. Who's takin' Stinker's place?'

'Bardoe.' Sheer surprise kept Nick silent. 'He's a changed man, but still feared, an' I think he'll make good. Bein' peace-officer is no picnic; I've had some.' He smiled reminiscently as he recalled hectic months in a tough little town on the Mexican border, months of almost daily danger.*

Nick was silent for some moments, and then, 'Jim, how did you make Towler put Cullin in the dock?'

He nodded sagely when he had heard the explanation. 'Guessed you warn't an ornery cow-wrastler,' he said. 'Well, havin' cleaned up I s'pose you'll be hittin' the trail soon?'

'Not till yo're in the saddle again, ol'-timer.'

'I'll be damn lonely in the Valley,' Nick said gloomily.

'Time's more than through,' came a voice from the door.

Outside, Mary was waiting, anxious enquiry in her eyes. 'He's lookin' better'n I expected,' Sudden promptly lied. 'A mite depressed, mebbe. I guess it's on'y heart trouble.'

'Only?' she gasped in alarm, and then the dawning smile made his meaning clear. 'Jim, you're a—dear,' she cried, and hurriedly retreated.

She found her patient lying back, eyes closed, face pale as the pillow on which it rested. He seemed dreadfully still, and her heart missed a beat. Had the visit been too much for him? Oppressed by the fear, she sank on her knees by the bedside, and spoke his name. Slowly the heavy lids lifted.

'Must 'a' dozed,' he muttered. 'Why, what's wrong.'

'Nothing—now,' she replied, as the colour drained back into her cheeks. 'I was alarmed. I thought. . . .' A shudder shook her.

* Related in *The Marshal of Lawless*.

157

'Would it 'a' mattered all that much?' he asked.

The barriers for her were down now. 'I think—I would have died too,' she said huskily.

For long breathless seconds he lay silent, trying to realise the joy that was coming to him. Then, 'If I tell you life can't give me a sweeter moment than this, Mary, you won't—laugh at me?'

Her head drooped. 'So you knew?' she said shamedly.

'I suspicioned,' he smiled. 'My dear, you were wastin' yore time; I reckon I loved you—unknowin'—right from the start. When I found out what you meant to me, I was scared to show it, in case. I couldn't blame you, after——'

A small hand closed his lips, and a passionate voice said, 'You should have used your quirt; it might have brought a vindictive little fool to her senses. Oh, I hate myself when I remember. You were kind to me, and in return I've——'

'Saved my life—yeah, I've the doc's word for that—an' given me the greatest happiness I have ever known,' he finished tenderly. 'The past is done, the future to face, together, just the two of us.'

A rosy face burrowed into the hollow of his shoulder.

He drew her closer and pressed his lips to the golden curls, as he whispered:

'Girl, girl, but I'll be mighty good to you.'

THE END